Risking Love

Malcolm stood looking down at her. "I was afraid of you—I had to consider whether I wanted to be a man alone, following one arrow-straight line, or if I wanted to be a man complete."

"You wanted," she said softly, "to decide if you could risk making love to me. . . . You sound like a man who has fallen in love. Doesn't it make you happy?"

"Not yet it hasn't."

She went to him and put up her arms, her hands clasped behind his head. "It will," she promised. "It will."

Then he kissed her, surprising her by the strength of his passion and the extent of his surrender. . . .

Other SIGNET Books You'll Enjoy

Doctor's Kingdom

by Elizabeth Seifert

A SIGNET BOOK

NEW AMERICAN LIBRARY

TIMES MIRROR

SIGNET TRADEMARK REG. U.S. PAT. OFF. AND FOREIGN COUNTRIES
REGISTERED TRADEMARK—MARCA REGISTRADA
HECHO EN CHICAGO, U.S.A.

SIGNET, SIGNET CLASSICS, MENTOR, PLUME AND MERIDIAN BOOKS
are published by The New American Library, Inc.,
1301 Avenue of the Americas, New York, New York 10019

FIRST PRINTING, DECEMBER, 1974

1 2 3 4 5 6 7 8 9

PRINTED IN THE UNITED STATES OF AMERICA

Chapter 1

This is the story of a dozen people, as for a year they lived on Kimberlin Lane, in the houses which Arthur Kimberlin had built at one end of his estate. A wide, circling roadway, the Lane, served these houses, and then led to Dr. Bennett's home, and finally to his own.

Arthur Kimberlin had engaged upon the building of the houses when he decided to retire as active president of Kimberlin Chemicals. He was named Chairman of the Board, but he considered himself too active, mentally and physically, to rest upon that honor. The idea of building the homes intrigued him; he spent a full year happily engaged with architects, forestry experts—he wanted to preserve the trees, the view, the air of quiet withdrawal which he himself had enjoyed about his home.

Dr. Bennett thought he should not bring in a "lot of strangers."

"I let you build a home out here," Arthur pointed out to his old friend.

"That was thirty years ago. You wanted your physician close, to give you paregoric after one of your banquets."

"You built that house *forty* years ago, my friend. And I have found neighbors to be a good investment." His brown eyes twinkled at the doctor, who also was getting old. He should retire, thought Arthur Kimberlin.

"If he ever does, he'll die," said Dr. Bennett's wife.

Arthur Kimberlin began to build the four houses, and spent another happy year climbing over stacks of lumber, skirting piles of brick, watching, and envying, the skill of carpenters, bricklayers, tilesetters. He wanted the houses to be individually different, and to fit into the contour of the land. He expected to sell the homes, and he did, except the one which he rented to Dr. Anderson.

Malcolm Anderson, a bachelor, thought he should not buy a house. "When I marry," he said, "the girl should have a say about her home."

"She might marry you for your house."

5

"Yes, she might," agreed the doctor, serenely puffing on his pipe.

Arthur rented him the house he wanted, the first one around the circle from the red brick solidity of Dr. Bennett's home. Anderson's house was low and white, spreading itself among the trees of the orchard, and looking quite content to be there. Next around the circle was the redwood and brick house which Christopher Kendrick bought for himself and his son. Nathan, he agreed, would marry and leave. Meanwhile they liked their low, comfortable house.

"All bachelors!" Dr. Bennett pointed out.

"Chris is young enough to marry again. So is Malcolm."

"Strange women can mean trouble."

"As can the ones we know."

"That's true," agreed the doctor. "I suppose you know that Kendrick bought your house to insure his job as plant manager."

Arthur smiled. "He has other insurance," he pointed out.

Crossing over, ready to come back along the other side of the circle, one found the much larger house of Dr. Aubuchon and his bride Susan. That house was built of brick, and it was expensive. "You should never have let that man in," Bennett told his friend.

"He has a lovely wife."

"She should never have married him."

"Joe . . ." Kimberlin protested. "You object to bachelors, you object to Rupert Aubuchon . . ."

"The best thing he ever did was to marry Susan. But Aubuchon—he wanted to get buddy-buddy with Malcolm Anderson. That's why he came in here."

"They're both heart specialists."

"Not in the same class."

"You should know. You're in the racket yourself."

Dr. Bennett's sense of humor did not cover such terms used concerning his profession. The discussion of Dr. Aubuchon veered off and away.

Beyond his home was that of Felix Lynch, a chemist for the company; he also was a bridegroom. His marriage had taken place after the contract to sell him the house was signed and delivered. Mr. Kimberlin readily admitted that he had been glad to sell the house to Felix and his mother. Alma, Italian-born, had for years been the housekeeper for Arthur Kimberlin. Felix was like a son to the Board Chairman. His education, his training, his job with the company as first assistant to Dr. Ottolini, had all been a matter of plea-

6

sure and pride to the Kimberlin family. Arthur was glad to have Felix and his mother, and now his young wife, living just down the drive from his own home.

"I'm going to enjoy the Lane," he assured Dr. Bennett.

On a cold and snowy night in January, Arthur Kimberlin could lie, warm and soft in his bed, and think with comfort of the homes which he had gathered closely about him. Before getting into bed, he had looked out of the window and seen the lights burning, the lampposts before the front doors and the lighted windows. They all meant people close by, their pleasures and their pain; those things came together. When a man reached the seventy-fifth year of a busy life, he wanted not to be lonely. He wanted life—any kind of life— to go on about him, to involve him if possible. If that was not possible, he wanted to be where he could see it.

Margaret had opened his window a threadlike crack, and he heard the car. It would be Malcolm Anderson, which was good because Malcolm could probably navigate the snow-covered Lane and reach the highway.

Malcolm himself was not pleased. Gladly he would have surrendered his place to anyone who came along. The snow was deep, wet; the only markers for the Lane were the humped, white-covered hedges, the juniper at the Kendrick drive entrance. The snow was blue-white, unmarked except for the deeper blue of the shadows cast by the hummocks of the shrubbery. The lampposts and the mounted mailboxes were topped with bread-loaf heaps of marshmallow white. The whole world was snow, and in that waste the only moving thing was the black automobile; behind the blooming headlights, the man behind the wheel was the only living thing.

Malcolm, too, saw the lights of the houses, and envied their owners. They made the night darker, the trackless snow more hazardous. "Why I ever thought I wanted to be a doctor . . ." He said that a hundred times a year. It didn't take snow, but snow helped make the statement fervent.

He shrugged more deeply into his heavy coat, and leaned forward across the steering wheel. If he could make it to the main road . . . The rear tires slipped, spun—then caught. He kept a bucket of sand and a small shovel in the car trunk; tonight well might be the occasion when he would use those things.

Doctors were not supposed to make night calls.

He could have quarters—he did have quarters—right in the clinic! On nights like this . . .

But Saturday and Sunday, alone out in the "country," were tempting. He had enjoyed his open fire, the steak he had broiled for himself, his books. He had even enjoyed the snow coming down, covering the trees, the roofs, and—the damned road!

The car lurched, tilted, righted itself, and the tires gripped firmly, reassuringly on the scraped, packed main road. He increased speed.

The team would be waiting; they wouldn't have called him if the emergency were not great. Maybe the team, individually and as a group, were also asking why *they* had chosen to be doctors—technicians, nurses.

He passed a car gone into the ditch. Poor devil. Malcolm could not safely stop to assist, but he lowered the window. ". . . send help," his voice called back into the cold night. Maybe the hapless driver would see his M.D. insigne on the license plate and understand.

But doctors did not make night calls. Everyone knew that.

The team . . . The surgeons, the senior resident, the anaesthetist Bill Alt at the machine . . . Good men, all. They probably could take care of this emergency without Anderson. Should he have told them to try? Because of a little snow? A team worked as a *team!* One man away could make a difference, and in heart surgery there was small room for difference.

He reached the hospital and parked his car in the almost empty lot. And he slipped as he walked toward the hospital door. Fine thing. Drive fifteen miles through snow up to his ears, and slip and break his fool leg in the clinic driveway! They'd call some luckless orthopod out of his warm bed to take care of him. He had better be careful. He stomped his feet, he wiped his boot soles on the mat, he wiped them again on the rug spread inside the door. The hospital was quiet, and warm.

"Good evening, Dr. Anderson. A nasty night."

"Not in here," said the doctor, pulling off his gloves and his coat as he walked, fast, down along the wide corridor. He stopped at a phone and reported the car in the ditch.

The Department of Thoracic and Cardiovascular Surgery was on the tenth floor of the big hospital. Malcolm's resident met his elevator. "I've been afraid of an aneurysm, sir," he said softly "Holman?" asked the Chief.

"Yes, sir. His wife . . ."

The lines deepened beside Dr. Anderson's chin. Charlene Holman had complicated this case from the start. She was a nervous woman; she anticipated trouble; she put the patient into a bad state of nerves.

"I've tried excluding her," Dr. Anderson murmured.

"I know, sir."

Mrs. Holman had read everything she could on heart valves and cardiac troubles. She—

She was a small woman, dark, and tense. "He is in so much *pain,* doctor!" she greeted Malcolm.

The doctor nodded. "Will you please wait in the hall, Mrs. Holman?" he asked, kindly enough. "Please?"

"You didn't alert the team?" He spoke below his breath to Dr. Mitchell.

"No, sir. It's such a bad night."

"It is."

Mrs. Holman had gone to the bedside; she was assuring the sick man that she would be just outside; she would wait. "Don't worry, Elmer. You must not worry!"

Malcolm glanced at the nurses, who firmly removed Mrs. Holman. The doctor went to work. His examination was thorough, and patient.

When he came out of the room, he could smile reassuringly at the sick man's wife. Holman was a very sick man! If he needed surgery, he must be built up to a chance of surviving that surgery.

The situation's difficulties were doubled and redoubled by the fact that Mrs. Holman had fallen in love with her husband's doctor. She had used extraordinary measures to bring Elmer to the clinic. She came with him prepared to worship the famous heart surgeon; no other doctor would even consider surgery on Elmer. But Dr. Anderson had said there might be a chance . . . So she worshiped him, she loved him.

"There may be an aneurysm," this man told her now. "But I think we can wait for a while. I am going home. Don't you think you should?"

"I'll wait in the sunroom, doctor. It's such a bad night."

"Yes, it is," said the doctor firmly.

She looked up at him; she clasped her thin hands together. "Oh, I do thank you for coming!" she cried tensely. "Dr. Mitchell . . ."

"Dr. Mitchell would not have operated without me."

"I know *that,* Dr. Anderson! But Elmer was in crisis!"

"He had pain; he still has pain. We'll evaluate the situation comprehensively on Monday. For tonight . . ."

His jaw was squared, his brown eyes were steady, his hand on her shoulder was warm and strong.

Tears welled into Mrs. Holman's eyes. "You are the most wonderful . . ." she gasped.

Malcolm patted her shoulder. "I wish you would get some sleep," he told her.

"Do you know what I wish?" she asked, almost pertly. "I wish I could go home with you, wherever you live, and see that you had a cup of hot chocolate, and a hot water bottle at your feet when you get into bed. So that *you* would sleep!"

He laughed. "I'd be so excited by all that attention I couldn't settle down," he assured her. "Goodnight, Mrs. Holman."

She watched him go along the hall, his reflection moving shadowlike along the gleaming floor. She went back to her husband's room and told the nurse there that Dr. Anderson was perfectly wonderful. "He instills strength just by being here."

"It was a shame to bring him out in the snow," said the nurse.

"Perhaps he should live in the hospital, where he'd be close."

"He has to get away from things. All his patients, you know, are so sick. A heart surgeon . . ."

"Yes, yes, I know," agreed Mrs. Holman, bending over to see her husband's face through the oxygen tent.

"I'd let him sleep," suggested the nurse.

"I just wanted to see . . . Is Dr. Anderson married?"

"I don't think he ever had time," said the nurse. She sounded a bit cross, and Mrs. Holman glanced at her. "I heard him tell you to get your rest, ma'am," the nurse added.

Charlene Holman smiled. "I know I should. I'll be in the sunroom if you need me."

"Yes, ma'am."

Meanwhile Dr. Anderson was checking out and putting on his galoshes again. He could have offered to take Mrs. Holman to her hotel, motel, or wherever she was staying. She should have selected a more sympathetic doctor. Somebody like Rupert Aubuchon. Dear Hannah, yes! That man knew how to charm and comfort the ladies. He'd built up a large, rich practice that way, and was able to buy old Kimberlin's biggest house. If Malcolm had known he was going to do that . . .

He fastened his coat buckle under his chin and went

toward the doors. His face was scowling with anger at himself. He wondered how many times Aubuchon had been able to raise his blood pressure this way. He should not let the man get to him. Mac Anderson could not possibly take care of all the cardiacs. There had to be Aubuchon, and old Dr. Bennett, beside the hundred other, and *good*, heart men in the city.

He got into the cold car and started the engine. He should stay here at the hospital, but, dammit, he still had Sunday coming to him.

The snow continued long enough after Malcolm's return to his home to blur the tracks his car wheels had made along the Lane. When the gray of Sunday morning revealed the world, and then the sun turned it to gold, that world was a beautiful place. "Have to shovel our way out," grumbled the householders.

"And beat the phfitzers," agreed the women.

Bush and shrub, tree and lamppost, were all turned into fairy tale creatures, dwarf and gnome and giant.

Too bad there were no children to frolic in the snow as the dogs were doing, helping and hindering the men who must, by contract, get the private road clear. They could have hired help; it was more fun to do it themselves, more neighborly to greet one another in a holiday spirit. And certainly it should be healthful. Where else did a man get such lifting and bending, for free, in the open air? So, each one of them would set aside his various interests and problems and come out into the crisp, clean air. Some might carry a problem or two with them, wearing them like the assortment of knitted caps and scarfs, for all to see.

The first home to show signs of life was the Kendrick house of rosy redwood and rough, sand-colored brick. Before eight, smoke began to circle upward from the big chimney. Chris opened his front door in what he knew was a futile hope that the Sunday paper would have been put into his mailbox. Except for some smoothed-over wheel tracks, not a soul had been along the Lane since the day before. The tracks—probably one of the doctors had gone out, and probably that doctor had been Mac Anderson.

Chris yawned and stretched his arms above his head, the fingers touching the open beams of the hall. Through the clerestory windows the sky showed a tender blue. But it was cold outside, a forbidding eleven degrees. No hope that the

11

snow would melt of itself, and there must be better than a foot of the stuff.

He went back to the kitchen, poured coffee into a big cup, broke two eggs into the hot grease in the skillet, pushed the lever down on the toaster.

"Hey, Nathan!" he shouted. "Will you be ready for breakfast?"

No answer. Chris nodded. He'd guessed right, and cooked only four slices of bacon. He drank his orange juice standing beside the stove, his eyes going to the view of the snowcovered woods. He had windows for the full length of the house, to the rear. The front was blank. A guy who managed a manufacturing plant employing more than two thousand workers did not always want to see people at home.

The toast popped up, the eggs were done; he took his small tray to the fireside. On the terrace outside the window a cardinal was already chipping for seed. Chris would fill the feeder before taking up his shovel.

He enjoyed his breakfast, and listened for sounds of life from his son's bedroom. Nathan had heard his call, Nathan had the nose to smell bacon cooking, Nathan knew there was snow to shovel. Christopher had mentioned it the night before. "We'll start at the gate," he had said at bedtime.

Nathan had made no comment then. He knew that the "old man" was angry at his son. Well, that was a father's privilege, his duty even. If a man had to raise a son, well, he should raise him! From the time the boy was seven, Chris had had to do the job alone. There were those who said he was overly possessive, and warned that Nathan was not learning self-discipline.

But he was a good kid. Infuriating, of course, at times. This happened to be one of those times—and one of those times when Chris was justified in being angry. Not like his disgust and protest over the way Nathan had wanted to paint the walls of his room. There he had given in to the boy, and only smiled in a sickly way when a visitor said their home was "amusing."

But this was a different thing. Swirls of green and yellow paint could be covered over. But the wrong girl . . .

Probably on Friday night Chris had shown how he felt. He was too big a man, too forthright, to conceal his feelings. He had not flared up at the boy. All yesterday afternoon he had busied himself in the study, unpacking books, arranging them on the shelves. Out in the workroom, Nathan had whittled away at a sailboat mobile he was making. There had been

12

almost no conversation between father and son. A televised football game took care of the evening.

But today Chris was going to say something. Nathan would expect him to. He was too much like his father, not quite so tall, six-foot-two to Chris's six-foot-four, and of course not so solid. At twenty, there had to be a difference from forty-four. Nathan's hair was brighter, his cheeks smoother, but in many ways he was like Chris. The others he must have learned about by now. The boy must have known, before bringing that chickadee to the house, that Chris would not like such a silly girl. My word!

He saw Nathan glide along the hall, heard him in the kitchen. Boys these days never wore shoes except when shoes were needed for warmth or protection.

"There's bacon and eggs, orange juice," Chris called.

"And no newspaper?"

"No. The radio says the snow is over."

"Not soon enough." He brought the percolator and filled his father's cup.

"Thanks," said Chris. "We'll have to shovel."

"I can wait."

"Only you won't wait."

Nathan said nothing.

The bacon sizzled and popped, the eggs hissed. The toast popped up, and Nathan was eating at the counter. Chris gathered his dishes, and took them out to the sink and the dishwasher.

"We ought to get at it pretty soon," he said shortly. "I'll dress."

"I'll be right out," Nathan agreed. He was playing with the radio. "Want to get last night's scores," he mumbled.

"Celtics won."

"They would."

"Don't put the bacon grease or the coffee grounds down the disposal."

"You've told me before."

"I've told you a lot of things before."

Nathan lifted his head. "All right," he said, "get it said."

Chris started away, then turned back. "Maybe you have more to say than I have," he suggested.

Nathan shrugged. "I thought the idea of this house was that we could have our friends out here."

"Our friends," repeated Chris.

"Well, gee whiz, dad . . ."

"I know. Your friends, and my friends. They are sure to

13

be different. But in one smallish house I'd hope they could be—er—compatible. Which means that they could be of a certain type, and standards."

"And Brenda wasn't."

"Brenda," Chris repeated, tasting the name. "Brenda Dishbein. What right have people named Dishbein to name their daughters Brenda?"

"Look, Dad, intellectualism can be just as damned snobbish as money."

"It can be more. It should be more."

Nathan slammed the door of the dishwasher. "These can wait until our lunch things," he said.

"They can. This Brenda, son. I don't think I ever met a sillier girl."

"But girls are silly. Or have you forgotten?"

His father's eyebrows went up. That girl, long, straight black hair, knowing eyes, a plump figure, a short skirt over well-filled black panty hose ... "I remember girls like that," he agreed. "They never were to my taste. How old is Brenda?"

"Good Lord, I don't know. Eighteen, maybe nineteen. We met. I brought her out. It was you who made a federal case out of it."

"I don't think I made any kind of case. I was polite to your friend."

"And you thought she was silly."

"I did, and I wondered how she managed to eat without getting hair in with her sandwich. I believe you made hamburgers."

And laughed, and shrieked, and laughed. And played the hi-fi deafeningly. And then were too silent before the fire. When Chris had begun to stir in his study, they had departed.

"Does Brenda go to the university?" he asked now, courteously. It was the tone he had used to Brenda.

"She takes courses in the School of Music."

Chris was surprised, and looked it.

"Anyway, the university hasn't anything to do with it," said Nathan. "I met her at an off-campus thing. She plays the organ, and is very interested in the electronic effects one can get."

Chris said nothing eloquently.

"The School of Music doesn't teach her that." Nathan agreed, laughing self-consciously. "But I've already drifted out of the academic orbit."

The way kids talked ... "What orbit are you in now?" his

father asked, getting a cloth and wiping the counter. "We'd better dress."

But Nathan had something more to say. "I've about decided," he told his father, "to leave school and get my military service over and done with."

Chris dropped the dishcloth. He bent to retrieve it. "You—what?" he cried, straightening.

"Well—I knew you wouldn't like it, but—"

"You're damned right I don't like it. Here you are, within a year and a half of graduating— You're just crazy, Nathan Kendrick. Stark, raving crazy!"

"I'm going to have to put on one of their uniforms sometime."

"And sometime will be soon enough! This close to your degree, if you keep your grades up . . ."

Nathan shrugged. Grades had never been a problem to him. "It's this marking time," he said. "Knowing that I am marking time. I want some action, Dad. I want to be doing . . ."

Chris turned full about. "If you dare," he cried, "to use the word *relevant*, I'll paste you one!"

Nathan laughed. "You mean, you'd try. Look—do *you* know the meaning of that word?"

"Relevant?" asked Chris. "Do you know what it means?"

Nathan went down the hall, shucking out of his robe as he went. Chris went to his own bedroom, his eyes on the snow-heaped shrubs, the trees, the sweep of white down the slope. A rabbit had made tracks.

"You'll complete your year and a half at the U. and then do your obligation," he said to his son, quietly and firmly. "And then you will come to work at the plant as the chemist you have trained to be."

"The boss's son," growled Nathan.

"You'll work under Felix Lynch, and you'll have to be good to please him. If you do good work, he'll be a big help to you."

"Isn't he out of town?"

"He was to have come back this week end. But what difference . . . ?"

"No difference. Because I don't think you or I should plan on any part of that particular career for me, Dad."

Chris stamped his foot into his boot and came to Nathan's door. "For Pete's sake, why not?"

"My grades at the U. this semester aren't good, Dad. I'm flunking in all the sciences."

15

His father stared. "But—why?"

"I told you. I'm not interested. I haven't been interested. I have not attended lectures nor done the lab work. They are sure to drop me. That's why I said I might as well enlist."

His father stomped back to his own room. "You won't enlist," he said. "Rather than have you do that, I'll take you into my own office where I can keep my eye on you."

"And my girls?"

"And your girls. Really, you had better try again on that score, son. Now get dressed and come out and help me." Chris ran up the coat zipper with a tearing sound. He was, he confessed inwardly, more scared now than angry. That damn boy . . . throwing his future out the window!

"Do you know what Brenda said about you?" Nathan asked as his father went down the hall.

"Let's get outside. Some hard work will clear the air for both of us."

"She said . . ." Nathan's voice was muffled by the sweater he was pulling over his head. "She said she had always wondered what God looked like. After meeting you, she knew."

Chris slammed the garage door behind him. Nathan shrugged and hunted for his heavy gloves.

The Kendricks worked from the gates west along the northern curve of the Lane. Soon, others were out in the snow, and working. A red coat, a yellow stocking cap, Susan Aubuchon's black cocker, dotted the scene. There were shouted greetings, and laughter.

At ten o'clock, Abby Bennett and her dog appeared at the far end of the Lane. She swept the snow from the porch railings and the steps. She used her broom to beat the snow which weighted the branches of the Scotch pines, getting that same snow all over herself. Her Scottie dog leaped and bounded through the whiteness, and Abby chased him.

"She's as cute as a button," decided Malcolm Anderson from the seat of his yellow snowplow. "Whoever she is."

He didn't know; he kept himself somewhat aloof, and he was generally too busy . . . He had thought he knew the Lane people by sight, but this girl in her black and red snowsuit, the bobbing pony tail of dark blonde hair, her gay greeting to the man on the plow . . . She had beautiful eyes, large and dark, a provocative mouth.

He cleared one wheel track of his own drive, turned up along the circle to Bennett's. The old doctor had a yard man, who probably was too old to shovel snow.

"Isn't a plow cheating on the shovel brigade?" the pretty

16

young woman called to him. For all her figure, that beauty was beyond any young girl's prettiness.

"I'm the best cheater in the world," Malcolm called back to her. He swooshed past her, and made a neat turn. Showing off like a ten-year-old, he told himself.

The snow flew behind him, he came back. The Scottie barked fiercely at the yellow monster, and the girl gathered the little dog up into her arms. His pink tongue lolled amiably at Malcolm, who took off his dark glasses and shut off the motor.

"Aren't you new here?" he asked.

"I'm a visitor."

"And they make you shovel snow?"

"I'm not really shoveling. You're Dr. Anderson, aren't you?"

She had seen his name on his mailbox. She had seen him, and his tracks, come away from that house.

He started the machine and swooshed away, back to his own drive, and again to the Lane itself, widening the path, doing the work precisely, clearing a good roadway. He'd get this end cleared, then move down toward Kendrick's. They were hand-shoveling the gate end.

Each time he approached Bennett's, the dog barked, and the girl said things to him. He couldn't hear, really, above the noisy motor. "It's really a lawn mower," he confessed to her, shutting the thing off. "And I'm afraid it's running out of gas."

"Can I get the can, or whatever, for you?"

"I'd have to show you . . . but come along if you like. I'd want the motor to cool before putting the gas in."

"It will do that quickly today." She ran to catch up with him, tucking her mittened hands under her arms to warm them. "Are doctors always so cautious?"

"No, but they should be. And at this early stage I'd hate to blow my little tractor all over the landscape."

"Not to mention the eminent heart surgeon."

He cocked an eyebrow toward her, and raised the garage door, found the red can of gasoline, and came out again.

"Of course I know who you are," she assured him. "I've read about you and the work you do, about your famous team, too."

Malcolm frowned. "That bunch of thugs?" he asked. "Me famous, oh, of course. But those guys!"

She chuckled. "I can see they are a team. I've heard as-

17

tronauts and football players talk the same way about their co-workers."

"You travel in fast company, lady."

She nodded. "I like men," she admitted. "Men who do things."

"Men on teams."

"That's right. So tell me about yours, and the work they do."

"Slavery," said Malcolm tersely. "The last pocket of slave labor in this country."

She began to laugh, then turned to look at him. "You're joking."

"Ask them."

"I'd love to. When can we arrange that?"

"And put me into competition for your interest? Lady, I'm great shakes at this game, but I know enough not to risk that."

"You think I wouldn't recognize them for a bunch of thugs?"

"Women are easily misled."

She was smiling, her cheeks scarlet with the cold.

"How many thugs are there?" she asked.

"Six per working unit. Twenty or twenty-one in all, what with replacements, relief, and so on. I am collecting thugs to train. Hungry interns, mainly. You know, a hungry intern will do anything. That is how I get my slaves in bondage."

"Doctor, I certainly have to know more about these slaves. Are all your team members interns?"

"Oh, no. No! Residents, staff—but I like them to begin training as interns. They are hungrier then, ready to learn; they have to stand still when told."

"I can't believe you are very fierce."

"I am fierce. Now, may I fill my gas tank?"

He filled the tractor's tank; he drove away from her, and returned. He showed her how to use a small shovel and help him make the road edge neat. And they talked. She knew, she said, a great deal about the work he did, and where he did it. She called him a pioneer.

He laughed at her.

"Yes, you are," she said earnestly. "You have a pioneer's instinct to do something no one else has done."

That was not entirely true, he said. Hundreds of brave surgeons had paved the way for him. The first man to open the chest, to remove a lung, to touch his knife point to the forbidden territory of the heart . . .

She knew, she said, about those men. Of course she did!

She asked again about his team, and he told her of the units he trained to go out and do his work.

"Myocardial revascularization," she said carefully.

He chuckled. "What big words Grandma uses! What else do you know?"

"Not enough," she admitted ruefully. "But I am interested. Especially in the human side of the work you do. You and your team."

He used a larger shovel, and his breath came frosty white as he wielded it.

"You're a strong man."

"A surgeon has to be."

"Does he? Why?"

"Have you ever cut through the human rib cage?"

"Certainly not!"

He laughed, mounted the tractor again, calling back that he'd clear the road . . . Kendrick's . . .

She watched him. She shoveled a little, and watched him. He went away, came back, and went away again.

After an hour of this hard work in the cold, she signaled him to stop. "I think you've earned a break," she called.

He turned off the motor and stepped down. He looked back at what his plow had done. "Your dog gave up quite a while ago," he conceded. "I can make you a quick cup of coffee in my kitchen."

"*I* can give you a well-perked one, and an open fire," she offered.

"Sounds better, but if you're visiting . . ."

"In my parents' home." She smiled at him over her shoulder, and led the way, her bright curl of hair bobbing.

He was too surprised to protest, to do anything but follow her along the drive to the Bennett front porch. He had not known that the Bennetts had a child, a daughter. He wouldn't have suspected it, either. This girl—this young woman— pretty, clever—He'd been had.

But, no, he had not. She had never claimed anything but what she was. A daughter visiting her parents. He should have known his neighbors better.

Of course he knew Dr. Bennett. As one doctor knows another. As the Chief of Thoracic and Cardiovascular Surgery knew the referral doctors. Bennett was on the staff, listed as a cardiologist. Exceptions were made for his age, and his peculiarities.

Mac stamped the snow from his boot soles. "I can't take this mess into a proper home," he told Miss Bennett.

"It will be fine. Come in." She opened the storm door and the inner door. A fire did indeed burn upon the hearth of the long and pleasantly outmoded living room. From the hall he had a quick image of red couch, Oriental rug, deep armchairs, all a bit faded and very comfortable.

"There's a powder room in here," said Abby quickly.

Quickly she left him, and was waiting for him beside the fire when he came out. She wore a sweater and her ski pants, but she had taken off the boots. Her hair was smooth and shining, the thick curl hanging over one shoulder.

There was a silver pot of coffee, a silver plate of small, nut-crusted buns, thin china cups. The chair was blissfully comfortable.

Dr. Anderson sank into its cushions and stretched his legs before him. "I've earned a half hour," he conceded. "Your parents . . . ?"

"Mother is cooking a huge dinner because I am home. She has her kitchen to herself on Sunday. Dad is in the basement painting yard furniture. He can get paint on his hands on Sunday."

"Yard furniture *today?*" asked Malcolm, smiling.

"He's a man to keep a list of chores ahead."

Yes, he would be. Bennett was a bustling little man, devoted to detail.

"This is very nice," he said, eating his second bun. They were delicious. "We don't get stuff like this at the hospital."

"Do you eat at the hospital?"

"Oh, I cook things at home. A steak—instant coffee—fruit. I don't have a cook, just a woman who comes in three times a week and tidies me."

"You are a lonely man," Abby decided.

"How could I be lonely with the work I do?"

"I can answer that when I know more about the work you do."

And to his own surprise—amazement, really—he did talk some about the work he did. He admitted to a humanitarian desire to do "something about one of the somewhat neglected fields of medicine."

Yes, myocardial revascularization was a fairly new field. He disclaimed individual credit. But the department of cardiovascular surgery at the Clinic did aim to reduce the toll of coronary artery disease.

"Half a million Americans die of it each year, six or ten

times that many are incapacitated—and there probably are twenty-five million people who have symptoms." His voice rang with earnestness.

"And what you do . . ."

He laughed.

"But you do help those people!"

"Well, yes. And what we do, simply stated, is to bring more blood into their hearts."

"You do that!" Her voice, her wide eyes were awed.

"Not for all those millions," he disclaimed. "Actually, very few patients have direct lesions which would lead them to undergo direct coronary artery surgery. Few, in a relative sense, you understand."

"But those others . . ."

"There are ways to help them."

"And you do help them?"

"Well, actually—" He shifted in the chair. "The selective coronary arteriogram led the way, you know. We figured out at least three techniques to use. The implants I've worked on are one of the three. And now—we talked about teams, remember?"

She nodded. She was leaning toward him, her hands clasped between her knees.

"Now my work— Our dream is to make this surgery feasible for every qualified team in the country. The procedure must be standardized. Each operation cannot be an adventure. You are not doing the patient any service if it is. You know, dramatics, suspense, miraculous accomplishment."

"And you train teams."

"Not really. I train my own teams. I demonstrate, and work with other men who will eventually form and train their own teams. The implant technique has the greatest application, and if we can train other units to perform some sort of internal mammary procedure . . . It is very successful, you know."

"How successful?"

"In my case, ninety-five per cent."

"But that is miraculous!"

He shook his head. "Reasonable. The result of careful selection and procedure. Which can be taught and learned."

She smiled at him. "You make it sound easy, but I know, from being my father's daughter, the work, the study, the dedication it takes."

Malcolm leaned forward to put his cup on the low table.

"Of course, my father . . ." said Abby gently, smiling into

21

the fire. "He was almost fifty when I was born. Did you know that?"

"I didn't know you had been born at all. I'm new on the Lane. Though of course I know Dr. Bennett."

She nodded. "He's old now, but he keeps going. Did you know it was only ten or twelve years ago that he decided to become a heart specialist? And the way that man studied! I was in school, then college, and I could appreciate the studying he did. At his age! But it didn't hurt him. In fact, I am sure it revived him. Don't you think it was a wonderful thing to do?"

Now this would take a direct answer. "We badly need G.P.'s," Malcolm said thoughtfully. "They have to have a much wider spectrum of information than the single-specialty guys require. They are important, because they get the patient first."

Saying these routine things, he was thinking: "I won't let old Bennett work on my team. How did I ever let myself in for this cozy twosome? It is embarrassing enough to live on the Lane with the old man, whom I can expect to retire, and Rupert Aubuchon, who won't do anything of the sort!"

He drew his boots toward his chair, ready to stand up. "This has been very nice," he said. "I am really surprised at your interest in my profession."

She laughed. "Oh, I plan to put everything you've told me to good use in my next article."

He chuckled and started toward the hall where he had left his outer wraps.

"I'm going to write that article, you know," she told him.

He glanced down at her. "About the stuff I've said this morning? It wouldn't cover a page."

"You stick to your profession, doctor. I'll stick to mine."

His eyebrows went up; he wrapped his scarf around his throat.

"I've material enough," she told him pertly, "to write a very comprehensive article. Even if I never saw or talked to you again. Which of course must not happen."

He smiled. "Are you staying long?"

She stamped her foot, and the thick curl bounced up and down. "Don't be polite to me, Dr. Anderson!"

"Oh? Why not?"

"Because we know each other too well for small talk."

He picked up his gloves.

"I know it's been a matter of hours only," she conceded,

22

walking with him toward the front door. "But we did get a lot of talking done."

"Yes, we did. About me."

She shrugged.

"Are you actually a writer?" he asked.

"I am, and I do have enough material to do an article about you."

He laughed. "Me, perhaps. I'm a simple man. But my work . . . Why, even if you faked it, you could not possibly give a creditable account of that field."

"Do you mind if I try?"

He shrugged. "I couldn't stop you. And I'll want to see the results. Thank you for a most interesting morning. I find you a charming combination of brains and beauty."

She smiled and extended her hand. "It's been delightful."

She watched him stride across the porch, down the steps, out to his little yellow tractor and snowplow. The morning, she told herself, had indeed been delightful. She was entranced by that man, not only by his physical strength and attractiveness, but by his intellectual naïveté. He said, and really thought, that his medical teams did the work which so interested him. Abby believed it to be a matter of his own calm confidence in his work, and his warmly kind devotion. She would so slant her article.

She went back to the fireside, set the screen in place, gathered things tidily upon the tray, and realized that she was smiling. It was amazing, of course, and, yes, amusing, but she really liked that man. Malcolm Anderson, M.D.

As she passed the window she saw his tractor, in a cloud of snow, pushing its way down the Lane. She went on to the kitchen.

"Has your young man gone?" asked her father from where he sat at the table before the windows, drinking a cup of coffee and eating one of the buns.

Her mother turned from the stove to smile at her daughter. It was good to have that daughter at home, and to have her entertaining boys—men—in the living room.

"My young man, as you call him," said Abby, emptying the silver coffeepot, "is out shoveling snow again. Your neighbors make quite a lark of that job."

"Are you going out again?" asked her mother.

"I may, later. Just now I have some notes to work on—if you don't mind."

"Of course we don't mind. We hope that you can and will

23

do your work here at home. We wouldn't ever interrupt you, dear."

"I found Dr. Anderson quite interesting," said Abby.

"He's a smart young man," her father conceded. Dr. Bennett was as small, and as quick of movement, as one of the chickadees busy on the feeder tray outside the window. "I am going to have to give in and work with him one of these days, I suspect."

"Are you a surgeon, too, Dad?" Abby asked, not turning from the sink where she was washing silver.

"Any doctor worth his salt is a surgeon as well as physician," said her father. "We are trained to be. Didn't you know that?"

"No. But I'm learning," said his daughter. She went out of the kitchen and up the stairs, still pleased with her morning. Her encounter with Dr. Anderson had given her a lift; the future possibilities were many, and exciting to contemplate.

It was noon exactly when Felix Lynch entered the Lane, shouting at the Kendricks, and driving carefully on the snow which still remained on the roadway. He was bringing his bride home.

"I thought he was coming last night . . ." murmured Chris.

"We didn't have the road shoveled for him," Nathan pointed out. "Is that chick with him . . . ?"

"I hope she's the bride," said his father gruffly. "In fact, I know she's the bride. She worked at the plant."

"Doin' what?"

His father growled something about impudence and chicks. But he, too, was disappointed in the girl whom Felix had chosen. He didn't know her. She was young. Nineteen. Girls with long, straight blonde hair, knowing eyes, and trap-tight mouths were not to his taste. But after all, Felix was a grown man.

Old enough—thirty, or even thirty-one. A good biochemist. Making good money. He had bought this house for his mother, but it was big enough—bedrooms upstairs as well as the master suite downstairs which Alma occupied—and Chris would bet she would continue to occupy. Alma would be a match for any chick!

Now there was a rare combination. Felix's Italian mother and his Irish father, dead now for twenty years. But he had bequeathed his son his height, his straight back, and probably his handsome, cleft-chin face. The dark eyes, the dark hair were Alma's. His— Well, yes, he was a rare combination.

24

Chris looked along the Lane. Felix had stopped his car at the front path of his home. He would have to shovel out his own drive. Now the chick—the bride—was out on the snow, as slender as a bread stick, her long hair blowing; she wore shiny boots up to her knees. Her coat was of black fur, and short. She was looking up at the house—red brick, spreading its wings, white shutters at the windows, a gracious white doorway.

"Ritsy," she confirmed.

Felix smiled at her, and carried two bags up to the door; he opened it, shouted "Hey, Mamma!" into the house, and came back. "You're beautiful," he told his bride, who smiled at him. She was looking out at the Lane and at the big, white-painted brick Kimberlin home down the slope of the hill. At Aubuchon's red brick to the east, then across to the Kendrick redwood ranch house, where a cute guy was shoveling snow in the drive. . . .

"Do you know all these people?" she asked, her voice high and childlike.

"They are friends. You know Mr. Kendrick."

"The boss. Oh, yes, sure I know him!"

"There are a couple of doctors live here. No, three."

"Brains," said Esther breathlessly. "I don't have brains, Felix."

"Who needs brains with your looks? Come on inside. Mamma will be waiting."

Mamma was waiting, with a large cloth to wipe up the snow they tracked in. "You got to shovel the drive," she told her son, submitting to his embrace.

She was a small woman, round, dark hair drawn back into a bun at the back of her head.

"Mamma, you remember Esther," said Felix, smiling down at his women.

Alma wiped her hand on her large apron, and held it out to her new daughter-in-law. "Esther," she said.

Esther managed a thin-lipped smile. Straight from the old country, she was telling herself. But this house . . . She turned about. The wide center hall, the stairway curving upward, the wallpaper, or maybe it was a painting of trees and clouds and little white houses. The big living room with wide, wide windows, the shuttered doors of the hall closet where Felix was hanging his coat. It was really a beautiful house. Like in the movies, or on TV.

"It's a swell house," she told her mother-in-law.

Alma shrugged. "Too big, too fancy. Too much money."

25

"Oh, but, Felix . . ."

"He spend too much money. That fancy decorating woman—such wallpaper, such carpets and glass chandeliers—they make work, work, work, You'll see."

Esther was examining the large religious painting which was hung, squarely, on the wall which faced the front door. A woman with a blue scarf, and a large, red, exposed heart. Had the expensive decorator chosen that? She smiled. No more than anyone but Felix's mother had prepared the food which was wafting its rich scents through the warm house. Tomato sauce, garlic, cheese.

Well, Esther liked Italian food. In moderation. But there was no need to pollute the air!

Felix brought in the last bag, and said he must get cracking.

What was *cracking?* asked his mother.

He replied in Italian, and evidently asked something about their room. "Upstairs," Alma said, pointing. "All upstairs yours now. I stay down, kitchen, washing machine—all down."

Felix smiled at her and hugged her. "You two girls will work things out."

Work, he heard Alma say below her breath.

Well, they would adjust. There were two pleasant bedrooms upstairs, a bath tiled in sunny yellow. He'd been more than comfortable up there. Esther would be. She would have a means of privacy apart from his bustling mother, should she ever want that.

He carried the bags up, Esther following him, but saying little.

Felix began to change clothes, and she asked him what he was doing.

"I can't shovel in my wedding suit," he pointed out.

"Are you going to shovel snow?"

"Sure I am. Clear my drive and walks, help on the road."

"There's a man out there with a plow, clearing your drive."

Felix plunged for the window, leaned out, yelled, grabbed a sweater and raced for the stairs. He threw open the front door. "Hey, *paisano!*" he shouted to Malcolm, who had run the tractor around Felix's car, and was busy on the rest of the drive.

"Come move your car," the doctor shouted to Felix.

"I'll get my boots."

He did get them, out of the hall closet. He went outside,

26

his dark hair blowing. Upstairs, Esther knelt on the window seat, watching. That was a good-looking guy on the tractor. From the way he'd pounded her new husband, they must be friends. Men being that way.

She opened her larger bag. Should she put on slacks, go out, too?

She shook her head. Felix would bring his friend in. She would make sure that her face was in order.

Felix did bring Malcolm in, though not really. The garage door was opened, and the little tractor roared in to turn and go out again. Alma was in the basement, and greeted him. Evidently she was fond of him; they yelled at each other, and laughed. The strange man mentioned the smells. "You could eat?" offered her mother-in-law.

He said something about goofing off. "But don't throw any of it out," he told Alma. "I'll bring a bucket."

There was laughter, and evidently Mamma Lynch was in the habit of sending a "bucket" of ravioli or chicken over to the doctor.

The *doctor?* thought Esther.

"He should get married," came Felix's voice, above the scrape of his shovel on the driveway. Esther had moved to the kitchen door which opened to the stairs down into the garage.

"Not the way you did!" said Alma, with feeling.

Well, that came as no surprise. Alma had just barely attended the wedding; she had terms for the bride which, not translated, plainly showed her feeling.

"You don't think it is good things, doctor?" she now challenged the tractor-riding doctor.

"Well . . ." said the man's voice. "I hope she proves to be the right wife for Felix, Alma. That son of yours can go far, and at his stage, the right wife would mean everything."

So he disapproved, too. Well, Esther could take that, or, even, do something about it. Before now, she had made men aware of her charms.

Alma was talking. This Esther, she said, was not the right wife for Felix! She mentioned her youth, her hair—every which way! She talked—Alma imitated Esther's high, childish voice. Her dress was too tight, she said, her heels too high. *Aghhh!*

The doctor laughed deeply, warmly. "You'll get to know her, Alma. Give her a chance."

Alma was most dubious. The right wife, yes. A man

needed a wife. Oh, yes, she would be good. He was a grown man, and he was the head of his house. That was right. His women, his wife and his mother—they had to learn to get along and do what Felix would wish.

Ha! said Esther, going back to the front of the house.

Felix came dashing in for gloves and a knitted cap. He kissed Esther. Wouldn't she come out, too? It was fun. Everyone got to know each other.

She would not go out, and he left again, ecstatic. As he had been ecstatic throughout the honeymoon. He at least approved of his bride. So what else mattered? Esther stood at the front window and watched him join the snow shovelers, laughing, talking—calling out. Having the time of his life, evidently. He and the blond young man across the circle were even throwing snowballs at each other.

Esther went upstairs and explored the two large bedrooms, the closets under the sloping roof, the pretty bath. She could make out very nicely up there, but she still planned to have a look at the downstairs quarters of her mother-in-law. If they were nicer, if Felix and his wife should have priority, she was ready for a fight, anytime, and with anyone.

She began to unpack, and to arrange her belongings. She was still busy with her cosmetics at the dressing table when she heard men's voices in the front hall. She went out, leaned over the railing, could not see, so she crept down, one carpeted stair, two . . .

Felix was there; she was looking directly down upon his thick black hair. And with him, wearing a light gray hat, was a small man—Esther could not see his face, and she dared go no farther down. With that open, wrought-iron railing, one of the men surely would see her. She tucked her bare feet under the folds of her housecoat and listened.

The man visiting was really small; he came only to Felix's shoulder. His overcoat nipped in at the waist. He wore light-colored gloves; she could see them as he talked and gestured.

He certainly did wear fancy clothes out into the snow; probably he had a car out in the roadway; she could look out and see. Just now she wanted to listen. The man was talking very fast, and in Italian, she supposed. Anyway, she heard Felix tell him to speak English. He did, after a fashion, but Esther couldn't, even then, make out much of what he said. He did seem to be calling Felix *Don*, and that was strange. Felix was telling him that he should not have come "out here." And *that* was strange!

"Not good!" pronounced Alma, the minute the front door

28

had closed on the fellow. She had a very bad opinion of Felix's caller, and the way he talked. "You no *Don!* You Mr. Lynch!"

"Oh, Mamma," said her son, going into the room at the other side of the hall. Like the coat closet, it too had shuttered doors. Esther gathered her full skirts about her, ran down the stairs, and followed Felix. She looked in surprise at the room. The walls were lined with bookshelves, there was a fireplace and deep leather chairs.

"What's all this?" she asked.

"My office, or study," said Felix, going to the desk and sitting down. He laid his cap and gloves to one side.

"It's nice," said Esther.

"Yes, it is." He was writing something. "You can use it, though don't bother things here in my desk."

"Who was that man?" she asked. She picked up a paperweight, put it down.

Felix was preoccupied and did not answer her. After a few minutes, she asked again.

Felix lifted his hands. "He was nobody, Esther. Just a guy."

"Your mother was upset."

"It doesn't take much to upset Mamma."

"But—"

He closed the book in which he had been writing and returned it to the desk drawer. He stood up and came to her. "Your feet will get cold."

The floor was of wood, set into a pattern, crisscross, forming squares. There was no carpet. "Don't bother about my feet," Esther bade him. "Tell me about your guy."

"He was just a guy, sweetheart."

"A foreigner."

"Well, a foreigner, yes. But I often help these fellows with their citizenship papers, you know, or sometimes I write letters for them when they are not too sure of their English. Things like that. See?"

"Would this fellow come clear out here—in the snow—Where does he live, Felix? In the neighborhood?"

He put on his cap and came toward her. He tweaked her nose. "Questions, questions."

"He looked like a gangster," Esther told him. "Is he one?"

Felix kissed her cheek. "No more than I am," he told her. He went outside again, and Esther decided she might as well go upstairs.

In the last house on their side of the Lane, Dr. Aubuchon and his bride of six months did not arise until noon. Sunday mornings were luxurious privileges to doctors and schoolteachers, said Susan, coming back from letting Mandy, her cocker spaniel, out into the snow. "She looks like an ink blot," she told him.

Her husband stretched his arms and grunted amiably.

"Everyone else is out shoveling snow," Susan told him.

"Without breakfast?"

"Perhaps they got up earlier."

"They don't have my privileges."

Susan flushed and laughed. She came back and bent over the bed to kiss her husband, with whom she was very much in love.

He pulled her close, and she reveled in the scrape of his rough cheek, the desire in his eyes, the strength of his arms.

"Get up, lazybones," she told him. "I'll make coffee."

"If I shovel, you shovel."

"All right," she agreed, "but I'll still need coffee."

She wanted to shovel, if that was what Rupert wanted her to do. She connected the percolator and came back. Her husband was in the bathroom, and she found stretch pants and a pullover for herself. This with her red coat, galoshes, a cap, would do. She had never done a lot of snow shoveling. For Rupert, there were corduroy trousers—he'd worn them when he'd gone duck hunting. A heavy sweater, dark blue, and his fleece-lined short coat. He would not wear any sort of head covering. He was a big man, with a sun-browned skin, and thick hair which could get wild on his head. He had a smile. . . .

Smiling herself, Susan dressed. It was wonderful to have such a husband, masculine, big, sometimes as rough as his cheek. It was wonderful to be a woman, and, in her turn, precious to such a man. Rupert teased her about being a late bloomer, but Susan was glad that she had waited to find just this man, to learn all about love from him.

Mandy came in, shaking snow from her feathered paws, ravenous for attention and for food. Susan went to the kitchen and put a coffee cake into the oven to warm, poured orange juice and coffee. By the time Rupert came out, breakfast was ready. "We can take fifteen minutes," she told him. "I'll clear up after we've finished shoveling."

"Did Mandy say the snow was wet?"

"She did. And the cold air made her hungry. She's going to put both of us in the poorhouse with her appetite."

It was foolish talk, and precious. Married only six months, they had done a lot of foolish talking.

"I think," Susan said now, gazing out of the window at the snowy slope behind their house, "that we could have a trellis sometime, but at first I believe just a rose bed will do. A round rose bed. And a sundial, Rupert. A really nice one, on a column. I'd want the sundial bronze, but the pedestal could be iron—or maybe marble. Are they called plinths?"

Her husband chuckled, ate the piece of coffee cake in his hand, and reached for the telephone. He was calling the hospital. "On that snowy landscape we call our backyard," he told his bride, "I'd call any kind of sundial and rose garden an impossible dream." He spoke briskly into the telephone, getting the night's report on his patients. He was a very busy doctor, a popular one. Even the nurses must like him, the way he was polite, and joking, too.

Susan put a fresh piece of coffee cake on his plate, and filled his coffee cup.

When he set the phone aside, she was still thinking about, and talking about, garden vistas and something she called an axis of interest. And Rupert again laughed at her, assuring her that she could have any vistas and axises she wanted. "Or is it axes, my pretty schoolteacher wife?"

She flushed. She was a schoolteacher. Dean at an exclusive girls' school, the Institute, and she was proud of having achieved that post.

"We should go out ..." she murmured. "At least shovel our own drive."

"We're going," Rupert told her, going back to their bedroom.

He put on the coat but did not button it. No doubt he would be warm enough, for he had a white turtle-neck sweater under the heavy blue one. He was careful to pull on thick gloves. He nodded approvingly at Susan's white helmet cap and her fleecy red coat. "You take the big shovel," he told her.

She laughed and followed him. They had trouble getting the garage door open. In twenty-four hours the snow had drifted and packed against it. But Rupert was strong and helped the electric motor.

Their arrival outside was greeted with shouts—from Felix Lynch next door, and the Kendricks from across the circle, and Malcolm Anderson on his tractor. Dr. Bennett's daughter was out, using a shovel, but Susan thought she could do better.

Someone chided the Aubuchons for being late. "Wouldn't you be?" shouted Rupert in retort. Susan blushed prettily, as Abby Bennett pointed out.

They shoveled, they exchanged insults. Felix was ribbed unmercifully and asked about *his* bride. Hadn't he married a girl able to shovel snow? What kind of wife did that make?

Felix said he could tell them, but would not.

The snow was shoveled, the red coat, the yellow cap, the tractor and the two black dogs made pretty pictures. Abby Bennett engaged Rupert in a five-minute conversation. They were absorbed.

"They are talking business," Felix assured Susan. "I don't know just *what* business, but it must be important. Don't be jealous."

Susan laughed up at him. "I'm not," she assured him. "I am glad that other women—particularly ones like Abby—admire Rupert. And that he likes other women. You see, that makes it more important that he married *me!*"

Felix leaned on his shovel and pursed his lips, considering this. "He did, didn't he?" he asked thoughtfully. "Are you easily managing a career and a home?"

She laughed. "Not easily," she admitted. "I forget things in both spheres, thinking about the other. But that will straighten itself out, because I am planning to quit the job at the Institute at term end."

"What was that you said?" asked Rupert, coming up behind them.

She turned. "That I'm going to stop being a schoolteacher," she repeated.

"But that's nonsense, funny face. You'll miss your work too much."

"No, I shan't," Susan assured him. "I plan to keep myself very busy at my new job of being a wife."

"And mother?" he teased.

Now her cheeks were as red as her coat. "I hope so," she said staunchly. "I certainly hope so."

She wanted to say something to him about surprising him with her announcement, but the tractor was coming along the road again and Rupert ran out to intercept it. Dr. Anderson stopped and leaned down to hear what he had to say. He was suggesting that they clear the Kimberlin drive. "If they are depending on Lionel, they'll be snowed in until July. You know Lester Elis isn't able."

He talked Anderson into it, and Rupert found a foothold somewhere and went off with the tractor. And the plow. Ten minutes later Felix reported that Aubuchon was driving the thing, with Mac operating the hand shovel. "That's nice work," he assured Rupert's wife.

Susan quoted him when she and Rupert were back in the house, shedding their wet boots and coats and gloves.

"I know where my bread is buttered," Rupert answered her.

Susan turned back to look at him in surprise. "What does that mean?" she asked.

"Just what I said. Anderson is a great man. He can do things for me."

Susan frowned. "Is he, really? That great?"

Rupert laughed. "They don't come bigger in his field."

Susan knew that Anderson was a heart surgeon. "He seems so young," she said. "No older than you are, Rupert."

Her husband pulled his sweater over his head. "As a matter of fact," he said, "he is a bit younger. That's part of my trouble."

"Trouble?" asked Susan.

"Of a sort. It means that I didn't train under him, or with him."

"But don't you work with him now?"

Rupert laughed. "It's a complicated field, sweetheart. Medicine."

"I'd like to understand."

"You'd better stick to cleaning girls and cooking my dinner."

"Don't talk that way to me, Rupert," she said crisply. "Surely I am intelligent enough to understand a few basic facts. I know the medical field is complicated—but I also know that you work at the same Medical Center where Dr. Anderson does."

"Wait a minute, sweetheart." He was getting shoes out of his closet.

"You are both heart specialists."

"But not exactly in the same way. I maintain a private practice with attending and staff service at the Medical Center. Dr. Anderson is a heart surgeon, and is Chief of the Department of Thoracic and Cardiovascular Surgery at the Center. He is a very big wheel. He has developed techniques— that means surgical procedures, my darling—that have made him an authority on such surgery. People come to him from all over, as consultant doctors, and as patients. Right now he has a man—came in about Christmas—he wants, and probably needs, revascularization. But he is waiting, and will wait,

33

for Anderson to say the surgery is feasible, and that he and his team will do the job. That poor guy has been everywhere—Rochester, St. Louis, Houston. He's sold his business, and his wife is living here while they wait for the nod of this man. Sure, Anderson is big, and I wait for his nod, too. I'd give my back teeth to work with him."

"On his team? Whatever that means."

"It means a lot, sweetie. You see, when you go into the chest, when you undertake to handle the heart, lift it, turn it, cut away one of the vessels—artery or vein—you need a half-dozen people standing by to see that the patient gets air, that his blood circulates around the heart, that he doesn't go into spasm or shock. Also, the surgeon himself needs assistant surgeons, one of them at least smart enough to take over and continue should the Chief have a stomach ache, his own heart attack, or just plain get tired. These sessions can last for hours."

"Is Dr. Anderson the only surgeon who does his—what is it?—technique?"

"Revascularization? No. He has taught others, and is training people for his team all the time. He says he wants the technique to be known and practiced wherever it is needed, and it is needed in a lot of places."

Susan brushed her hair and studied herself in the mirror. She had changed into one of the "housedresses" she liked to wear when functioning as a wife and homemaker. This one was pink, and pretty. "As a surgeon yourself—in the same hospital center," she said thoughtfully, "I should think you would automatically work with another surgeon on the staff."

"But that doesn't follow, dear. I told you the subject was complicated. In a way, I do work with Anderson. He has the go-ahead-stop say on any surgical work I do at the Center. As Chief, you see. But as for working *with* him, on his team, he likes to train his own men, in diagnosis, surgical procedures, and research into future procedures. He takes a young doctor who thinks he wants to be a surgeon, a heart surgeon, and he hand-trains him in those things. I didn't come up through residencies on his service. I am not one of his 'slaves,' as the term goes at the Center."

"But couldn't you be? If that is what you want. You're not so old that . . ."

"I am already trained, and he knows that I am available. But so far I have not been given a union card to the closed shop which Anderson runs in his o.r."

Susan tied her dark hair back with a pink and gold striped

34

scarf and went out to the kitchen to clear away their breakfast dishes and to begin her preparations for dinner, still
several hours away. She was, she acknowledged, a "slow
cook."

Rupert urged her not to fuss. He was content with a steak
quickly broiled, or even hamburgers. They could always eat
out.

But Susan wanted to do the whole thing; she wanted to
feed her family properly, and a Sunday roast was part of the
program.

Rupert brought the Sunday newspaper and a bottle of beer
out to the breakfast table to watch her and to be companion-
able. She was still thinking about Dr. Anderson and her husband. She liked to get a subject neatly researched, the notes
in order, before she pigeonholed the matter for future refer-
ence.

"If Dr. Anderson's project is, as you claim, developmen-
tal," she worried, "couldn't he train a capable and mature
surgeon to go on with his work and be ready not only to help
here at the Center, but to go to other medical centers and
train teams? You say the need is great."

"For surgery, yes, it is great. There are vistas opening wide
for coronary surgery."

"Then couldn't he train you, both in diagnosis and procedures?"

Rupert pursed his lips and poured beer into the tall glass.

"Why don't you ask him?" Susan persisted. "Maybe he
doesn't think you would be interested, that you are too busy.
He must know that you have a big practice."

Anderson knew all that he needed to know about Rupert
Aubuchon. "Why don't *you* ask him?" demanded Susan's husband, a little testily.

She laughed and patted the rib roast she had put on the
rack. "I don't believe Dr. Anderson is a woman's man," she
said.

"Nonsense. All men are women's men. He probably ad-
mires you very much."

"I believe every word you say," Susan retorted. "But I still
think my appeal would be a strange basis for your medical
advancement."

"Ah-huh," said Rupert, his interest held to the sports page.
"Strange."

"I don't see how you could take on any more work," said
Susan, "but if this is something you want, I hope you will still
try to achieve it."

35

"I will," Rupert promised readily. "Sure, I will. There are lots of angles to play, you know."

By midafternoon, the snow was cleared. Cars were going out of the Lane and coming in. The Lynches had callers. Dr. Aubuchon's low, sporty car went out and returned. Nathan Kendrick went somewhere. It was still very cold, and the snow squeaked under a man's feet. However, with the sun against the roofs, enough melting had taken place to produce a curtain of icicles before Christopher Kendrick's front door. Seeing them when he came out of the house, he went into the garage for a shovel, and sent them flying, tinkling across the lawn.

"If I were ten," he said, half aloud, "I'd suck one of them."

His hands in the pockets of his fleece-lined coat, a plaid muffler at his throat, his head bare, he crunched up the road to the Kimberlin house.

This big house, of white painted brick, seemed to sink into the contour of the hill and the ravine behind it. Large deciduous trees and dark evergreens embraced it. It was a gracious home; its long windows and wide doors spoke of hospitality. In its time, parties were frequent here, with carriages, and later, cars, lined all the way up to the gates at the main road. In those days wide lawns had stretched where the new houses were built, and the stone gateposts had borne bronze plates which read "Kimberlin."

The house was old, the family was old. But the family had made its money through hard work, and the fortune had been amassed and dispersed for the good of the city. Hospital, park, youth center, many such establishments could bear the nameplate "Kimberlin," though few did. The Kimberlin diagnostic center at the Medical Center, a graceful fountain in the children's zoo, were all that carried the name.

Arthur Kimberlin, his father, and grandfather, were proud of the name but refused to exploit it. They had kept their industries abreast of the times, their chemicals and drugs had gone from the old basics—quinine to antibiotics, celluloid to the acrylic resins. Their research was widespread. Yet Arthur Kimberlin, by his fireside, could see his plant manager coming along the blue-shadowed snow, and say to his granddaughter, "Here comes the Chief of the Vinegar Works."

She smiled at him, and went herself to open the front door.

"I am Margaret Elis," she told Chris. "Grandfather saw you coming."

He kicked at the snow on his boots. "I should have gone to the back door," he apologized. "I'm a hazard to carpet and floors."

"Come in anyway."

"I'm Chris Kendrick," he said. "How is Mr. Kimberlin?"

"He's all right. Impatient about watching you younger men at play out in the snow."

"It got pretty heavy play before we finished. My shoulders will tell me so tomorrow."

Arthur Kimberlin was on his feet, hand outstretched to greet Chris warmly, and point to the chair which faced his own across the hearth. His skin was brown from a Christmas holiday in Florida, his handclasp was firm. His white hair was vigorous, and his eyes clear. There were a few telltale signs; Arthur Kimberlin was not a well man, and not anywhere nearly as healthy as he looked. His one capitulation had been to bring his granddaughter home to live with him, to "look after me, Chris. I decided that one thing I had been missing was a woman to fuss over me."

"It must be nice, sir," said Chris, sitting down as directed. Margaret still stood behind her grandfather's chair. She was a handsome woman who looked every inch a Kimberlin. Her dark hair was drawn into a smooth knot, her eyes were beautiful, dark ones. She knew how to dress. Chris admired the tailored dark dress she wore, with a soft white scarf filling its throat.

She's a real lady, he decided.

"Lester?" she said now, her gaze going beyond Chris's head toward the far door.

Chris turned, then got again to his feet.

"This is my husband Lester," said Margaret of the slender man who was advancing. He walked with difficulty and used a cane. He looked ill.

Chris shook hands with him, said something pleasant, and resumed his chair. Lester Elis chose to sit at the far side of the room. Margaret sat on a hassock beside her grandafther.

She suggested a drink. Or coffee? Tea, perhaps?

"Nothing for now, thank you," Chris said, feeling big, rough, and very healthy against this Elis. What ailed the man?

Chris turned to Mr. Kimberlin. "I came here on a personal matter, sir," he said. "I wanted to discuss with you the propriety of hunting for a job for Nathan. A job in the company."

Mr. Kimberlin pursed his lips. "Has Nathan finished at the University?" he asked.

"No, he hasn't, sir. He—" He turned to smile at Margaret, the small, neat, and lovely. "Nathan is my son," he explained. "Not quite twenty. I thought I was doing a fair job of raising him."

"How old was Nathan . . . ?" asked Mr. Kimberlin.

"He was seven when his mother died."

"You have done a good job with the boy."

"I'm afraid not, sir. He was planning on chemistry, and coming into the company. But he tells me he's dropping out of school now."

"He wants to do something relevant," said Lester Elis from across the room.

Chris turned to look at him. "He's decided that the University has nothing to teach him."

"What about military service?" Arthur Kimberlin asked.

"He's vulnerable, of course. Any job at the company would not be long-term, I'm pretty sure."

"Find him something," Mr. Kimberlin decided. "He's a good, strong boy. Six months of hard work in the shipping department may change his viewpoint."

"I hope so. He has agreed to stay at home."

"That's something," breathed Margaret.

"It helps me, at any rate," Chris agreed. "Do you have children, Mrs. Elis?"

"I'm sorry, no. And will you call me Margaret? I am going to live here now, and my feeling here is very young. I used to visit here, you know, when I was a child."

"That can't be long ago," Chris assured her. "And I'm glad you are going to be on the Lane. It strikes me there are several new, and young, women on our Lane these days. Susan Aubuchon. She comes with the new house, of course, but she's a recent bride, as well. Married about six months, I think. She's a dandy."

"And then there is Felix Lynch's bride," said Mr. Kimberlin. "They must be home."

"They are, but I haven't more than seen her as she got out of the car this morning. She is *really* young. She wears long, black, shiny boots. Blonde hair . . . Somehow I don't think she is what we might have expected from Felix."

"She isn't Alma's type, certainly," said Arthur Kimberlin dryly. "Felix's mother is quite upset. She said they didn't have a proper wedding. It took my persuasion as well as the boy's to make her attend the ceremony."

"I do love Alma," said Margaret softly.

"She's a great old girl," Chris agreed.

"For years she took good care of Dad and this house. I hope I can do half as well."

"You'll do what I want of you," said her grandfather. "Make this a home, and be company for me."

"Yes, sir," said Margaret meekly.

"And then there is Abby Bennett," Chris resumed briskly. "She seems to be here for an extended visit."

"Oh, but she's not new," Margaret protested. "She grew up here!"

"She did, indeed, and then she left."

"To go to school, college, to work. But I hope she will be around for a time. Her parents must be glad to have her."

"She's a writer, you know," Mr. Kimberlin said.

"Yes, I do know. She does clever books on things women don't usually write about. Lester had one she did on a football hero. I believe there was one about a safari she took. I'm going to go see her. She's younger than I am, of course."

"Not much," said her grandfather.

"Yes, she is. When I was twelve she was only nine, or ten. That's a big gap."

"When you're twelve and nine. But now . . ."

"Now it may be as much as ten years," drawled Lester.

Chris didn't like the way he said it, but Margaret laughed. "It well could be," she agreed. "But I know why she came back here to the Lane." She clasped her hands around one knee and gazed into the fire. Chris decided that he liked this young woman. That he liked her very much.

"Whenever I came here," she was saying, "when I came here last week, knowing that I probably would stay, I felt that I was being rewarded by a chance to live in heaven itself. I was so grateful to Grandfather for asking me to come!" She turned her head to smile at him. "I have always loved this place, the woods, this house, the garden with the slat house and the ferns. I used to come here when I was a child. Lately—we lived in California. Lester's health did not make long trips possible, or, at least, easy. But when Grandfather asked me, we did come. And it is all as I remembered it. Except . . ." She smiled shyly at Chris. "Now there are friends close by. Or people I hope will be our friends."

"They will be," Chris assured her, his deep voice earnest. "I'm number one on the list, and I hope I can stay there."

"I hope so, too."

For an instant their eyes held; for an instant they felt a spark, a warmth, between them.

"I was thinking of myself," said her grandfather, "when I asked you. Pure selfishness."

"Our coming wasn't entirely unselfish," Lester Elis spoke up.

This time Margaret glanced at him. "There wasn't *any* unselfishness in my coming," she said firmly. "To live with Grandfather, to do what I could to care for him and his home ... I've always adored him, and, as I said, this house, since my earliest childhood, has meant a place of celestial beauty and happiness. Oh, I remember ..."

For ten minutes she reminisced, with the men watching her indulgently—two of them. Her husband was actively bored with this babble of playhouses in the grape arbor, the stars to be seen from her soft bed at night, the smell of roses outside the windows at breakfast.

"And now," she concluded, "to come back here. The stars are still there, and the rose bed. The arbor ..."

"Under a foot of snow," growled Lester.

Margaret laughed. "It's there. And don't be sarcastic. You know what coming here meant to us." She turned again to Chris. "My husband has a spine ailment," she explained, her voice gentle. "It was caused by an injury, and affects his nerves and muscles. We have had to decide that he cannot work at any sort of employment, certainly not as a reporter on a newspaper, which he used to be. When Grandfather's offer came, it found me anxious to be here, as well as weary of the secretarial work I had been doing to support us. So we packed up—"

"Wheelchair, dogs, and all," said her husband's sardonic voice.

Margaret laughed. "You must meet the dogs," she told Chris. "Two of the zaniest cockers!"

"They will feel at home here, too," he said, rising. "Susan Aubuchon has a cocker, a black one."

"Mine are black."

"I am glad you are here, dogs and all," Chris told her. He nodded to Mr. Kimberlin. "I'll be seeing you, sir. Elis ..."

Margaret brought him his coat and woolen scarf. He said again that he was glad she was on the Lane; he was sure she would find the move rewarding.

"It will be," she assured him. "Everything is going to be rosy now."

"Then it is time," her grandfather called from the hearth, "to look out for trouble."

Chapter 2

There came a certain cold, and black, night in February. The January snows had melted, there had been several days of what Arthur Kimberlin called "January thaw." And then winter had tightened its clasp again on the Lane. On this particular night, the stars blazed overhead, a wind blew and sighed through the woods and cast strange shadows upon the lighted drives and walks which led to the homes. The windows of the houses glowed rosily, and the smell of wood fires was a comforting thing. It was a very cold night, and withal a peaceful one, each household preoccupied with its own affairs, when the long white car drove in, its red lights blinking and whirling. It stopped at the first house, and under the lights from the clerestory windows one could see the insigne on the side. The state shield, the gold letters. The man who got out and went up to the front door wore a hip-length light blue overcoat, a broad-brimmed hat strapped under his chin, black boots.

The door opened, and Christopher Kendrick stood in the rectangle of yellow light, talking.

The trooper returned to his car, drove on to Dr. Anderson's, then to Bennett's, where at his ring the yard lights sprang up as wide and white as at a party. Down the Lane, Chris still stood at the door and watched.

Every doorbell was rung, every front door was opened—by the houseman at Kimberlin's, with Margaret in a red dress also coming to listen and to answer questions.

Alma answered the front door of her home. The man of the house was out, she said. Yes, she would give their names. No. No one had called the police. She turned her head. "Esther," she called, "you did not?"

"Why should I?" asked Esther, coming into the hall. She wore a white blouse, leopard-printed trousers, full about her feet; her yellow hair was tied back with yellow yarn. She invited the trooper to come inside.

He refused. He had others to ask.

Dr. Aubuchon also invited the man to come in. "It's as

41

cold as hell out there. And you're running up my gas bill with that damned door open."

"I'll hurry it up, Dr. Aubuchon," said the trooper. "We had this phone call, seemingly from someone in the neighborhood. The Lane was mentioned as the location from which shooting had been heard. Did you hear anything of the sort?"

"Not me," said Rupert good-naturedly. "We were watching a TV western. At least I was. My wife is more intellectual; she reads."

He laughed; the trooper smiled, thanked him, and departed.

Aubuchon followed him along the walk, and stood there, watching his car depart, looking speculatively down the Lane, up and around the curve of it. Chris Kendrick came across the circle and called out. "Kendrick here, doctor," he said. "I'm going on to see if the Old Man is all right."

"Kimberlin, you mean? Is he sick? I could come along with you."

"He's not sick. But a caller like that can be disturbing. Did you hear anything?"

Dr. Aubuchon mentioned the western again. "A real shoot-'em-up," he said. And he laughed.

The sound of their voices brought Esther Lynch out, and Nathan. Dr. Bennett came down the road with an enormous bull's-eye flashlight. He thought they should have some mercury lights in the middle of the circle.

Esther thought perhaps she had heard shots. "It could have been backfire?"

The people, and their shadows, shifted about. Susan looked out of their front door inquiringly. "Has something happened?" she called. Rupert went toward her to reply.

Chris made his way from person to person, determined to get on to Kimberlin's. Malcolm Anderson called to him when he reached there. "What happened, Chris?"

"I don't think anything did, really. Someone reported shots up here. I didn't hear any. Did you?"

"Not me. Some young bright soul being funny on the telephone, no doubt. What possible reason could there be for firearms up here? We're all too comfortably stodgy and unexciting."

"I could argue that point, doctor."

"The shots or the stodginess?"

"Both."

"All right, we'll have a go at it sometime. Tonight I'm admitting stodginess and going to bed."

"I thought I'd check on Mr. Kimberlin."

The doctor's attention focused. "Should I go with you?"

"I've no reason for alarm. I just thought—"

"Tell me if he's been disturbed."

"I would. I would, indeed." Chris walked on.

Margaret met him on the stoop before the front door. "I've been peering out the window," she confessed. "I saw you all talking."

"Your grandfather?"

"I don't think he knew about the policeman. If he did, he was not concerned. A clear conscience, I suppose." She drew her coat more closely about her. *"Brrr,* it's a cold night! But look at the stars!"

"Keep looking at them, and come back to my house for a drink. I'll guide you."

She laughed. "And I'd let you."

"Bennett thinks we should put a row of mercury lights down the center of the Lane."

"Oh, Dr. Bennett! He couldn't do that, could he?"

"I don't know how much influence he has with the necessary authorities. But perhaps the rest of us could raise a voice. It would have to be loud. He's used to having his own way, I understand."

"Grandfather says he's spoiled. That no one ever crosses him."

"He's pretty old to be practicing medicine, isn't he?"

"He doesn't believe in retirement. He says it kills the men who do."

"Sometimes that seems to be so. But for a doctor . . ."

"I think he resents the fact that Grandfather has consulted Dr. Anderson."

"Oh, but Mac . . ."

"I know. He is a big specialist. But I'm afraid Dr. Bennett feels that he is a specialist, too."

"Well, the same could be said for Aubuchon. It's a bit strange, you know, that we have three heart specialists on the Lane."

"It just happened so. Grandfather thinks he should have been more choosy. Though he says he made concessions to get Malcolm Anderson here."

"He's really a fine chap. Stays a bit to himself, but that may be due to the intense life he leads professionally. Now, how about that drink? I don't like to stay too close to myself."

"You could come in here."

"And have Mr. Kimberlin stay up late entertaining me?"

She smiled. "No, that's not what I want either. I tell you, Chris. I'll go back, check on Grandfather. Once Lionel gets him to bed, I'll fetch his hot milk. Then if things are all serene, I'll run down to your house for a quick half hour."

"With all the shooting, you maybe should not."

"I don't think there was any shooting, do you?"

He nodded. "I'll watch for you."

"If I can't get away, I'll phone."

He watched her go inside and close the door. Slowly he walked back and around the roadway. Margaret had not mentioned Elis. Often, she did not mention him.

Lester, Margaret knew—or thought—was upstairs in bed. He had gone up early, and probably was still reading. He read stacks of books, and did some reviewing. His strength did not often carry him through an active day, though he seemed to enjoy reading in bed, and was often cross if Margaret interrupted him with an inquiry as to his well being.

She sighed and went to the kitchen to warm the milk for her grandfather. She could hear Lionel talking to him in the bedroom which had been made out of a sitting room and sun porch on the first floor. Her grandfather had a failing heart, a coronary insufficiency, and Malcolm Anderson had vetoed stair climbing. Arthur Kimberlin had accepted the edict, and seemed satisfied with his present quarters.

Margaret put the hot milk into a flower-sprigged chocolate pot, with a cup to match on the little tray. She varied the ways in which she served her grandfather's milk, a dull drink in itself. Sometimes she would use a heavy pottery mug, sometimes a shining crystal glass. Once she made the old man chuckle by unearthing a Peter Rabbit cup and plate, long ago owned by some child of the family. Margaret's father, perhaps.

She smiled down at the pink clovers on the dishes of her small tray, and thoughtfully selected a napkin from the drawer. Her mind was not on what she was doing; she was thinking of Christopher Kendrick. Within a short month, she told herself, it was not possible that she could have fallen in love with the man. But she had . . . She knew that she had. Everything she did these days told the story. If she went up the stairs, it was as if Chris walked beside her, quiet, strong, and kind. If she brushed her hair, it was with the thought of his approval, the clothes she wore—this red dress tonight. Did Chris like it? Would he mention it?

She had come to know him well in that month. He came

44

making his painful way up the stairs. He was in pain, she knew that. But pain in itself did not excuse . . .

When she had stopped trembling, when her breath came steadily and she hoped her face was composed, she went back to her grandfather's door and looked in. Perhaps he was already asleep.

But he stirred and switched on the bedside lamp. "Come in, my dear," he said.

"Oh, Grandfather . . ." She went over to take his outstretched hand.

"Tell me," he said quietly, "why you haven't killed Lester long before this?"

She stood gazing down at him, and her mouth smiled a little.

"Well," he cried angrily, "you could at least have kicked him where it would do the most good!"

Margaret bent over to kiss his cheek. "You're not to worry," she said.

"I hope I won't have to. Good night, my dear."

Felix Lynch had not been at home when the trooper paid his call. He did not come home until almost midnight. Esther didn't like the many times he was away at night, coming home at all hours. He had to check the night's shifts on a run, he would tell her. Or something of the sort. "We have a new process about ready to jell." That didn't make sense either. Couldn't he let old Ottolini, or whatever, be the genius research man? Esther would bet he didn't keep such hours. Though she didn't know. She had seen the famous scientist only twice, and spoken to him only once. He was not really "old," and he surely was a drag to talk to.

When Felix did come in that night, she made a great fuss over him, jumping at him, clinging to him, telling him about the police.

"Was there shooting here, Mamma?" Felix asked Alma.

She shook her head and shrugged.

"Nobody would admit any," Esther told him. "It was a good thing you weren't here with that gun of yours; they might have thought . . ."

Felix smiled at her.

"D'you carry it all the time?" Esther persisted. Her hands explored his body, pockets, under his blue jacket.

He took the snub-nosed gun out of his belt. "I carry it all the time," he admitted. "You know that I do. Ottolini has asked me to. I have a permit. But I don't shoot it more than twice a day."

"I don't think you shoot it at all," Esther pouted.

"I don't. But in the highly classified work we do, Ottolini thinks . . ."

"Well, put it away, now!" Esther cried. "It makes me nervous. I don't want to get near you."

"Well, we can't have that," said Felix, laying the gun on the mantel, grabbing his young wife and whirling her about. She clung to him, pressing her soft body against his hard leanness. Six weeks as his wife had taught her the full strength of Felix's passion and desire. Had taught her that she could use it, as tonight she used it, for her own purposes. She wanted a car of her own, not to share the one with Alma. She would get it, too, thought Alma, who sat knitting, watching a little, listening. Her fine, big son—he made her *sick!* And that Esther—why had he *married* her? He could have had everything Esther had to give him without tying himself down to a legal marriage. Without that legality, this craziness would calm down in time, and Felix could be free. Well, he would be free!

Alma had set herself that goal. She was going to get rid of Esther, her long hair clinging to everything, her pants, and her bare feet.

Felix thought she was in love with him. Love! That girl . . . Animal love, sure. In-bed love, Alma supposed. To get what she wanted. The car. She would get that. But the warm, rich love a woman could give, love for the sake of love itself. The babies, the home kept for her man, her thoughtfulness of him, and for him, no! Not from Esther.

Someone was tapping on the window beside the front door, and Felix went to see who it was.

Nathan Kendrick, of course! Who else? He had seen Felix's car come in. Had Felix heard about the police? he asked. What did he suppose they wanted—or expected to find?

Felix was trying to say that he had not been at home, but Esther was gladly welcoming the boy. She gladly welcomed him, every chance she got, and there were many. She announced that now they could have some fun.

"It's pretty late, baby," Felix reminded her.

"Late for what?" She turned on the hi-fi and pushed the hall rug out of the way. Felix could fix some drinks. While he was doing that, Esther danced with Nathan. The way young people danced nowadays, wriggling, not touching each other, but promising everything.

Alma, at the fireside, rolled up her knitting and watched the goings-on. Tomorrow there would be crumbs all over the floor, and Coke spilled ... And Esther would sleep until noon, not worrying about who would clean up the mess. Well, Alma would not want *her* to try! She probably didn't know one end of a mop from the other.

Out in the hall Esther and Nathan shimmied and gyrated, and smiled widely at each other. "I'm so glad you came," the girl told Nathan, bending over from the waist, rotating her hips, her stomach, her shoulder, as she struggled—it seemed—to stand upright again. "Everyone else around here is so *old!* Only you—and me—"

Nathan grinned at her. "Susan Aubuchon is a cute trick," he pointed out. "I like her."

The men did like Susan. Esther had noticed.

"But she's a schoolteacher," she protested. "For heaven's sake!"

Nathan put his hand about her slender waist. "Esther," he laughed. "You're really too much!"

Alma had started across the living room, toward the hall, on her way to bed. "Too much," she agreed, under her breath. "Too much."

Her head went up. She had thought Felix was in the kitchen, getting ice cubes and glasses. But she was sure now that she heard his voice. Yes! He was in the study, talking on the phone there. She moved swiftly to close the door. Others might hear him also.

Nathan did hear. And Esther. Felix was talking softly, his tone guarded. But the music had stopped while the record changed, and it could be heard that he was speaking in Italian.

"Do you comprez that stuff?" Nathan asked Esther.

She began to catch up the new beat of the music. "I sure hope not!" she cried, tossing her hair back from her face. She saw Alma go along the back hall toward her bedroom. Good! She ...

Felix's hand on her shoulder startled her. She had not known he was close. She screamed a little, and looked around. "You scared me half to death!" she protested.

Felix's gesture brushed this out of the way. "Do you remember what I did with my gun?" he asked brusquely. "I recall having it in my hand; we were talking about it. I have to go out again, and I must have it."

49

Esther sighed. "Why?" she asked, her tone flat.

Felix bit his lip.

But Alma was coming back along the hall. *"Basta!"* she bade the girl sternly. She crossed the room to the fireplace; the coals were rosy, there were no sparks or flames. She stretched her arm and brought down the gun, came back with it to Felix.

"Thank you, Mamma," he said, taking it.

"No need to thank me, my son. Go safely, and return well."

At midnight, the Lane was dark. Now lights shone only in the Kendrick house and at Lynch's. Behind Margaret, a lamp burned dimly on a table near the front door. She wrapped her dark coat closely about her, and hurried down and around the road, the wind tugging at her pink head scarf. Hearing her heels on the hard surface, she moved to the grassy border. She wanted to run—away from the big house, and Lester, though he was, finally, asleep—toward Chris and his warm patience, his kindness, his strength.

"Kick Lester where he needs it most . . ." Arthur Kimberlin had advised.

It was good advice, it was fair.

Margaret was not leaning on it. Her going down to Chris was something Lester expected her to do. He would not feel kicked. He would not care that much. In his sardonic way, he expected a wife to do that sort of thing. Under their present circumstances, he might even think Margaret a fool if she did not go.

But Margaret— She was going because she wanted to go. She wanted to, terribly. She had never expected this sort of feeling to come to her. Love like this. When she had married Lester, years and years ago, she had been an excited girl, a somewhat frightened one. There had never been this feeling of warmth, of trust, of safety—of joy.

Chris was waiting for her; he opened the door as she came along the flagged walk, and drew her inside.

"Nathan is off somewhere," he said softly, taking her scarf from her hair, bending to kiss her.

Her eyes searched his face. "Should I have come?"

He drew her close. "You should have come," he said.

He put her coat and scarf on a chair; he led her into the living room where a fire burned. He seated her on the couch, and indicated the tray on the low table before them.

"I don't really want a drink," she said softly.

50

He sat beside her, his arm around her.

"I want . . ." she began.

"Shhhh."

She sighed softly. There was no need to speak. She had what she wanted. This man would give it to her. Lester . . .

He is sick in mind and body, she told herself. My husband. I am stealing nothing from him. He—for five years—he has not . . .

Chris's hand turned her face for his kiss.

"I love you, Chris," she murmured.

"I know."

It was as simple, as right, as that. They loved each other, this man, and this woman. What could be wrong with that?

"Don't question it," he said to her in the next hour. "Don't ever question this."

"Dr. Anderson is in a hurry." The word had got around the hospital unit. He would check the floor, he would check the charts and the recording machines. But he would not want to stand about talking.

There probably would be no surgery that night. "There had better not be," Dr. Cameron told Dr. Richardson. "He's signing out. With a flower box delivered to his office at five P.M."

"A . . . ?" Richardson turned, unbelieving. "What sort of flower box?" he asked.

"A date kind of flower box. Remember? Junior prom? When you took your bride-to-be out on the town?" Dr. Cameron's hands measured off dimensions. "Orchids, son. Maybe a camellia. Or even two."

"*Anderson?*"

"I saw it myself."

"Well, go tell Chicken Little!"

It was a flower box. Tied in white ribbon, a transparent one. When Anderson came out of his office, struggling into his topcoat, he was carrying it. No charts, no books, such as he usually took home with him. Just that square white box.

"His hair needs combing," sighed the nurse behind the curving desk counter.

"He'll comb it. And change his clothes. That man has a date!"

"With a girl," sighed the floor nurse. "I'd like to see what kind he's finally noticed. He sailed right past Mrs. Holman without batting an eye."

"Oh, Mrs. Holman!"

"All right. So she's a pest. But she's a patient's wife, and Mac . . ."

"Don't call him *Mac!*"

"Who'll notice? If he's as steamed up about this date as I think he is . . ."

Perhaps Malcolm Anderson would not have agreed that he was "steamed up." If he would put his situation into words, no doubt he would say that he had seriously decided to court Abby Bennett—to see enough of her that he could, or might, ask her to marry him. He knew that to accomplish such a project, there were proper steps for a man to take; he knew, and would have admitted, his lack of practice in such endeavors. He hoped that he would not appear unpracticed to her. Surely another man, many men, had approached her with the same purpose in mind.

If Mac Anderson was to get anywhere, he must be serious about this thing, so serious he was. And he knew it. Naïve he was, too, which did not occur to him.

He had studied the situation, and had decided on the course he would take. His profession would interfere; there could be, and would be, many interruptions. But that was not entirely a handicap. Abby's first interest in him had been his profession. He remembered how she had talked about his work, and questioned him. She was a clever young woman as well as a beautiful one. She would make him a wife to be proud of—provided he could use the right approach to further the project, and to accomplish it.

He invited her to dinner, he talked to her whenever he saw her. Tonight he was taking her to a gala concert in the city. Proper in white tie and tails. He had them, because the eminent heart surgeon often addressed important dinner meetings. Carrying flowers in the transparent box, his hands a little damp from nervousness, he parked his car in the Bennett drive, went up on the porch, and touched the bell.

Dr. Bennett admitted him. Jovial, welcoming. The old doctor had been one of the things Dr. Anderson had thought deeply about before deciding that Abby was worth a few hazards.

She was not quite ready, the old man said. "Women never are on time. Come in and sit down. You may as well take off your coat. Getting themselves into shape for public exhibition takes a while." He bustled ahead of Malcolm, a little man, thin and brittle as an old stick.

He spoke of the weather, he spoke of a heart seminar

which Dr. Anderson was conducting for other medics in the city. Not heart specialists, but men who would probably encounter certain warning symptoms in their patients. Dr. Bennett thought the idea was just fine.

He was a talkative chap, and after five minutes he blundered into mention of the magazine articles which his daughter was writing. "That's why she came home," he said, "and stayed when she met up with you."

Malcolm stiffened in his chair and looked at his watch. Yes, he agreed, he did know that Abby was a writer.

Well, Dr. Bennett should hope she was! And if Mac only knew what it was she was writing about ... Wait a minute! He darted out of the room; he came back with a dozen sheets of white paper in his hand.

"Manuscript," he said importantly. "She works in her mother's sewing room. Has an electric typewriter—pecks away for hours at a time. Here. Read this!" He thrust the pages into Malcolm's hand and stood back, beaming.

"I don't think I should ..." Malcolm demurred.

"Well, sure you should. You'll be interested. Go ahead. Glance down the page."

Malcolm glanced down the page; he carefully read the second page, and the third. He moved closer to the lamp, and a knot tightened the line of his jaw.

But this was incredible! He glanced up at Dr. Bennett, who was beaming happily. "Great, isn't it?" he demanded.

Malcolm did not answer. He ran his eye down the rest of the typed pages. Why—the woman—Abby—was quoting back to him the things he remembered having said to her.

One night, over dinner, they had soberly, seriously, discussed the man-woman relationship. And here were his beliefs, his actual words!

They were things he believed, and would state again—but not down on paper, not in a magazine article, where the source could be traced.

Here: "How can one tell if there is a romantic match between a man and woman," he had asked, "until their companionship is thoroughly tested?" Sex response would be only a part of it. There should be a similar response in other areas. Laughter, hate, their seriousness about certain things ... Of course a marriage had a better chance if the sex impulse was simultaneous, but these other aspects must feature.

Word for word, she had set his contributions down on paper. Neatly typed between neat margins. Bold. Bald. Shocking.

"I am astonished," he said helplessly to the watching Dr. Bennett.

"Quoted you, eh?" said the old man. "That's the way Abby does. She's always bleeding some poor fellow's brain. Last year it was a corporation lawyer. Big man, smart chap. This year it happens to be Dr. Malcolm Anderson, that heart surgeon. Also a big man, and a smart fellow."

Dr. Bennett cackled with amusement. Malcolm Anderson felt sick. He again read the last pages. There she had set down exactly what he had said to her about his work. *Exactly!*

"Our dream is to make this surgery feasible for every qualified team in the country. It must be standardized. Every operation cannot be an adventure. You are not doing the patient a service if it is."

He said that often. He had said it to Abby. He said it almost every time he spoke of his work in public or to his colleagues. Anyone who knew him would recognize him and say so. The easily identifiable statements, the credo, coupled with his probably naïve pronouncements about sex relationships, things he had said to a woman. . . . Malcolm dropped the pages of manuscript on a table, took out his handkerchief and wiped his hands. This was a most incredible situation.

"Next year," Dr. Bennett was saying, "she means to get a story about the captain of one of the river towboats. Or she'll write a novel about Cosa Nostra. She'll use Felix Lynch for that, of course."

Malcolm was still frowning with concern about his own involvement; he only half heard what Bennett had said. Then it clicked clear in his mind. He turned sharply. "What?" he cried. "What was that you said? About Felix?"

"He can tell her all about it," Dr. Bennett assured him. "Of course he won't know he's telling her."

As Malcolm Anderson had not known. But Felix—The Cosa Nostra—Oh, that was entirely absurd! This gossipy old man needed to be warned about spreading such dangerous lies.

"She'll use him," Dr. Bennett said confidently. "She knows how to get men to talk and tell her the things she wants to know. She never bothers with women." He laughed. "I suppose, being women, they see through her pretty little tricks and schemes." He continued to babble on about the way, even as a little girl, Abby had been able to charm men and get what she wanted from them. She had charmed her father. And now she used that same ability to earn herself a good living. She knew what she was doing. She had come home for Christmas, and stayed on, especially to meet Malcolm Anderson and to get a story from him about the famous heart surgeon. To talk to him, and then to venture to touch the precincts of his profession! "You and your cardiac department will get to be widely known, doctor!"

Malcolm stood in the middle of the floor and let Bennett's words wash over him. Years ago, in a swift mountain river, he had been caught against a jutting boulder. He remembered this same feeling of panic and helplessness.

He had come out of that experience bruised and aching. Hurt. So, tonight he was hurt—with a pain which grew from a wistful regret at his need to abandon the plans he had made, the dreams begun and ventured upon, to a mounting cumulative anger. At Abby. At himself, for making himself vulnerable.

He had been dead serious. He was going to spend the spring courting this lovely, intelligent young woman. Gifts, thoughtful attentions, time spent getting to know her, and for her to know him. He had even planned a party in his home so that his friends could meet her.

But now—

Now there was only this aching, hollow hurt. A pain so great that it took real effort to conceal it, to make himself go into the hall and greet Abby, to put her fur wrap about her shoulders, pick up his own coat, and go with her out to the car.

The florist's box remained on the table, under the lamp.

Abby Bennett and Dr. Anderson went to the concert. She was beautiful in golden-brown chiffon, sequins, and furs. She was talkative and entertaining. The doctor, in his turn, spoke little, responded little, and at the end of the long, long evening, he made no plans to see her again.

The next day he was like a wooden man. There was no surgery scheduled. It was not his way to prepare for his delicate sort of work by a night on the town. But his day was a full one. He lectured at the medical school. He met and did an initial examination for a man who probably would be a candidate for revascularization. And, in the late afternoon, he assembled his team, asking for a dry run of their proceedings in view of surgery on the next day.

This he occasionally did, and the team was not surprised at the order. Usually even the dry runs were conducted before observers. Medical students, and—or—surgeons who wanted to learn his technique, nurses who might serve in his o.r., young doctors who perhaps could become members of a team.

He was as meticulous in these tests as he was during actual surgery. Every detail must be remembered. One of Dr. Anderson's own men was serving today as the "patient." And each thing was done as closely as possible without actuality—the vein "stripped," the tube attached—taped on rather than inserted—the detailed check of the heart monitors, all proceeded exactly as was done when surgery was imminent. No pilot flying a supersonic jet could check his valves and dials and lights more exactly. The doctors bathed, dressed—complete asepsis was maintained.

And pressure built up, just as it did if it were the real thing; each misstep or fumble would be noted, remembered, and talked about. A telephone call came for Dr. Anderson from so important a doctor in the southwest that one might think . . .

"I can't take it now!" he said sharply. "Tell him I've scrubbed in."

"I hope he remembers that I'm only a stand-in," murmured Hank Mitchell, the resident who lay on the table.

"You'll look good with a hole in your chest," the instrument nurse consoled him.

Dr. Anderson was approaching the table, and, as he probably would not do during a real operation, he looked up at the people who sat beyond the glass dome to watch. It had occurred to him, with a sick feeling in his stomach, that Abby might, through her father's influence, come to watch the great heart surgeon in action. If she were there . . .

She was not there.

But a woman was. A small, dark, tense woman in a blue dress and pink scarf.

The doctor's head snapped up. "Who gave Mrs. Holman permission to observe?" he asked.

"I think the Administrator did, sir. Since it was to be only batting practice."

And Malcolm Anderson blew up. He blew up completely. Mrs. Holman was removed from the observers' benches. Dr. King said, humbly, that of course he knew the term *batting practice* was out of line.

There was not much shelter, but each member of the team, each highly trained, privileged technician, sought to find shelter.

And Malcolm saw their search. He knew why. He realized what he had done, and he was shocked. A man disappointed

56

in love had no right to come into an operating room of this sort and let his disappointment ... He apologized. He apologized to the team as a whole, and to each member individually.

"We will continue," he said quietly. "But I do not, as a practice, want lay people observing. Please check with me, whenever the matter comes up. Dr. King, where were we in—er—your batting practice?"

"I'm sorry, sir," said the anaesthetist.

Malcolm nodded. "I am sorry, too." He was sorry. Truly sorry.

He was too young a man. The hospital, in talking about the episode—and would it *ever* talk!—would decide, or at best consider, that he was too young to have such responsibility. Was he? If he could not sublimate his personal affairs? He had thought he could. He had developed surgical techniques, and built up a team of co-workers, friends, men and women, some of them older than he was, who worked with pride in what they did, as well as in what Malcolm Anderson did. He would not have tolerated their bringing their personal moods to the operating table. Why, then, should he ... ?

The story did go about the hospital. Anderson had blown his cool. What happened? What had happened? Something must have. This was just not Mac's way of doing his job.

"A mighty big job."

"It's big. But he himself built it big."

"He takes care of himself. He approaches his work as an athlete does a championship game. He keeps himself fit, his hours, his appetites. He isn't married, so it could not have been domestic trouble."

"Does he have a girl?"

"Whichever way that's answered, you'll solve the mystery, won't you?"

"Will I?"

His colleagues were concerned, and generally sympathetic. Malcolm Anderson was a gifted man, a clever man. He was also a lonely man doing delicate work. Each day he was called upon to make hairline decisions. He was not the sort to become calloused, hardened, against the emotional side of such work. Each life he handled, each decision he made between hope and no-hope was a renewal of the whole burden he carried. He took his work seriously, he performed it seriously. It was work he enjoyed, and for which he had both ideals and hard-nosed plans. He was humble about his own abilities, but never undervalued the results attained by the team. This was known, and Malcolm was liked. By most people.

Of course, there were those, even among his colleagues, who should know what he did, who did know, and still were jealous of his position in the profession.

"Someone has to pick up the knife," these men said. "At least half the men on that famous team could carry on if Anderson's ulcer decided to bleed. And some not on the team, as well."

Such talk went on. Dr. Anderson knew that it did. He knew that men like Rupert Aubuchon resented the fuss made over him. If Aubuchon would study and work, and mend his ways a bit—quite a bit—he could be inside, looking out, instead of . . .

Fairly often, Aubuchon got in Malcolm's way. He wished he need not have to cope with him as a staff doctor. The man was what Menninger called an exhibitionist, a doctor who loved to operate because of the exhibitionist opportunity afforded. At least in part . . . No! With Aubuchon, exhibitionism was everything. It was why he had studied medicine in the first place. He foresaw himself, capped, gowned, the center of an operating theater. Not the patient, but the surgeon. Aubuchon had a good mind; he could have developed skills beyond those he had. But the picture of himself always got in the way—to the point that he just might be a psycho case. Really, instead of dressing himself up in a white tie and tails, the Chief of Thoracic Surgery should put some time on Aubuchon. Study his record more thoroughly, watch his work, get to know him personally. . . .

He winced at the thought. There was opportunity to know him better. Aubuchon and his pretty wife lived on the Lane. They might have bought in there to get to know Anderson better. It was the sort of thing Aubuchon did. There was much maneuvering, he knew, much funny business conducted, to get on Anderson's team, or even to get his job as Chief. In fact, certain doctors on the staff had suggested that Anderson's heart work be made a separate department.

There were all sorts of angles in the whole game of hospital politics. All sort of strings to pull, or to tangle. Why, the complicated game of publicity alone was a fascinating thing to watch. How Anderson avoided it, how a chap like Aubuchon courted it.

Naturally, no ethical doctor advertised himself or his profession. But it was fun for his friends to see how slickly Dr.

58

Anderson would slide into his seat at the last minute before a play's curtain rose, and melt away seconds before it fell. They were equally accustomed, and amused, to see Aubuchon's face on the society page.

"Dr. Rupert Aubuchon, heart surgeon, attended the benefit. He is shown here with Mrs. Million Gotrox, chairman of the affair."

He bothered Malcolm, somewhat, by his tactics, and much more by his behavior as a doctor. And he did wish that Aubuchon had not bought a house on the Lane. Though Mac had not felt free to protest to Kimberlin about the sale.

Just as he had not used as an argument against his own residence there the fact that old Bennett lived next door. He considered it an argument, but he admired Arthur Kimberlin; he liked most of his neighbors.

Aside from his irritation about Abby, he found old Bennett only a nuisance— On the Lane, and in the hospital. The staff men laughed about the man. Malcolm had used to laugh, too.

But Aubuchon was a different matter.

Aubuchon did live on the Lane—with his bride, who certainly was a pretty and clever young woman. She had, for a month or more, been devoting herself solely to her position as wife and homemaker, and so far, she loved it. Each day stretched beautifully before her. She could walk Mandy, she could dig flower beds. Bulbs planted in November were showing green shoots. She could clean her house, rearrange furniture, put ribbon bands around stacks of carefully folded towels on the shelf. She could practice cooking, which was not a natural gift with her. And all day she could look forward to Rupert's return home that evening when she would again be a bride—wife. His kiss, his embrace, the smell of his tweeds and his tobacco, the sound of his hearty voice—all these things built up into the thrill which the intimacies of marriage gave Susan Aubuchon. Just the sight of Rupert's big hand clenched lightly on a chair arm could turn her heart over in her breast. All day she looked forward to the time each evening, she cherished the time, when, together, they would turn out the lights through the house and go back to their bedroom. Here indeed was the altar, the ritual place, here the rites of marriage were at their most wonderful. The intimacy of seeing her husband take off his shirt, empty his pockets of keys and change, sit down and take off his shoes.

Oh, if Rupert only knew how she cherished these small things! Her own bedtime preparations became almost a liturgy. The turning back of the bedspread, the way she laid her gown and robe across the back of the little green chair. When she sat at her dressing table, she watched the room in the mirror as a girl—a very young girl—would watch a play on the stage, watch an actor on whom she had an all-consuming crush. That was the way she felt about Rupert Aubuchon. That she was here with him as his wife was almost more than she could bear. She knew that he was aware of her crush, and he sometimes teased her about it. He thought it wonderful that a woman of her somewhat-mature age— "All of thirty years old!" he would tease her—and of her mental capacity. "Dean of a girls' school!" he would point out. That such a young woman, that Susan, could fall head over heels in love intrigued and delighted him.

"Such pretty heels, too," he would say. "Did you know, Susie, that few woman have pretty feet?"

"And how do *you* know?" she retorted.

"I'm a doctor."

"But not of feet!"

"We consider the whole body. We get educated by studying the whole ... Well, no matter. Take my word for it. Women have ugly feet. Except you. Even in those awful slippers old lady Lynch knitted for you."

Susan wriggled her toes in the red and white slippers which Alma, indeed, had knitted for her and brought to her on one snowy afternoon of pleasant gossip before the fire. Susan had served tea, and even some cookies which she had baked.

"My slippers are as warm as toast," she now told her husband.

"Let's see ..." His arm swooped down and he had her feet in his hand, the slippers off. He stroked the white skin. "They are warm, sure enough," he admitted. "But, my God, these socks are ugly!"

"Not really, dear," Susan protested, all rosy confusion now. "Just—different. You wouldn't notice them with the tailored flannel robes I used to wear." Laughing, she ran the green ribbon of her negligee through her fingers.

"Tailored ..." He stared at her in protest. "Did you throw them all away?"

"I had only two. An old one which I wore, and an almost new one which I saved for possible trips to the hospital."

"I never saw you at the hospital."

She laughed helplessly at the way he could divert a conversation. "I am disgustingly healthy."

60

"That's why I had to marry you. I'd never have met you otherwise."

He went in for his shower, and came out, rubbing his hair with a towel. "Speaking of the hospital," he said, "our friend Anderson put on a show today. The great, the wonderful, blew his stack in o.r. just the same as we common mortals sometimes do."

Susan turned from the mirror to look directly at her husband. "Dr. Anderson?" she asked, unbelieving.

"Certainly Dr. Anderson. The big heart surgeon, with his o.r. packed solid full with machines, teams, observers on the benches. Something got to him, and he flew apart like last summer's bird's nest. I understand it was quite a sight to see."

Susan looked sorry. "That's too bad," she murmured.

He came to her and put his head down into the hollow of her neck and shoulder. He was damp, and big, strong and urgent.

"It's not too bad for us, sweetie," he said. "Not for the doctors on Cardiac. Because if Anderson wavers and falls— the schedules he keeps will almost guarantee that fall—I stand next in line, you know."

"Next in line for what?" She still was troubled.

"To be Chief, darling. To be Chief of Service." Rupert Aubuchon wanted to believe that he was next. Declaring such a thing to Susan made the position seem very real. He led his wife toward the bed. "You know what I think I'll do?" he asked a few minutes later, in the darkness. "I think I'll start a ball rolling. A big ball, striped red and white like your ugly slippers. Though the ball won't be ugly. No, sirree. It will be beautiful!"

Susan stirred uneasily. "I don't know what you're talking about," she told Rupert.

"I'd explain if I didn't have better things to do. For now I'll just say the ball I'm talking about will be a word, two words, then three, and so on, to the effect that our present Chief seems to need a rest, that he should take a vacation. . . . Oh, yes, sir! I can do that."

"Rupert . . ."

"Well, sweetie, for all we know maybe he does need a vacation. Blowing his stack in o.r. the way he did."

She caught at his hand and held it. "Wait . . ." she said. "I want to get this thing straight."

"You're sounding like a schoolteacher, my darling."

"That's all right. You said once that you married me be-

61

cause I was a schoolteacher. Now, tell me. Should you interfere? Should you play with red and white balls when it comes
to professional matters?"

He lay back on his own pillow. "Going ethical on me,
maybe?" he asked her.

"I know only a little about the ethics of your profession,
Rupert. But what you seem to be planning sounds like trouble to me. Troublemaking. And should you do that?" Susan
liked Dr. Anderson, meeting him only a time or two on the
Lane.

"Stirring things up a little. That's all I had in mind, Susan.
I only planned to place the thought of Anderson's going
away. That little thought would make some fine waves, I
guess. But I like to make waves. I like to see things stirred
up."

Susan said nothing.

"You mad at me, sweetie?" Rupert asked.

"No. But I am thinking."

"Well, don't do that. You stay close by me, and enjoy
things, too. For instance, the other night—when the Highway
Patrol was out here? Because they had heard some shooting
up here?"

"Yes," said Suan, "I remember."

"Well, guess who did that shooting?"

She sat straight up in bed. "Rupert!" she cried. "You
didn't!"

He laughed. "I sure did. And d'you know why? I went outside that night. Remember, I took your dog for a walk so
you wouldn't have to change your shoes."

"I remember." Her voice was without inflection.

"Well, I walked up and around the circle, and I saw all
those smug houses, back behind their little evergreens, their
curtains closing them in—and—well—I thought I'd get the
people inside excited a little. Make 'em open their doors. . . ."

"But, why, Rupert?" she asked. "I mean, why should that
sort of excitement please you? I presume it did?"

He said a few words she had never heard him say before.

"You're mad," he excused himself. "You're mad because I
had a little fun."

She lay down again. Yes, she was angry. It surprised her
that she should be, but there it was. It did anger her that Rupert should act this way, that he should behave like a child.

Susan slept poorly that night, lying awake for long
stretches, holding herself rigidly still lest she disturb the rest

of her husband. He slept. With his broad back and shoulders turned toward her, his rumpled head buried in the pillow, he slept soundly.

As early as half-past six, unable to stay in bed any longer, Susan slipped out, found garments, and went down the hall to the guest bathroom, where she showered and then dressed. From there she went to the kitchen, made coffee and set things ready to prepare the hearty breakfast which Rupert usually ate. Fruit juice, eggs, toast, a bowl of cereal. Coffee. At least three cups of coffee.

The alarm would waken him at seven-thirty.

Susan sat down at the table, read the newspaper headlines, and drank her coffee. She felt tired, as if she had quarreled with Rupert. She had not, actually. He had said things that made her unhappy. Uneasy. But surely she had not scolded, nor preached.

Her head lifted. There was a knock, and then another, at her kitchen door. Who . . . at this hour . . . ? She got up and opened the inner door.

Lionel, the Kimberlin gardener, houseman, chauffeur, stood on the walk. In the past months, Susan had come to know this kind man well—through Mandy especially. Had the dog . . . ? Susan had let her out, unleashed, when she first got up. And then, frankly, she had forgotten her. Now, Mandy slicked in ahead of Lionel, who came, smiling, into the kitchen. Her coat was wet, she shook herself vigorously.

"Did she do something?" Susan asked. "Good morning, Lionel."

The tall man shook his head. "She didn't do anything 'cept be friendly. But her being out told me you folks was up."

"Well, me, at any rate," Susan agreed. "Would you like a cup of coffee, Lionel?"

"No, ma'am. Not this mornin'. I just stopped to bring you these."

He held up a small brown-paper sack. Susan took it, first studying Lionel's friendly face, then opening the sack.

"Tomatoes?" she asked, in disbelief.

"Yes, ma'am. I raise 'em. In the greenhouse, you know. Mr. Kimberlin, he brings me all sort of chemistries and things. He bein' in that business." Behind his large, thick glasses, Lionel asked Susan for understanding.

She took out the round, smooth tomatoes. They were temptingly red and perfect. "They are beautiful!" she cried. "Thank you so much, Lionel. We'll really enjoy them."

"Yes, ma'am."

63

"Sit down, won't you? And tell me . . ."

"I can't really tell you how I raise 'em. Mr. Kimberlin could, but the old gentleman, he ain't so well this mornin'. The doctor is there with him, right this minute. Miss Margaret, told me. Course you know his heart ain' so good."

Susan nodded. "Yes, I had heard. Well, thank you, Lionel, for thinking of us. Maybe you should get back; you might be needed."

"Yes, ma'am. Could be."

He faded through the two doors, and into the shadows of early morning.

Susan put the tomatoes into the refrigerator, folded the sack neatly, and glanced at the clock. The alarm would go off in a minute. She went out to the hall and to the bedroom where she snapped on the lamps. Rupert stirred, groaned, looked at the clock. "You up?" he asked groggily.

She laughed. "Of course I'm up."

The alarm went off sharply, and his hand came out to still it. He sat upon the side of the bed, rubbed his head, frowning, glanced at Susan. "Shoes," he mumbled. "Striped shirt . . . What goes on?"

He was commenting on her loafers, her striped blouse and her gold-yellow skirt.

"You going back to school?" he asked, standing up and stretching.

"No. I just—woke early, and decided to dress. I didn't disturb you."

"Oh, no." He went into the bathroom.

"I'll fix your breakfast," Susan called to him.

"Yeah. Do that."

She was careful to get things exactly the way he liked them, the bacon strips uncurled, the toast a golden brown, when he came out, carrying his suit jacket, a scarf tucked into the throat of his white shirt. He bent and kissed her cheek. "Still mad at me?" he asked.

She shook her head. "I haven't been 'mad,' Rupert."

He sat down and picked up the newspaper.

"Mr. Kimberlin is ill," Susan told him, putting his plate before him. "Lionel brought me some tomatoes."

"Hydroponics," murmured Rupert.

"Yes, I think that is the way he raises them. I was wondering if you shouldn't go up there before you start for the hospital."

Her husband folded the newspaper, drank some orange juice, and took up his fork. "Certainly not," he said crisply.

"But, dear . . ." She sat down and filled the coffee cups.

"If he needs a doctor . . ."

"Lionel said the doctor was there."

"Well, that answers your suggestion. Old Bennett probably was called; he probably is still there. Has Mandy been out?"

"Oh, yes. For a half hour."

"Good." He put marmalade on a piece of toast. He always ate quickly, but with enjoyment. "Kimberlin and Bennett are old friends," he said, "and I do mean old."

"But, as a neighbor . . ."

"I'm a doctor, too. Remember? And if the family wants Dr. Aubuchon, they will call Dr. Aubuchon." He picked up the newspaper again. "Not that they ever will call him," he added. "You can bet on that, sweetheart." He disappeared behind the paper.

Susan sat thoughtful, nibbling at her toast. "Why?" she asked then.

Rupert peered around the edge of the newspaper. "Why what?" he asked, his mind not on what she was talking about.

"Why wouldn't the Kimberlins call you?"

"Oh, that." He held his coffee cup toward her. "Thank you, sweetie. Well, they won't call me because I'm not their sort of doctor."

"Is Dr. Bennett?"

"I tell you: old Bennett and Arthur Kimberlin fought the Civil War together." He laughed at his own humor and said something about spring baseball practice.

Susan put her hands on the table. "Answer me, Rupert," she said firmly. "Why aren't you the Kimberlins' sort of doctor? I mean the sort they would call."

"Because rich guys like that, they settle in, sweetheart. They carefully select even their shoeshine boy. As for doctors . . . Well, they just don't call in a doctor because he lives in the neighborhood. That's a valuable heart up there, you know. Kimberlin decided some time ago which doctor was going to take care of it."

"I see . . ." said Susan, though she did not see at all.

"You're a good doctor, aren't you?" she asked thoughtfully.

He did not reply, and she put the question another way. "Why do you decide for yourself that the Kimberlins would not choose you as a doctor? You do heart work. Don't they know that?"

"They know. But to them I am what is called a slick doctor."

"Now, Rupert ..."

"I am a slick doctor, Susie," he assured her, beginning to take an interest in the conversation. "I know the necessary things, and I work hard to get patients, the right kind of patients. I have my office in the right building, I am on the staff of good hospitals. I do charity work where it will be noticed by the right people."

She did not like this sort of talk, and her face showed it.

"Oh, Susie ..." he laughed. "I know what your trouble is. I knew when you said you would marry me, it was because you thought all doctors, all practicing physicians, were noble characters. Hippocrates in a Brooks Brothers suit. That belief was appealing as well as naïve. But by now you must know that doctors are not saints."

They were talking about Rupert Aubuchon, not "all doctors."

"I thought they were honest men," she said stiffly.

Rupert looked at her keenly. "But you don't think that, do you?" he asked. "Not really? You can't believe that."

"But I do!" she cried. "I believe that you are, that you should be ..."

"Oh, brother!" He shook his head and brushed his hair back with his hands. "You're talking about ethics, aren't you? And of course we do have ethics. But you can't be so innocent ..." He was laughing at her.

And Susan was as frightened as she had ever been in her life. "You told me once," she said faintly, "that you married me because I was innocent."

On their wedding night, he had said that.

He remembered, too. "I did say that," he agreed. "But I wasn't thinking of ... Well, there are limits to innocence, Susie. You're a grown woman, thirty years old. You've taught school, made your own living."

She was still frightened. And stubbornly sure that doctors could be—should be—honorable men.

Rupert was still talking. He went to great lengths to explain the folly of her idealistic beliefs. Doctors were human, he said, with all the frailties of any human man. Yes, sure, there were dedicated men. Self-sacrificing men. Ones who would kill themselves to save or help a patient. He just didn't happen to be that sort, and to tell the truth, these days the biggest proportion of doctors were not that sort. They went into the profession for some pretty sensible reasons. The prestige it gave a man, the chance to make money—good money. He quoted statistics. The proportion of medical students who considered the money to be earned. The amount of money that was earned.

"Money . . ." said Susan softly.

"Sure, money, sweetheart. Lots of money, to be earned, to spend. It bought this house, it bought my car—which reminds me. I have some payments coming due. What with income tax, they are overdue. Have you some funds available?"

Susan agreed to transfer a thousand dollars from her savings to his account. It didn't matter. Nothing mattered.

Rupert departed for the hospital, and his wife attended to her household duties. She straightened things in the kitchen, she made the bed and restored the bedroom to its orderly prettiness. There was no joyous daydreaming on this morning. She changed to a tweed suit and a white blouse. She tied her dark hair into a club behind her neck, found gloves and her purse. She let Mandy out for ten minutes, put her back into the house, smiling at the little dog's readiness to accompany her.

"Not today, sweetheart," she said.

She thought of Mr. Kimberlin as she drove out. Should she have inquired for him? She would, that evening. She and Margaret had become friends.

She stopped at the bank, and then went on to the school, to the Institute, where she had used to be dean. She should have made an appointment, but the president was an old friend. She might have to wait, but she could visit any number of old friends. After all, she had been away from the place only for a month or two. It gave her a peaceful, safe feeling to go into the main building, to feel the quiet fold about her. There was sunlight through the high windows, the sound of distant voices, a ringing telephone.

When Rupert returned home, late that afternoon, he seemed relieved to find Susan her usual self, ready to accept his kiss, to bring him a drink, and to sit beside him on the couch to watch the evening newscast.

"What did you find to do today?" he asked her.

Susan smiled a little. "I found a lot to do today," she said quietly. "I got through my housework quickly—with Mrs. Heep coming in twice a week, there isn't too much to do. And then I went back to the school and asked them if they might have a job for me."

Rupert sipped his drink. "Did they?"

"Yes. As a matter of fact, they said I could have my old

job back. They had done very little toward getting a replacement. Dr. Younger—everyone—seemed happy to have me there again."

"I'll bet they were."

"I should have asked you . . ."

"It's all right. I think you did the right thing. You like to keep busy, and the contacts can be valuable to me."

She thought about what he had said. Then she turned on the couch to look at him. "What contacts, Rupert?" she asked.

"Oh, you know. Those girls—or rather, their families—top-drawer stuff, aren't they?"

Yes. The Institute was an old school, an exclusive school. The girls were, many of them, enrolled at birth by their families. Their mothers and grandmothers had graduated from the Institute. The families were the cream of the city and county society. Usually there was money. But she still did not see . . .

Rupert realized that she was puzzled. "Look," he explained. "If the girls like you, their families will like you. And if they like you, and need a doctor . . ."

Susan stared at him.

He pushed at her small, straight nose with his forefinger. "You're being innocent again, Susie," he teased.

"Is that why you married me?" she asked, her lips stiff. The contacts . . . ?"

"It's why I first made a play for you. But then you were so cute, and smart, and—like I told you—innocent."

Susan looked down at her hands, clenched in her lap. She felt sick. His grammar, even, was bad. Popular, but bad. Like him. Like her husband. Oh—dear Lord. Dear Lord.

He had been, he was being, frank with her. And, for all her talk of honesty, she wished he would not be frank. People needed the decency of polish, of manners, to hide their ugly nakedness.

She stood up. "When I came back this afternoon," she said, in a quiet, unemotional way, "I went down to Kimberlin's and asked Margaret about her father."

"How was he?"

"She thinks they will be taking him to the hospital for tests. I like Margaret."

"She's a handsome woman. Kendrick likes her, too, I understand."

"I'll get dinner on the table," Susan said. "It will take a half hour."

It was their usual evening proceeding. Her welcome, Rupert's drink, the brief time during which he sometimes changed, sometimes followed Susan to the kitchen, sometimes just sat with the TV and a magazine.

Tonight he did not follow her, and she was glad. She was greatly disturbed, and hoped to be able to recover herself before she must talk to him again. Not that she planned any talk. She already had done too much of that. But just to face him, to look at him, realizing that she was seeing her husband more clearly and truly than she had seen him when she married him. Then he had been only a big man, rather handsome, saying that he was in love with her.

Did all wives go through this time of enlightenment, of renewed vision? Perhaps they did. After eight or nine months of marriage, they must come to know their husbands, and the revelation could be a good thing—if a girl had married a man of—of quality.

Susan broke lettuce into a wooden bowl and shook a tear from her cheek.

Was it only now that she knew Rupert was a weak man? Hadn't she always guessed that? And perhaps known it?

She sighed. She had, and even guessing it, she had fallen in love with this male creature questing for her. She still loved him physically—protectively.

Because if that big, boyish man in there was a scoundrel, really, as he did seem to be, she must do all she could to protect him from himself.

Perhaps she should leave him. Now. Before there were children to complicate matters. That, really, would be the sensible thing to do. She had her job again, she could get her little apartment. . . Yes, it would be sensible.

But, oh, dear, she would hate to acknowledge her failure to the world, to have to live the rest of her life in the knowledge of that failure. She was too young.

Besides, she loved Rupert. She loved marriage, being Rupert's wife. She could not give that up without an effort to change things enough to make her marriage endurable. If she watched him, and talked to him . . .

He was the only man who had ever called her pretty. That alone . . .

Before the chops were quite broiled, he came out to the kitchen and he bent over to look into Susan's face. "Have you been crying?" he asked.

She shook her head and tried to smile. It was no use. She looked up at him, and then threw herself into his arms.

69

"Don't hurt me, Rupert!" she begged. "Please don't hurt me, darling."

The next morning, the tenth floor of the big hospital, the Department of Thoracic and Cardiovascular surgery, seemed to be going about its business as usual. It was, in fact, doing just that. But no one, from cleaning orderly to the nursing head, was unaware that the coronary o.r. was in full service. An undercurrent of tension rippled in waves along the corridor. The patients knew what was going on. They had seen the teams the day before, they knew of the preparations being made the night before. This morning Dr. Anderson had made early rounds, gowned in white, a cap on his head.

"Is this a big day, doctor?" one patient asked.

His dark eyes smiled. "Up here," he said, "every day is big enough. Today—you are getting better, aren't you?"

"Yes, sir. Just as you predicted, I am beginning to fuss about my wound, the scar, and to notice other things besides me."

The surgeon laughed, and his hand pressed the man's shoulder. "You're making strides," he said, going swiftly out of the room and down the hall.

The heart surgery o.r. was a medium-sized room, crowded with panels and switches, beeping oscilloscopes, tanks and tubes, a dozen men, all very busy. The table, the lights, the patient, on his left side the surgeon, beside him his assistant.

The team—the teams—moved in, they stepped aside, they moved in and out again. The doctors not really busy at certain stages would stand on tiptoes to see over the shoulders and between the bodies of the surgeons gathered about the table. The observers' benches were full. When Anderson operated, it was a sight to see. Today he was doing an implant—an internal mammary artery implant. It was one of the techniques he had perfected in revascularization, an important one because implants had the greatest application on the greatest number of patients.

It was delicate work. Dear Hanna, yes! Malcolm knew that it was. He was thankful for everyone who helped him, the patient himself, the nurses, the prep workers, the men now busy, and the women who stood so reliably by.

He worked. He knew that this one was going to come out well, and the frown smoothed from between his eyes. "Good!" he said. "Good work, you beautiful people. Would someone please swab my forehead. I seem to be sweating."

Someone swabbed his forehead. "It was a beautiful operation, doctor," the nurse told him.

He nodded. "It was, wasn't it? You know, team, I think we can just about say that the implant operation has passed the experimental stage."

Someone laughed. The surgeon nodded. "Now," the Chief added, "we can break our backs developing it."

When he was finished, he was tired. But, before he changed his clothes, he asked about the patient they had for surgery on the following day. He wanted to talk to the man. . . .

The team understood. They knew, and each one wished he could acquire, Anderson's ability not only to inspire his team to top-level performance, but to inspire, to uplift the patient's morale. He was able, always, to make these sick people amenable to rehabilitation. He did that by assuming, and making the patient assume, that there was no possibility of failure. He showed each one this firm encouragement, which was different from, and better than, coddling sympathy.

"But it takes it out of a man," said Dr. Cameron in the lounge where the doctors of the team had gathered for coffee, food, and relaxation.

"Who takes what out on which man?" asked Malcolm as he came in through the door.

Someone tried to enlighten him. He listened, and nodded. "I get tired," he admitted. He stood at a high desk, writing on the report sheet, already filled out except for his contribution. "Who checked last on Joe?"

He called all his patients "Joe." Or Josephine. Someone answered him. He nodded. "Got to keep at those vital signs. Why I keep a team," he said. "To do my leg work."

There were knowing smiles around the cluttered room. Nobody did any of Anderson's work.

He got himself a cup of coffee, considered the Danish left on the tray, and asked what sort of sandwiches were "hiding behind the wax paper."

He took a sandwich and found a chair. He sat down, and the springs groaned. "Next endowment we get, I move for new furniture in here." He said that at least once a day. He drank his coffee, made a face at its bitterness, and unwrapped the sandwich. "I'm tired," he said again. "Could be I'm getting old."

"We all are," said Dr. Mitchell, the chief resident.

"Go check on Joe, will you? Anderson asked the young doctor. "And bring me another ham sandwich while you're up."

"When I learn to keep my yap shut, I'll be staff," murmured the resident.

Anderson nodded, and accepted the sandwich. "Find I'm hungry, too." Someone filled his mug with hot coffee, and he stretched his legs still farther along the floor. "When I chose my specialty," he said, "I thought it would be a matter of trained hands. Maybe eyes."

"But you've learned . . ."

"Yeah. Legs. Every damned vertebra, and both feet. That's what it takes." He ate his sandwich, he closed his eyes. And no one spoke to him for a long time. Men left the room, some returned. He was thinking about himself. And Abby Bennett.

For so many years—resident, staff doctor, surgeon, Chief of Service—he had devoted his whole life, his strength, intellect, and an interest that amounted to absorption, to the lives, the *living,* of other people. To poor Joes like that guy Holman in the cardiac care unit, that quiet, cheerful world of man and machine. Holman's wife *knew* that her husband had a distinct lesion. Dr. Anderson was not yet sure that he did. Mrs. Holman wanted him to take a chance. . . . *She* would take a chance! So he must think about Holman, and the other Joes for whom he lived. Them, and their arteries.

But lately a change had come about. Not a change in what he felt, thought, and did for his patients. Never that. But a change in himself. A softening, an opening of doors. New vistas presented themselves, new hopes and plans.

What had happened, of course, was Abby Bennett. Abby.

Malcolm pressed his shoulders against the cushion of the creaking chair, and thought about Abby. Her big, dark eyes, her soft mouth, the way her hair curled, thick and shining. The manner in which she spoke, the things she said.

With one half of his mind, the doctor, seeming to sit relaxed in the surgeons' lounge, continued to think back over his day's work. The surgery had been entirely successful. Joe's lesion had been right where it should be. Anderson could not always be sure things would work out that way, and when he was not . . . Holman certainly was a sick man, and a frightened man. But Dr. Anderson was not sure at all that Holman could be helped by his surgery. Other good heart men had said that he could not be. And Mac would *not* be pressured to operate against his own judgment!

And then, Arthur Kimberlin. Now, there was a case. Malcolm wanted to help the man. He really did. But—

He sighed, and crossed his legs at the ankles. Ninety per

cent of his implants survived, but only because the surgeon was meticulous in his diagnosis. He did not agree to operate when the odds were too long. He saw no benefit, no sense, in subjecting a patient to long and rugged surgery unless he was pretty sure he could be helped. No surgeon "played things safe," but he could, Malcolm felt, weigh the chances very carefully.

The other half of his mind stayed with Abby.

Only two months ago, she had come into his sphere of interest. And through her a new life had reached out to touch the dedicated surgeon he had been for so long, had involved him in its fascinating complexities. Not too readily, he had accepted the thought that his life could be broadened and enriched. There simply was not time, nor strength—and all the time, each time, he was with Abby he could see a change. Beyond his conscious will, he began to see himself and a woman building a life, a home, for two people. He had begun to see the shadow of himself as the father of a child, with still another new life in his hands.

The vision had surprised him, awed him, and then excited him. He became anxious to get at the realization.

And then—on the night of the symphony gala . . .

It had been like throwing a shovelful of dirt on a blazing fire. In an instant, the thing was gone. Nothing was left but dark emptiness.

The doctor drew his heels up toward his chair, he raised his head, straightened his back, stood, and walked out of the room. He would go see how Joe was doing, and get things lined up for tomorrow's work.

He returned with a glass of orange juice in his hand, and said, well, they might as well plan on what came next—while he had the whole team available.

Those not already in the room quickly were brought in. And Dr. Anderson, all surgeon now, all teacher, talked about the case. He used a blackboard; there were X-rays to examine, a history to read, EKG tracings. He asked questions, he answered others. He assigned duties for the rest of today, tonight, the next day.

"And get yourself some sleep somewhere," he concluded.

"You, too, doctor," suggested the anaesthetist Dr. King.

Malcolm frowned.

"You look bushed."

Malcolm nodded. "I believe I am bushed," he agreed.

"You're working too hard."

The Chief smiled a little. "Me, and who else?"

"We change off, and don't have your responsibility."

That was true. It wasn't good, but it was true.

"I can think of three men who could have done that job for me today."

"It isn't only the surgery, sir."

No, it was not.

"But the surgery is the reward of the diagnosis, the tests, the planning," said someone.

Dr. Anderson was thinking. "No man should be irreplaceable," he said aloud. "And I believe we are going to replace me."

Everyone in the room looked alarmed. No one thought it could be done, no one wanted the spot.

"The patients would never stand for it," said Dr. Alt.

"They'd have to stand for it," Malcolm assured him. "And they would, if it were giving them a chance at life."

"Do you think for one minute," asked Alt, "that Mrs. Holman would let anyone but you operate on her husband? Say, Dr. Aubuchon?"

Malcolm looked as stunned as the others. "Aubuchon?" he repeated.

"He'd do it in a minute."

Malcolm nodded. "I'm afraid you are right. I'd better get my vitamins and stick around, hadn't I?"

"You'd better arrange your schedule to allow you a vacation, doctor."

Malcolm took a turn around the room. He stopped at the desk and signed the p.o. report. "I could take some time off," he agreed.

"You sure could, sir. Get a change, a rest."

An escape . . . "I believe I'll do it!" Malcolm declared.

The team stared at him, unbelieving. They had not dreamed he would ever . . . Oh, he took short trips. He gave the team members breaks. But a vacation?

"Where will you go, sir?" asked the resident. "For how long?"

"I'll work something out," the Chief told him. "As Alt said, my schedule must be flattened down. Then I'll take off. I don't think I'll say where. Just some quiet, secluded spot where I can't be found, where not one of you birds can get in touch."

"If it means Aubuchon in your shoes, we'll get in touch," drawled Dr. Cameron, standing up. "Or even Bennett."

The men burst into laughter. And, the tension released, they left the room, going off on their own affairs, tomorrow's job, their own reports to make. Some went home for the time free.

And the word quickly began to go about the big hospital complex that Dr. Anderson was going to take a vacation. At least, he *said* he was.

Dr. Aubuchon heard the word, and shrugged. He had not had to lift a finger. Meeting Malcolm at the nurses' station on ten an hour or two later, he asked boldly about the vacation. "Anything romantic involved, Mac?" he ventured.

"Jeeze," said the resident who had been standing near. "I wouldn't ever want to make the Chief that mad at me!"

Chapter 3

On the fifteenth of March, to celebrate what he called his tenth wedding anniversary, Felix Lynch gave a party. Not Esther and Felix. Not Alma. But Felix. He issued the invitations, he made the plans. "I'm the one who's been married ten weeks. I'm the one who wants to celebrate."

He was enjoying the whole thing, and his friends indulged him. Certainly they would come. Felix gave good parties. He invited the neighbors on the Lane, some of whom had never been to one of his parties, but almost everyone planned to attend this one. Alma cleaned the already clean house. Esther bought a new outfit. A pants suit, of all things. Alma sniffed loudly at the very idea.

"She looks cute in it," Felix told his mother. "As little as she is . . ."

"She's big enough," Alma declared. Esther did not look like a man's wife in that slim suit of champagne-colored crepe, dangling gold chains, and high-heeled slippers that, miraculously, had no backs to them, but stayed on to click, clack about the hall. "She'll fall and break her neck," promised Alma.

"Don't count on it," said Felix.

He was arranging his buffet at one end of the living room.

At first mention of the party, Alma had happily assumed that he wanted to have a "feast"—the traditional Italian feast of which she had been cheated at his wedding. She began to plan.

"No feast," Felix stopped her.

"No—feast?" asked Alma, her eyes wide, her lips trembling.

"No feast. I'll tend to everything. You'll see. I've ordered flowers. I'll fix them, too."

Alma shook her head. "What kind of man are you?" she asked. "With two women, you'll cook the food and arrange the flowers?"

He laughed and caught her up into his arms, whirled her around. "You know what kind of man I am, Mamma. And I do not plan to cook anything!"

"You'll not feed your friends?"

"Oh, sure I'll feed them. I am having Bommarito cook the ham and roast the turkey. He is sending a man to slice it and generally keep things going."

"You think I cannot slice a turkey?"

"I think you can do anything you want. But tonight, no. You are to be one of the hostesses. You and Esther."

"Do I have to put on a pants suit, too?"

Even Esther laughed at that idea. The little brown ball of a woman . . .

"You wear your good dress," said Felix, "with the lace I brought to you from France."

"I'll wear it," Alma agreed. "But it will be a funny party."

"Good. That's what we want. Fun."

Esther sighed. She could only hope he was right. A tenth anniversary was not measured in short weeks for her. She was beginning to wonder how much longer she could endure the boredom of her life. It wasn't Felix; he was all right. Sometimes. He still was the best-looking man she had ever known; he could make exciting love to her. When they were alone together, things were not too bad. He even would sometimes take her to the places she liked to go—the young, *in* places. He did not enjoy those evenings. He was as bored with them as she was with the older people who were his friends, the "brains" who thought it a big deal to sit around the fire for hours at a time and talk about things like books, and trends, or listen to the music Felix put on the hi-fi. They *enjoyed* that!

Esther did not. And tonight the party would be more of the same. Already, soft, harmonious music was drifting through the house. There were flowers, a silver vase of yellow roses in the hall—the religious picture had disappeared without comment. There were spiky red glads in the study where Felix had set up a bar, with the second man from Bommarito's in charge. On the buffet table single gladiola flowerets floated in a shallow bowl of water. There were tall candles.

And this sort of thing, the restrained, polite music, the restrained, even if rather pretty, flowers, were all the same thing as the snobbishness Felix's friends felt and showed toward the mentality of people like Esther.

She sometimes pointed out to Felix that he had known, when he married her, that she was not a brain. Lately he'd countered this charge by reminding her that *she* had known she would live in the same house with Alma, his mother.

77

She had known that. And it was not entirely her fault that she did not get along with Alma. Oh, yes, she could have learned to scrub and clean, she could learn to cook spaghetti, and eat the fattening stuff, too. But Alma should get used to the idea that she was old and a foreigner, and that Felix and Esther were young. Tonight, Alma should stay decently in her room, and not try to spoil things for Felix by the way she looked.

"My God, her dress is halfway to her ankles! And I suppose her head would crack if she'd ever put a curl into her hair! Let alone lipstick . . . !"

Alma was slyly adding things to Felix's buffet, too. Something she called antipasto—tomato sauce, and olives, and sliced mushrooms, and tiny fish. Cauliflower slices, even. She'd put a tall compote of candy there, a sort of nougat, or hard divinity. She called it Torrone. It was good, but— Any minute, Alma would bring in a great bowl of spaghetti. Esther would bet on it.

"How does it look, sugar?" Felix asked, coming up behind her, his hands on her slender shoulders.

"It looks like a bachelor's party," she answered.

And he laughed. "I've given it many times. People like it."

On the coffee table before the living room couch there was a great wooden tray of crackers and all sorts of cheese. On a small tray-table there were several bowls of dips, with all sorts of things to use. Cauliflower pieces again, and sliced mushrooms.

On the buffet itself was a silver platter of country-cured ham, tender and sweet, another platter of sliced turkey, plates of every kind of bread, a shining urn, and stacks of coffee cups.

The guests began to arrive and they were of all sorts, of all ages. Generally they knew each other, though some of the Lane people were strangers to others of Felix's friends. That big, noisy Dr. Aubuchon, and his little wife. Esther wondered how those two ever had got together! Susan was attractive, with smooth, creamy skin, large dark eyes—but she was so quiet! Still, she could sit on the stone ledge before the fireplace and laugh companionably with the young Negro couple, the blonde girl who also wore a pants suit—hers was red—and Nathan Kendrick.

It got to be fun, watching the Lane people, how they looked and acted. Twice Esther caught Susan out on the porch with Felix. Her dress was the simplest sort of straight sheath, but it had huge flowers of red and white splashed across its green background. Felix evidently liked to talk to her, and laughed at things she said.

Then there was Mr. Kendrick, the plant manager. He was there, in a brown dinner coat, and he talked to everybody, but especially to Margaret Kimberlin. No, not Kimberlin . . . Her name was something else, but she was Mr. Kimberlin's granddaughter.

Even the mysterious, and famous, Dr. Anderson came to the party. Felix had wondered if he would. No, he was *not* snooty! he had contradicted Esther's charge. "But he is a very busy surgeon; and he takes care of himself, the way a prize fighter or a baseball pitcher does. You know—he gets to bed early, is careful of what he eats, stays out of crowded parties." But tonight he came, and his dinner coat was gray—his whole suit was gray, with a brown tie on the large side, and a brown silk handkerchief. Esther could have enjoyed making a play for that man, but Abby Bennett kept him close. She was a girl who knew what she wanted, and how to go about getting it. Esther wondered what Alma would have said if *she* had worn that dress, and shown that much cleavage.

It would seem that the Lane people could step out, but, except for Nathan, they still were not, any of them, Esther's choice.

Felix liked them all. He went about happily with his pitcher of daiquiris, laughing and talking.

Susan Aubuchon asked him how he made the daiquiris. And he said he would tell her. "Do you want the recipe for a big party? Or just two people for an evening?"

"I haven't dared give any parties, yet," she told him, her eyes lifted to his face.

"Then you do this. If the doctor doesn't appreciate them, find yourself another man who will."

"Mr. Lynch . . ."

He smiled at her. "I am only giving you the recipe for my daiquiris. But the name to put with them is Felix."

"All right. Incidentally, they are delicious."

"Of course. And so easy to make. You see? You take one can of frozen lemonade—concentrated. One can of rum."

"Rum, in a can?"

He leaned toward her. And he spoke softly. "You measure the rum in the can that once held the lemonade." "Oh," said Susan, confused, her cheeks rosy. "How stupid of me."

His dark eyes softened. "Not stupid," he said. "Then you add one half can of water."

"The same can?"

He smiled at her. "And eight ice cubes. No can. You mix this all in the blender—and—" He lifted the pitcher. "They are easy, they are good."

She sipped from her glass. "They are—delicious," she said again. But the becoming color had faded from her face.

That was the first time he took her out on the porch, still carrying his pitcher. She seemed quite ready to go with him. The evening was a pleasant one, and the porch was cooler, not so noisy as the main part of the house. Through the glass doors she could look back at the party. Felix set his pitcher on the table and put his hands under Susan's elbows so that she must face him.

"Is there something wrong?" he asked gently.

Susan tried to laugh lightly, she tried to say no. There was nothing wrong.

"I would help you if I could," said the tall man quietly.

She turned away. Then she turned back and looked up into his face. "You are a very kind man," she said softly.

"I watch people. I see you walk your little dog, and stand, thinking. I know you have returned to work."

"There was not enough to keep me busy at home."

"In that large house, no, there would not be."

"Mr. Lynch . . ."

"Felix."

She tried to smile.

"I know the doctor is the one who fired his gun up here last month."

Susan nodded. "He told me that he had. For fun, he said, To see all the doors pop open . . ." Grinning like a mischievous boy, he had told her.

For several minutes, Felix let her stand there beside him, quietly, comfortably. Then he spoke hesitantly. "I would want to help," he said, "where help may be needed, Susan. If trouble has come to you, if it should come, I know that you would not be to blame. I live next door, and I want you to count on me, should you ever need help."

Susan stepped back so that she could look up into the tall man's face. That face was grave, and almost stern. It was a very handsome face, the chin deeply cleft, the features regular, the dark eyes fine. She knew little about Felix Lynch, except that he was a chemist, that the Kimberlin Company thought highly of him. Mrs. Lynch, his mother, was a privileged person with the Kimberlin family.

Why should he say such disturbing things to Susan, and be-

80

wilder her? He was talking about Rupert, but she knew of nothing her husband had done, really. Felix knew about the shots, fired irresponsibly.

"I know Rupert should not do irresponsible things," she said uncertainly. "It isn't behavior that fits into the proper image of a doctor. Doctors have troubles enough without that. You know?" She began to speak more hurriedly. "They keep strange hours, women call them excitedly. But don't let yourself judge my husband by such things, Felix. Nor by any gossip you may hear. He is a doctor and any doctor is subject to gossip, just as he is subject to strains beyond our imagination. At least, beyond mine. Here at his home—because Rupert has such a large practice, you know—he may be excused if he lets off steam a little. Now he laughs about the shots, and thinks it is remarkable that not a door did pop open because of them, but did open when the police came. He talks about that, quite a lot. Just letting off steam, Felix. You know?"

Her defense of her husband had been fierce, defiant, protective, then it shredded away into a timid plea for understanding.

Felix picked up his moisture-beaded pitcher. "I am sorry I spoke as I did, Susan," he said gravely. "I was only offering you a friend—another friend—should you need one. I had also forgotten that women can love men in that blind, devoted fashion."

He held the door open for her to go back into the house, to the party. She shook her head and clasped her hands together.

"Could I stay out here for a little time?" she asked. "You must not, of course. Your guests will miss you."

"I have upset you."

She smiled at him. "I am upset," she agreed. "You may not be to blame."

He was not to blame. For Susan Aubuchon was upset to realize how relieved, how greatly relieved, she was to have the assurance of a friend close by.

In the big house at the far end of the Lane, Margaret Elis dressed for the party which the Lynches were giving. She was going to be late—later than she had hoped to be. But Lester had made things rather difficult. He refused flatly to attend. He said, sure, sure, she was to go. But he would not. Yes, Lionel could push his chair down the road, and help him inside—where all the heads would turn toward him, and away again.

This last year Margaret had stopped protesting with Lester in his moods of self-pity and bitter resentment, though they no longer, really, were moods. He was engulfed in bitterness most of the time. The move to her grandather's home probably had been a mistake, though she had had small choice. She could not, alone, have supported the invalid and herself, cared for their home, and Lester.

Now she shook her head, as if to cast off this sort of speculation, half regret, half self-vindication. Things were as they were, and chewing over the facts was always an unpalatable task.

She did not, especially, want to go to a party, though she did not, especially, want to stay at home, either. Chris would be there. . . .

Fastening her tiny pearl earrings into place, she saw, in the mirror, that her lips were smiling. She nodded to herself. Yes. She would be glad to see Chris—to go to a party and see him.

She examined her turquoise-blue gown. It was of chiffon, hanging from a halter of pearl beads. It was simple, but very pretty.

Her grandfather had insisted that she have something pretty. "We will want to send our girl off looking her best," he told Margaret.

"I wish you were going," she said when she came downstairs to show herself to him.

He touched the material of her gown with his fingertips. "I won't go," he said reflectively. "If I did, and got tired, Malcolm Anderson would make it an excuse to send me back to his hospital. It's worth any sacrifice to avoid that."

"They treated you well when you were at the hospital."

"They did, my dear. Very well. But I told Mac that I wanted to die in my own home."

Margaret smiled, shaking her head at him. "And what did he say?"

"He told me if I did that, it would be a reflection on him. People would think he was not doing everything he could to help me."

"But he is doing . . ." Now her eyes were anxious.

"Of course he is," said her grandfather. "And when I know the chips are really down, I'll do anything Mac tells me to do."

"We are lucky to have him—doctor, neighbor, and friend."

Her grandfather agreed. He extended his hand to Margaret, and she took it, bending over to kiss his cheek. She loved her grandfather very dearly.

"I'll have Lionel drive you," he said now.

"I can walk."

He looked at her slippers, silvery white, but not too high in the heel. "You'll need a wrap."

"I have one. A silk shawl." She pointed to the heap of rosy silk and long white fringe on a chair.

"Good. And there is another thing, my dear. I count on my oldest grandchild for so many things, you know."

"But that's what I'm here for."

"You're here to please my senses, a pretty woman in a pretty blue dress. But—well, this isn't so pretty. Sit down a minute, will you?"

She dropped to the wide hassock. "What is it?"

"I heard . . . You know, the key personnel of the company are good to come out here and gossip with me about business affairs."

"Yes. They come for your advice, and your suggestions."

He patted her hand. "They get that, often enough," he conceded. "Yesterday—I think it was yesterday—the office manager was out here. He is always a good source of gossip, and I enjoy his visits. I find out about the girls in the stenographic pool, what the key punchers are up to. But yesterday—well—I didn't enjoy the gossip he brought with him yesterday."

Margaret waited, feeling her fingertips go cold. If someone connected with the plant had seen her and Chris— She waited.

Her grandfather took a deep breath. "He told me," he said, "that the nice blond boy, Nathan Kendrick, is stealing money from the company. He's working in one of the offices, you know. Time and payroll. And some cash is kept on hand. The boy—he hasn't taken much, but enough. I can't imagine why he should need it. He quit college and came to work for us. He is earning enough to care for his needs, since he lives at home."

It was Margaret's turn to take a deep breath. "Why do you tell me, Grandfather?" she asked.

Her grandfather's hand went out, and his fingertips under her chin lifted her face to his.

She flushed. "I wouldn't tell Chris such a thing about Nathan," she cried. "He worships the boy."

"He is going to have to know, my dear. The thing will

come out sometime. Perhaps you could be there when it happens. The wrench will be a bad one in any case. Chris has not faced up to the fact that a father can hold a son too long. He does worship Nathan, he is too wrapped up in the boy. And that is not good. A time comes when a son steps out on his own, loosens the strings, the swaddling clothes. When Nathan dropped out of school, Chris might have done better to let him find his own job."

"He thought Nathan would resume his studies."

"He would have, without Chris watching him, treating him as if he were ten and needing a father's hand to help him cross the street. The boy is a man now. At least he thinks he is one, and wants to act as one. Chris should let him find out for himself how much of a man he is."

"I think Chris knows that, Grandfather. He is not a stupid man."

"No, he is not, and I wish this were not about to happen to him."

Margaret stood up. "I'll think of something to say," she promised, "something to do. Maybe Nathan could be approached. If he would tell Chris himself . . ."

She left then, enjoying the short walk up the Kimberlin drive, and then down the curve of the road to Lynch's brightly lighted house. She was glad that Dr. Bennett had received no encouragement to install mercury lights around the circle. Without them, she could tip her head back and see the stars. There was a young moon, too, already going down the western sky. She hurried her step.

But, perhaps, being late, she would get to talk to Felix a little. She had decided that she would speak to him about Nathan, and her grandfather's concern. Felix, too, was employed at the plant.

She went into the house without ringing the bell, and hung her shawl in the hall closet. There were a lot of people; the noise of their voices and laughter met her in surflike waves. The house was so large that there was no feeling of a crowd. Margaret stood for a minute deciding which way to go. She could see Felix's dark head at the far edge of the living room. She looked into the study, and nodded to Dr. Aubuchon, who seemed, maybe, a little "under the influence." His face was shiny, his hair tousled. He was laughing loudly at something or other.

Margaret moved on and was almost immediately taken over by Felix's mother. Had Margaret eaten? Alma asked.

"No," said Margaret, "I just got here."

"Then come . . ."

Margaret "came," and was rewarded with a heaping plate of food. Yes, she said, she was hungry. The ham was delicious, and the antipasto! She selected French bread, with a thick, crispy crust and a tender, moist center to the slice. Alma trotted off, promising that she would bring "Miss Kimberlin" cheese.

Margaret talked to Abby Bennett and some man, she talked to some of the strangers and enjoyed them, she took her plate into the main part of the living room and ate the food, talking to those close by. Not about anything in particular. About how delicious everything was . . . Had she had one of Felix's daiquiris? No . . . "He'll be around. He has a pitcher of them."

Margaret drank coffee, cleared her plate, and took it toward the kitchen. A white-coated man relieved her of it. She began to hunt for Felix. She could see Chris, and hear his big laugh. She would see him later. Dr. Anderson was talking to Susan Aubuchon who looked lovely—but Felix had disappeared. He was probably out on the glassed-in porch.

Margaret began to make her way along the wall. He was her host, seeing her as a late arrival; he would greet her and, free somewhat of his other obligations, he would talk to her.

She opened the glass doors, and slipped through, and almost fell over Nathan Kendrick who—well—he *could* have been dancing, but since there was no music out there, what he was doing was holding Esther Lynch in his arms, or vice versa. And they were kissing each other, but really!

Margaret put her hand over her mouth and slid back through the doors again. They had not seen her. They would not have seen anybody. Any number of anybodies! Well.

She took a long minute to compose her face and her feelings. Those two . . . That had been an embrace. That had been a kiss! Anyone could have gone through those doors. Chris, or Felix . . . Margaret had been the one, and she knew . . . Why, this was worse, much worse, than stealing the company's petty cash!

Margaret had heard a little talk about Felix's quick and, perhaps, unsuitable marriage. Chris had laughed about a man who waited a little longer than usual to get married and then fell for a girl who would not have had a chance with him at twenty. "Oh, he might have given her a *chase*. But marriage? No, sir. You've got to wait ten years or more to get caught by someone like Esther."

But what about Nathan? He was twenty. Was he giving

that girl a "chase"? Perhaps. But the thing was: now Esther was married. She had a husband. She had a husband who was a brilliant young scientist, who worked for the company where Nathan had a job, where his father was plant manager, and both men could probably get hotheaded about poaching young men!

Margaret had said she could not tell Chris about the till-pilfering. Could she tell him about this development? Darn Nathan, anyway! Why couldn't he fall in love with some girl in the proper manner? Well, maybe not *proper* in this day and age, with the young folk what they were, but must he stir up a scandal on the Lane by selecting someone who was married and had obligations elsewhere? Margaret stopped short, her eyes flared wide. She felt her cheeks flame. Wanting to run, but not quite doing it, she cut across that end of the room and down along the hall to what she knew was Alma's bedroom and bath. She went into the bathroom and locked the door. A night light burned brightly enough so she could see herself in the mirror above the vanity. Smooth dark hair, large dark eyes, her pretty chiffon dress, and her crimson face. Of course she blushed! She was glad she still had the grace to blush. For who was she to criticise Nathan and Esther? She too was a married woman, and in love with the wrong man. She too—

Lester was right. He had warned her. Situations like this could do much to dim the light of heaven, to tarnish the shine of the paradise where she had thought to live.

Abby Bennett's father had not approved of the dress his daughter was wearing to the Lynch party. It was too pink, he said. Mrs. Bennett and Abby both laughed at him. "If I put on a sweater," his daughter teased, "you'd like the color better."

"It is too low, dear," said her mother. "Isn't it?"

"Not to be stylish. And a girl has to get attention. You know? Twenty-four is pretty old not to have caught a man."

"I thought maybe you had caught Anderson," said her father. "What happened? Did you scare him off with a high-collared shirt?"

Abby laughed fondly. "You two are priceless," she told her parents. "Why aren't you going to the party?"

'We don't go to any parties," answered Mrs. Bennett.

"I have a couple of serious cases," said her father. "I may be called."

Neither excuse was valid. Abby shrugged. She didn't espe-

86

cially want to go to the party, either. She could imagine what it would be like. A lot of strangers. If they were Esther's friends, heaven to Betsey! If they were Felix's—or Alma's— she smiled. In any case, the evening would be spent talking to one man after another, not caring about any of them. The long, dark-haired, very young man who would bring her a drink, and tell off-color jokes. The two men, not so young, who would, by their own admission, gang up on her and suggest a move into the city; one of them would know a really good place! Had she been to the Pavilion—or whatever the local, popular saloon was named? Then there would be the toothy man who liked to hook arms and draw a girl close, while he smiled and smiled. No! She would not go!

She told her parents that she would not. "I have no real gift for small talk," she confessed. "The saying nothing, over and over. And sometime, maybe tonight, there may be others with the same lack, and think what a disaster could result!"

"I'd count on you to find something to say," said her father, holding her fur jacket for her. "You should have a scarf . . ."

"And tuck it into my bosom when I take off my jacket?" she teased.

"It wouldn't hurt."

"She's going," said Dr. Bennett, as he watched her go down their driveway, "thinking that she will see Dr. Anderson."

"He seems to like her," said his wife.

"Seemed, not seems. Something happened the night they went to that concert. Abby must have said something. He's the one who stays away."

"You're full of ideas," his wife told him. "Come sit down and watch the movie."

Abby's parents were right. She was going to the Lynch party for their reason only. She expected to see Malcolm there. He was doing a very good job of avoiding her lately, but if he was there . . . and he probably would be. He was Felix Lynch's friend. Older than Felix, he liked the young man, liked to talk to him. Yes, he would come to the party if that was possible, and Abby would see him.

He was there, and she did see him. He first saw her from across the room, nodded to her, but made no effort to cross to her. He was not exactly rude. But he certainly could not be called cordial or eager. Abby was more determined than ever to talk to him; men did not rebuff her. Something must have happened, perhaps only Dr. Anderson's arrived-at decision to stay clear of female involvements—but she could at least make him regret his resolve.

She talked to various people, to the young man with the dirty jokes, and told one herself that made him blink. She then refused a suggestion to move on to someplace really exciting. Yes, and here was the guy who put his hand on her shoulder and then about her waist. He wore a wide-striped shirt and a rose-colored tie.

"It's like a dog show," thought Abby. "We didn't bring our dogs, but we each one jockey for position, for a favorable stance and appearance. We struggle to meet the judges and gain their interest."

She became intrigued with the idea, and moved through the rooms with interest. She leaned against the bar and talked to Rupert Aubuchon, who had every grace of the practiced charmer. How had he been lucky enough to marry a genuine lady like Susan? Well-mannered, friendly, and smart! What was their home life? Dr. Bennett did not speak well of this Aubuchon; Abby had a vague impression of shady ethics.

Now this Kendrick was another thing. A big man, perhaps a bit rough—but a gentleman, withal. There was no wife in evidence. Did Abby remember something said about two bachelor households on the Lane? His could be the second one. Malcolm's was certainly the other.

It was their group that Dr. Anderson ventured to join. Abby said, "Hello, doctor," to him softly. He said, "Hello. How are you?" And immediately engaged this Kendrick in an argument about writers, big writers, famous writers, yes, he would admit, good writers. But ones, he said, who did not always wear well.

"I used to admire Eliot," said Dr. Anderson. "I admired him immensely, and I have been known to quote his poetry from memory at what must have been boring length." His brown eyes sparkled, and Chris Kendrick chuckled.

"Lately, however," Dr. Anderson continued, "his writings, like those of Ernest Hemingway, have begun to seem incomplete. At least to me. It just is not enough to complain exquisitely."

"Here, here!" Abby applauded. Malcolm glanced at her, but immediately turned his attention back to Kendrick, who was ready to defend Hemingway.

"Oh, you thick-necked men all identify with Hemingway!" Dr. Anderson argued.

They soon were at it, tooth and nail, with their group growing. Margaret—Lester, was it?—came up, and Susan Aubuchon. Felix stopped to listen and declare that he still read the Disney books. Abby said a few things but found that in this group she was not going to be deferred to as she was in the purely egghead literary, cultural circles which she had known elsewhere.

This gave her something to ponder, to think about. Here she was in what she had been thinking of, and speaking of, as a restful pocket where she could hibernate, rearrange her busy schedules, and replenish her physical strength before going back to the pressures and excitement of the rat race.

But the darned "pocket" seemed to be saying something to her, even teaching her something. These men here at this party—she really liked the "thick-necked," blunt-spoken, kind man, Chris Kendrick. She liked and admired the hard-working, straight-thinking doctor who knew what he wanted to do with his life and went after it. She even liked the tall, and extremely handsome Italian-Irishman, Felix Lynch, who could be charming and still mean every word he said. And even the slick Dr. Aubuchon, while a familiar type, was intriguing. She cared about what the man might do.

Oh, yes! She had some thinking to do. She had explored and traveled in the intellectual world, and she had returned to find these good things in the home where she had been born and had grown up. Which she had left ... What had she left behind? What had she missed? Did she need to miss it longer? Could she at least study the lesson which the past months had offered to teach her?

She listened to the talk going on about her. Susan Aubuchon was well involved in it. And, listening, she thought about Malcolm Anderson. She had been attracted by him, to him, from the first. He was a new sort of man to her. Not only because of his professional accomplishments. Abby had interviewed and come to know a lot of men who "did things." But this man's overall character, his personality ... He hewed to the line, he set his feet on a road, he—he—*flew right* was another expression. Those phrases were not trite clichés when applied to Malcolm. He did have that quality, that integrity—to the point that he could make other men seem silly and futile. Abby wanted to know such a man better, to know him very well. He had shown interest in her, then had lost it, set it firmly aside. Why? Knowingly, she had done nothing. She liked him, honored him.

What could she do to get him to talk to her, to let her

prove her good intent? She would try almost anything. She had come to this party to try to make some effectual gesture of open friendship. What else . . . Good heavens, must she lay siege to the man, actually *court* him? She glanced quickly at him. His strong face, he looked well in that gray silk suit—he liked to talk, to argue. He was laughing now at something Susan had said, something which Abby's self-preoccupation had caused her to miss. He could be reached; she had reached him once. And yes! She definitely would court him, if that was what he wanted, what would be necessary.

She gave him a half hour. She danced with Dr. Aubuchon; she talked for five minutes to Alma Lynch. She watched Esther and Nathan Kendrick; they were dancing, too, out in the wide hall. She drank one of Felix's daiquiris. And, glass in hand, she asked Malcolm Anderson if he knew how they were made.

He offered to find out.

"I'll go with you. Together, we should remember."

Felix was only a few feet away. He laughed at their request, and said he planned to have the recipe printed. "I'll send you a copy."

"And then we'll give as good parties as you do," said Abby sincerely. "Now, doctor, if you are ready to go home, perhaps we could walk up the road together?"

Alma Lynch spent a busy evening at her son's party. In spite of all his arrangements—and the money the boy had spent!—she felt responsible for the guests in her home.

She kept her eyes on things, in the kitchen, in the dining room—even in the bar. Some of Felix's friends drank a lot, some did not. They all ate a lot. And Alma had no reason to regret putting out some extra food for them.

She watched the people, hearing the tone of the talk and laughter, making no attempt to understand what it was all about.

She kept her eye on Felix; he was the host—but young. She must be sure he attended to all of his guests.

He did a pretty good job, she decided. For a time she thought he was devoting too much attention to Mrs. Aubuchon; he took her out on the porch, and he stayed there a long time. Alma peered at them through the glass curtains. They were talking, very seriously. That young woman looked troubled. When they came back into the main part of the house, Felix kept watching her, and often went near her. His mother decided that he was only being kind—as he should

be! Naturally! Though if his interest were of another sort, Alma would approve. That slender, ladylike woman was exactly the sort Felix should have married. He still should have that sort of wife. She was smart, but not bold. She wasn't pretty, though there was real beauty in her dark eyes, and in the way she held her head.

Yes, Felix should have that sort of wife.

And Susan should have a good man like Felix. Surely by now that smart schoolteacher must realize that the husband she did have was a scamp. A rascal. A no-good! Someday he would probably walk out on her.

As for Felix—he was already married, too. And he was not the man to desert his wife, or put her out of his house, however wise he might become about her. There, Alma would have to do some work. Esther must be the one to leave.

That girl had things pretty nice in this house—clothes, a fine home, the use of a car, no work to do. *Maria mia, no!* And whatever the priest had to say about divorce, Esther must go! Alma would work on that. There were loopholes. Felix and Esther had not been married in the church. And if that girl became unhappy enough to look around for a man she liked better . . .

Now, of course, no man was better than Felix. But if she thought— Alma would think up some faults for Felix. He worked hard, and was often away at night. He—*ha!* He talked Italian to his mother! Esther hated that. She hated everything Italian. The smell of garlic and good cheese. She said *pasta* would make her fat. Tonight Alma had heard the little pullet apologizing for her antipasto. Esther was ashamed of it. Alma's head nodded up and down. Yes, she would think of something.

The next day was a busy one for Alma. Certainly she would clean up after the party! Who else? Let the men from Bommarito's take their platters and their sharp knives, their bottles and their glasses and depart. This was a home! The women of the home would clean up.

"Esther, will you help Mamma?" Felix asked anxiously.

She shrugged. "If she'll let me."

"Mamma, you let Esther help you."

"Of course."

The next morning Esther did not appear until almost noon. By then Alma had the rooms aired, and the doors closed again. The cigarette trays, the plates and glasses, the crumpled napkins had all been brought into the kitchen.

Alma was vacuuming the carpet, plumping pillows, finding bits of food and coffee cups in strange places. She was down on her knees, tidying the fireplace when Esther came down, yawning, and saying it had been a big night. Was there any coffee?

"In the kitchen," said Alma. "I'll be out there in a minute."

"I can get it." Esther drifted kitchenward. She wore a robe of bright red corduroy; her long yellow hair was tangled, her face had no make-up. She did not bother about her appearance when only Alma was at home.

Alma followed her to the kitchen and cleared a free space at the table. Did Esther want toast? Eggs?

At the suggestion, Esther frowned as if in pain. "Just coffee for now," she said in her childish voice.

"You ate too much last night?" asked her mother-in-law sympathetically.

"Everything was too much last night. My head aches."

Alma put a cup of coffee on the table, and a glass of tomato juice. "You eat, you feel better," she said, putting bread into the toaster.

"Why Felix ever wanted to give a party like that . . ." said Esther.

"He wanted his friends to know his new wife."

"But, good Lord, the people here on the Lane already knew me!"

"Yes, they did. And even some from the plant knew you. But Felix has still some other friends. . . ."

Esther frowned, trying to remember. "Those colored people . . ."

"No. That man works in the laboratory. But there were some from La Cosa Nostra."

Esther still struggled to recall—then her attention fired. "What did you say?" she asked.

Alma shrugged. "My Felix is a big man in La Cosa Nostra," she said proudly. "He is important."

"But the Cosa . . . That's *gangsters!*"

Alma shrugged. "They are all sorts. They do all sorts of things."

"I've heard," said Esther heavily. "Good God, do you realize . . . Why, that's a dangerous thing! Should you even hint that he belongs?"

"You are his wife. You will not talk about this."

"I don't even want to talk about it here," said the blonde girl, shuddering. "I'm not smart, but that thing—gangsters,

crime syndicates ... I'll take such things on TV, but not in the family, if you don't mind."

Alma shrugged and began to wash dishes in the sink.

"Why don't you use the dishwasher?" Esther asked petulantly.

"These are thin glasses, they could be nicked. Felix has nice things in his home."

"Yeah. Nice. Like gangsters. That old man—his boss—Ottolini. Is he a gangster, too?"

"I do not know. The names are not known."

"So you tell me that my husband belongs."

Alma did not turn. Esther stared at the woman, at her plain, dark gray dress, with the strings of her red apron tied around her waist, her iron-gray hair twisted into a tight knot at the back of her head.

"Dagoes!" said Esther, under her breath.

Alma put a thin, stemmed glass carefully into the drainer. "Felix is only part Italian."

"I know, I know. And the part that is belongs to a thing like— Mrs. Lynch, that gangster-stuff scares me cold!"

Alma shrugged.

Esther was thinking. The men who sometimes came to the house. She remembered, on her very first day here, a little man—he wanted to talk Italian. Last night—maybe even the waiter from that restaurant— "Do all Italians belong?" she asked, breaking off a bite of toast.

"To La Cosa Nostra? Oh, no. Me, I do not."

"Well, me neither. I am going on record, here and now. Whatever Felix does or belongs to is no skin off my nose. I'd not— Why, that thing is dangerous! You know that!"

Again Alma shrugged. "It is dangerous," she agreed. "Felix has to be very careful. And of course you must not speak of it. I do not speak of it—to him."

"I don't believe he belongs," declared Esther.

Another shrug.

"He wouldn't be such a fool."

"You asked if maybe Dr. Ottolini belonged. He is a smart man."

"Okay. Okay. But me—I'm out of it. I'm as all-American as hot dogs."

"Hot dogs, maybe," Alma agreed, polishing a daiquiri glass with a linen towel. "But you are Felix's wife, no? And as his wife, if Felix ever should get into trouble with the law, or with La Cosa Nostra, you would find out what that means.

The law would question you. The organization would suspect you."

She ventured a glance at Esther's face. It was white, and her eyes were wide.

"Of course," said Alma comfortably, "we both know how smart Felix is. He would never let a dumb American catch him at anything." She mounted a stepstool. "Hand me those glasses," she said. "They go on the top shelf here."

"I'd break them," Esther protested. "You've got me shaking like a leaf."

It was an early spring. By the late days of March, the world was a lovely place of new green leaves, perfume and flowers. Birds were busy, and lyrical. The air had a silken softness. And the woods down behind the Kimberlin home were delightful. Each step into them was a new adventure and offered treasures. A thick patch of violets, a beautiful white mushroom, the flowerlike unfolding of the leaves on a tall hickory tree, the gold-varnished buds splitting, the new leaves unfurling. There were ferns, and any number of wild flowers unknown to Margaret Elis. She had determined to have a wild flower garden close to the house, and this afternoon she had put on a sturdy denim dress, and even sturdier shoes, selected a good-sized basket, a trowel, a small spade, and ventured down the hill, going in under the tall trees as reverently as she had ever entered a church.

She would not go too far, she had promised Lionel and the cook. A good, hearty "holler" would summon her. With her grandfather not so well, getting whiter and more silent each day— She wished Malcolm Anderson would decide he could have surgery, and then perform it. She could not face losing him. It was he who had urged her to get out of the house.

"I am going to rest in bed until five," he announced. "You shouldn't be around with your chatter."

Margaret gave him the smile he wanted, and agreed to go for a walk. She had already discussed the wild flower garden with him. "I won't be far away," she promised.

"Good. You know? I like you with your hair down."

Margaret felt the red plaid scarf which tied her dark hair behind her neck. "Then I'll wear it this way more often," she promised. Chris, too, liked the way her hair fell into big, rich curls when released.

Thinking of Chris, happy to be out of doors if her grandfather would safely rest, she went down the hill and into the woods. She did more enjoying than she did working, but she was determined to get some violets from the large patch behind the Bennett house. They were so thick that a few would not be missed. The woods were Kimberlin land, she knew that. But the view from any of the windows surely belonged to the householders.

The Bennett house rose abruptly from the hillside here, its sturdy brick walls planted firmly upon piers which, she hoped, were bedded on rock. The screened porch jutted out, really, into the leafy treetops. It must be a delightful place on which to sit in the summer, or on such a warm spring afternoon. Just enough sunlight would filter through the new leaves.

Margaret knelt among the violets, selecting a square of strong-seeming plants, and reveling in the beauty under her hand. She took her trowel from the basket, and paused.

Above her—less than ten feet above her, less than ten feet away from her, someone was talking to someone else. She lifted her head. If it were Mrs. Bennett and her maid, she need not worry about eavesdropping. She could distinguish Mrs. Bennett's voice; like the lady herself, it was delicate, pretty, well-bred.

And the other voice— Oh, it was Alma Lynch! Margaret smiled. She did love Alma, that honest, good soul. For all the years she had kept the Kimberlin house and made Grandfather comfortable. Never really a servant. A friend, rather, glad to help. Visiting children and grandchildren all came to cherish Alma.

Mrs. Lynch wanted Margaret still to call her that. Even at the party. . . .

And now, the harmless gossip of two nice, elderly women was nothing to worry about. She would get on with her gardening. Because once she had dug up some plants, she must take them immediately to her prepared bed.

The two women were talking about her grandfather's illness, as they would. . . .

Margaret marked off her square of violets, ran her trowel down and carefully under the plants, getting enough soil, not disturbing the roots. She was very careful, thinking about the moss she wanted to transplant, and after that the trillium she had seen farther down into the woods.

Mrs. Bennett was saying that she didn't think there was anything wrong with Mr. Kimberlin except his heart. "But of course, that's enough, Alma. My husband explained it to me. His trouble is that not enough blood comes to the heart. It is like trying to run your car with not enough gasoline."

Coronary insufficiency, due to an arterial lesion. Yes, that was one way to explain things.

Carefully Margaret transferred the patch of violets to the sheet of foil which she had spread in the bottom of her shallow basket—dirt, roots, the perky flowers and their rich, heart-shaped leaves.

She glanced up at the porch thinking that she would wave to the women if they saw her. They evidently did not. Mrs. Bennett sat on the glider, her face in profile. Alma sat in a rocking chair, its back to the woods.

"Is Dr. Anderson caring for Mr. Kimberlin?" Alma was asking.

"Well, I think so. My husband is very close-mouthed about medical affairs, you know, Alma. But I have seen Dr. Anderson going in there a couple of times each day. Now, though, he is away. Out of town."

Margaret lifted her head.

Alma must have asked a question, too.

"Yes," Mrs. Bennett was saying, "he left three days ago for a vacation. I don't know where he's gone—or how long he will be away. He makes these trips, to lecture or do what the doctors call demonstrate. But this seems to be different. Dr. Bennett called it a vacation, and sounded as if there were some mystery about it."

Margaret moved to the nearby bed of moss, as green as emerald, each minute plant delicately perfect. Her grandfather would know; Malcolm Anderson would not go anywhere without telling Arthur Kimberlin. The doctor was a fine man. Chris liked him.

Margaret rested her hands to think for a minute about Chris. He would come to the house tonight to see Arthur Kimberlin. As she admitted him, his hand would touch hers, and something would stir in his eyes as he searched her face. She would flush.

She flushed now, and cherished the warm glow of knowing that she was a woman beloved. Chris . . .

Margaret loved him. Their love should be a clean and simple thing between a man and a woman. But—it was not, because there was Lester Elis to be considered, to be counted on.

She was sure that a change must come, that a change must be made. But how? Certainly her grandfather could not be subjected to the scene which Lester would make at any suggestion of a divorce. He could be extremely nasty.

It certainly was not true that suffering enobled a man's

96

©Lorillard 1974

Micronite filter.
Mild, smooth taste.
America's quality cigarette.
Kent.

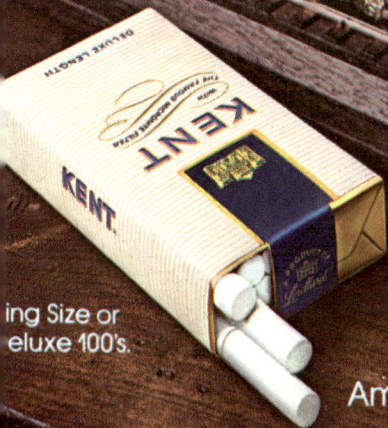

ing Size or
eluxe 100's.

Kings: 16 mg. "tar," 1.0 mg. nicotine;
00's: 18 mg. "tar," 1.2 mg. nicotine;
Menthol: 18 mg. "tar," 1.2 mg. nicotine;
av. per cigarette, FTC Report Mar. '74.

Try the crisp, clean taste of Kent Menthol.

The only Menthol with the famous Micronite filter.

nature. Generally suffering revealed only what that nature was, and had always been. Still—could a woman, could Margaret, divorce a crippled man?

Would Chris want her to do that?

Chris . . .

Again she sat smiling, and dreamy. If only . . . If only . . .

Arthur Kimberlin would buy Lester off. And Lester would sell. But Margaret could not let either man know she would bargain. Or Chris. Especially Chris!

She sighed heavily. Something would happen, something would come.

Meanwhile she would plant her wild flower garden, and tell her grandfather about it. He seemed to enjoy her enthusiasms. He was a very kind man.

The women up on the porch were still talking about him, and about Dr. Anderson. Alma did not think a doctor had a right to go off. . . .

Mrs. Bennett was explaining that doctors had to have some relief. She mentioned the tension of their lives, the pressures upon them.

And she said again that there was some mystery attached to Dr. Anderson's vacation. He had told no one where he was going, and it seemed that he could not be reached. The hospital, or his office, had said that he was going to an Oregon ski resort, but he had never arrived there. Dr. Bennett had phoned the lodge and was told that he had not registered.

Alma suggested that some woman might be in the picture.

Mrs. Bennett discounted this, and vigorously—so vigorously that Margaret smiled. At the Lynch party there had been a little talk that Abby Bennett had set herself the hitherto impossible task of catching Malcolm Anderson. If so, she might succeed. She was a beautiful woman, and clever.

But where could Malcolm have gone? Where could he be? Would her grandfather know? He might. She would ask him that evening. There could have been an accident, or even foul play. These days, a traveler, between airport and hotel, could be waylaid.

Margaret knew that Malcolm had not been to see her grandfather for several days; yesterday she had called his office about some medication, and was told that Dr. Anderson was not available. His office nurse gave her directions which she knew would "be all right with Doctor."

Margaret had thought little of the doctor's being away. But this morning she had begun to worry that a doctor was not seeing her grandfather regularly, and debated whether, in an emergency, she should call Dr. Aubuchon. Or Dr. Bennett? Should she, perhaps, ask Rupert Aubuchon to stop in and see the sick man regularly while Dr. Anderson was away? Wouldn't Malcolm have told her to do that? Or even have spoken to Dr. Aubuchon? She would ask Chris what to do.

Up on the porch the women were following a parallel line of thought. Mrs. Bennett was saying, rather forcefully, that the Kimberlins should have called Dr. Bennett on the case from the first. He would have devoted himself . . .

Should they have done this? Margaret asked. The choice of doctors had been made before she had come to the Lane to live. And she had not questioned it. Her grandfather and Dr. Bennett were friends and had been friends for many years. But did friends, to that degree, make good attending doctors? Wouldn't it be like caring for a family member?

Dr. Bennett came to see Arthur every day; he would sit and gossip with him; never once had there been any medical service, not even the use of a stethoscope. Of course, in an emergency, though, Dr. Aubuchon might be the one to call. Dr. Bennett was old. And before Malcolm had disappeared, during the brief time her grandfather was in the hospital, Dr. Anderson had spoken of surgery as a possibility. Surely Dr. Bennett would not be the one to perform such delicate surgery. In Margaret's childhood and girlhood he had been a general practitioner. It was only lately that he had narrowed his work to that of the heart, probably to cut down his activity.

Margaret could talk directly to her grandfather, if she thought he would not become anxious over Malcolm's absence.

Thinking about these things, she went down the steep hillside for the trillium; she did not take her basket; she could bring the plant up in a bit of newspaper and have a hand free to catch herself should she slip. Clutching at the bushes, at the trunk of a young tree, she went down, and came up again, more careful of the plants she carried than of herself. Once she fell and skinned her knee on a rock. Again on safe ground, she sat down to investigate the damage. Perhaps she should go home now, wash the injury with soap and water, and put some sort of antiseptic on the cuts.

She lifted her head, frowning. The women above her were talking in a more spirited way. Abby's name was mentioned.

"Such a beautiful girl," said Alma.

"I thought you might be shocked at the dress she wore to your party," suggested Abby's mother.

Alma had better not agree with her, Margaret said to herself.

She could imagine the way Alma shrugged. "After Esther, what's to shock me?" she asked. "These young women!"

"Abby says they wear clothes like that to attract the men."

"Then they succeed. The men at the party thought she was beautiful."

"Dr. Anderson, too?" asked Abby's mother. "Or did you notice?"

"I notice everything. But Dr. Anderson . . ."

"I know he's standoffish," agreed Mrs. Bennett. "But for a time I thought there might be hope for a romance. He took Abby to a concert, brought flowers; they saw each other at various times, and talked."

"I knew that they took walks," Alma agreed.

And a romance between those two would be wonderful, decided Margaret. Handsome, clever people. Dr. Anderson showed himself for a reader, a thinker. At the party he and Chris had had a most amusing round about Hemingway. He'd called Chris "thick-necked," which he was. Strong, sturdy, reliable.

"The trouble with Abby," said Mrs. Bennett sorrowfully, "is that, while she is pretty and men are attracted, she then shows herself to be a *smart* woman. Smarter than most men. And the men just don't want that in a woman. I've tried to tell Abby this."

Margaret bent her attention to putting the trillium safely into her basket. She could not support herself on her injured knee, and this made her awkward. She must concentrate; she wondered if she would be able to plant the things in the bed. Lionel would help her, of course, but she wanted this garden to be her own.

She managed, though not tidily. She stood up and brushed dirt and leaf mold from the front of her skirt. She had better go home with the plants she had, come back tomorrow, or the next day. She—

Her head went up. She had heard her own name.

"Margaret is the nicest sort of a girl," Mrs. Bennett was saying virtuously, "and I know it cannot be easy for her, as young as she is, to live with an invalid husband."

Alma said something, and Mrs. Bennett's high, clear voice came again. Margaret listened, rubbing her hand against her skirt.

99

"I've heard he has a bad temper," the woman agreed. "But with pain—and if he even guesses his wife is having an affair with another man ... That could drive an invalid like Lester Elis crazy. I just wonder if Arthur Kimberlin knows what is going on?"

"Do you know?" asked Alma, her voice harsh.

"Well, there is talk, Alma. Among the people who work on the Lane. Doris Kendrick has a housekeeper who is cousin to Lionel— Oh, one hears things. And sees them, too. Dr. Bennett himself saw her going down to Kendrick's very late one night."

That one night. That one hour of warm love and singing joy. Never since. Neither Margaret nor Chris wanted a hole-in-the-wall love. But they did want love! And they should have a right to more than touching each other's hand in greeting, or their eyes meeting across the room at a party, more than a word or two of conversation.

And who were these two old women to sit in judgment? Margaret was shocked, and very angry. She was ready to shout at them, to ask them why they should dare to talk about her?

It was that sort of talk which made the world ugly—more ugly than any love affair could do. She did love Chris, and he loved her. Someday they would be together.

But even now there was this sort of talk, which spoiled the heaven in which she had hoped to live. Lester had said that heaven would be spoiled. And it did seem— Why, these two old women, surely not meaning to hurt anyone, could even drive Margaret out of this paradise of violets and green moss and— A tear fell like a jewel into her basket. She knelt on the ground, not noticing her hurt knee, and wept.

Life was so short. She loved Chris Kendrick. Other women had love, and could realize their love. Women like Esther Lynch took love where it was offered. From their husbands, from other men, without any apparent agonizing or moralizing.

Margaret wondered if Alma knew about Nathan and Esther. That embrace on the porch had not been a first, nor accidental, encounter. Even in the short minute that Margaret had watched them, she had seen Esther move against the man, tightly; he would have felt the pressure of her body. Her mouth opened under his, and for a second she lay slack, letting him hold her. Excitement grew in him and he kissed her with a franker urgency. . . . Margaret shivered just to remember.

Did Alma know?

Margaret had decided at once that she could not tell Chris anything about his son. But she had thought, perhaps, she might speak a warning word to Nathan. But not now. If the Lane was talking about her and Chris, her position was not such as to make it possible for her to take a virtuous stand of protest to the boy. Or to Esther. Oh, if she could just talk to Chris about all this! How on earth had paradise tricked her into such a messy situation?

Three days later, Arthur Kimberlin was taken to the hospital by ambulance. It was at his own suggestion; he had awakened that morning knowing that he was a very sick man. And he had promised Malcolm Anderson . . .

Lionel made him ready. Margaret accompanied him in the ambulance. She was frightened, but appeared calm. She had nothing to do but sit on the jump seat and present a quiet countenance whenever her grandfather opened his eyes and looked at her. He spoke only a word or two—once to ask why there weren't sirens, and to essay a smile to go with the question. Another time—they were going through the city park, with the fountains shooting bright spray up into the sunshine, and men carrying golf bags across the green grass—he said something that sounded like "Malcolm said surgery . . ."

"They'll take care of you," Margaret assured him, not at all sure that care would be enough.

They reached the hospital, and doctors, nurses, attendants, took over. Stubbornly, Margaret insisted on staying within sight of her grandfather. Yes, she knew that she could go upstairs in another elevator, but she preferred this one, with him.

She was a small woman, with smooth dark hair, a neat suit of brown plaid worn with a white blouse. She was pleasant, and firm. She went with her grandfather. Yes, she would answer questions. She met Dr. Mitchell. She had met him on a previous occasion, when her grandfather had come in for tests and examination.

"Dr. Anderson . . ." she said.

"Dr. Anderson will see him. I am the resident doctor."

"Yes, I know. But if there is to be surgery . . ."

"That will be decided, Mrs. Elis, I promise you that Mr. Kimberlin will have every possible care."

She expected him to get such care; the hospital expected him to have it. Word reached the newspapers that Arthur

101

Kimberlin was a patient in the Medical Center, expecting to have heart surgery. Dr. Malcolm Anderson was scheduled to perform it. When? asked the reporters. Where? What did it involve?

The hospital could not speak for Dr. Anderson.

Would he speak for himself?

Possibly. Just now, he was not available.

Where was he?

On vacation.

Would he return?

It was certainly hoped that he would.

Mention of Oregon was made. Within hours, the reporters returned to the hospital. The Oregon ski lodge had no record of Dr. Anderson's having been there. If he had planned to, he had not arrived. What went on here, anyway?

Serious concern was expressed. At once it was asked who would ever replace Anderson? Overall, and immediately. There began, at once, a fevered jockeying for position. Of course his team was on duty, trained by him, skilled in every aspect of his techniques.

Oh, sure, but the team needed a leader. A quarterback to call the plays, and to execute them. Who, who, *who* would go in for Anderson? Heart surgery could be done, but not *Anderson* heart surgery.

The families of patients were disturbed, particularly little Mrs. Holman, whose husband was one of Dr. Anderson's cases. She went all to pieces to know that the surgeon had disappeared and so completely that he could not be found to care for a big shot like Arthur Kimberlin.

To begin with, she was a nervous, apprehensive person. Secondly, she had, from the first, slavishly worshiped the miracle-working doctor, a name she had attached to him, and which the surgical floor repeated as a joke. One never appreciated by the Chief. Now—

"She's all over the damn place!" cried the Administrator in anguish. "Here, she's brought her husband to our hospital to have Dr. Anderson. Somewhere she's acquired the term 'patient abandonment.' She is going to talk to the press, and to other patients' families. Can we exclude her from the hospital?"

"I'd try to quiet her fears," said the Medical Director.

"Ha!" barked the Administrator.

Everybody in that unit of the Center became on edge. The members of Malcolm's team went into hiding, too, as best they could. *They* didn't know what was going on, they said.

They had their doctoring jobs to do, but— They never had talked about the Chief. Why start now?

All they knew, all little Mrs. Holman could find out, was that Arthur Kimberlin had been installed in the penthouse suite of the heart unit, entirely isolated, with no visitors except his granddaughter.

As she waited for the elevator one day, Mrs. Holman ventured to speak to Margaret. Wasn't she crazy with worry?

"My grandfather is seriously ill," said Margaret. "Yes, I am worried."

"Have you had word about Dr. Anderson?"

"Excuse me, please?"

The persistent reporters came to know the slim, pretty woman in her dark suit with the fold of her white blouse against it. But they got little from Margaret. She was pleasant; she said nothing. Not even to Dr. Bennett, who came over to the house one evening to complain to Margaret about his being kept away from Arthur.

"I'm sorry, Dr. Bennett. I don't have any authority at the hospital."

"You have more than you are using, my dear. You are the patient's next of kin."

"Now you know better than that! There's my father, Aunt Cecily, and four other grandchildren." Her father was in California, her aunt in Switzerland.

"I mean, here. Locally. In the home."

"Yes. Here I suppose I am the closest."

"You could make a few demands. I'm a doctor. I am Arthur's old friend."

"Yes. I know that, and I am sorry."

"But you won't do anything about it?" The wiry old man was deeply hurt, especially in his professional pride. Margaret was sorry for him.

He turned to leave. At the door, he spoke as cattily as any woman could have done. "I just wonder," he demanded, "if Dr. Aubuchon may be privileged?"

Margaret sighed. "I don't know, Dr. Bennett. The doctors come and go. I hope my grandfather's welfare is everyone's first concern."

Dr. Bennett repeated his complaint to the Chief of Medical Services. And he asked that doctor, too, if Aubuchon had been allowed to attend Kimberlin.

The Chief answered him grimly. "I certainly hope not!" he said. "He had better not try to step in. They seem to be having trouble enough over at Cardiac."

"Yes, they do," admitted Dr. Bennett. "With a lot of patients expecting to have surgery from Anderson—not only Kimberlin—everything disorganized. Shouldn't you at least name an Acting Chief, doctor?"

The Chief of Medical Services, like Margaret, was sorry for the old man. "Mac left orders on his patients," he said. "I think your friend Kimberlin will be all right for a time, doctor. He is getting excellent care. And if surgery is needed, it won't be a matter of acute question for a few days."

"I hope I'll be told," Dr. Bennett managed to retort. It helped his vanity a little to be waspish.

Of course the Lane was disturbed. Dr. Anderson's dark house was a constant reminder of the situation. Susan asked Rupert keenly about his knowledge of the affair. "You said . . ." she reminded him.

"I said I'd suggest he needed a vacation. But he went without benefit of my advice."

"Did he, really?"

He laughed. "Now, what do you mean by *really?*"

Susan blushed, and turned away. He might want to know what she meant; she did not. Later she was to remember that last brief conversation as Rupert was getting into his raincoat, ready to go to the hospital, to his day's work there and in his office. He had laughed and teased her—and she had been ashamed—not only of herself.

That morning, she had, as usual, cleared the breakfast things away, and tidied the kitchen. Now that she was again working, she had her cleaning woman, but she always went through the house, straightening magazines, emptying ash trays, smoothing a chair cushion. That day, she dressed absent-mindedly, but as carefully as always. Her dark hair was neat, her rosy red suit and figured scarf carefully put on. She took up a raincoat, though the sun seemed to be coming out.

She drove to the school, she went to her office, and from there to the assembly hall. Later she remembered that the magnolia tree was in bloom, and that its pink and white blossoms made a picture of beauty against the gray sky, seen through the square panes of a tall window.

The day progressed as usual; the Dean was always busy. She saw students, she talked to the librarian and to one of the teachers. She ate lunch, and dictated to her secretary for an hour. She found time to make one of her tours about the school, this day covering the gymnasium and the lower floor of the dormitory. The school's main enrollment was in day students, girls whose families lived in the city or in the suburbs. Only recently had a dormitory been built and girls admitted from out of the city. Often these were daughters of former students. And sometimes a local girl was accommodated because her parents were to be away, traveling, or for business reasons.

The dormitory was a pleasant, Williamsburg-style building, with attractive reception rooms on the main floor, a dining room, the housemother's apartment. Susan stopped for a minute to visit with this woman, a poised, interested person who knew how to dress well and keep an even approach toward the young people in her charge. She was a strong woman, and laughed easily. Susan liked her, and felt sure that the girls did. Today the housemother reported that everything was pretty well with the dormitory section of the Institute.

"Of course the girls all want to know when we will admit boys."

Susan clapped her hand to her brow. "As if we needed that!"

"Do you have troubles?"

"No more than usual. One girl is flunking, another won't take part in activities ... Well, I can see the end of the day coming up. I'd better check in on my appointment sheet."

She crossed the gravel drive to the side door of the main building. The wide halls and the circular lobby were becoming shadowy. She touched a couple of switches as she went through, liking the way the lamps and the prismed chandeliers cast new shadows on the walls, glinted on a bronze memorial plaque, and picked out a girl seated on a bench outside her office—a dark-haired girl, the picture of dejection.

Susan hurried her step. "Bonnie?" she asked in concern.

The girl's head turned. Like most of the girls, she wore her hair long, always ready to fall front and conceal her face. "Oh, Mrs. Aubuchon," she said. "I wanted to see you."

"All right," said Susan. "Why didn't you wait in the office?"

"Because—I wanted to see you alone." The girl stood up; she was pale, and looked ill.

"Is something wrong, Bonnie?" Susan asked.

"Yes, ma'am."

Susan touched her elbow. "We'll go inside," she said. Within five minutes the wide lobby would be swarming with girls.

"Please don't disturb me," she told her secretary. She

opened the inner door, and Bonnie preceded her. The girl was shivering; she must be in real trouble.

Susan seated her, and looked at her in concern. "Are you really sick, Bonnie?" she asked.

The girl gulped. "Yes. ma'am. I think so. I—I'm afraid I am."

"All right. Then we'll get you right over to the Infirmary. Can you walk that far?"

The Infirmary was in the dormitory. Bonnie thought she could walk.

She did make it, but just barely. She was shivering, and as white as the nurse's cap on the desk with a sign propped against it that read, "Back soon."

The nurse's hours were flexible, and like Susan, her duties took her all over the school. Well, Susan had decided that what ailed Bonnie was a chill; she probably was coming down with the flu. She could get her into bed as well as the nurse could.

There were no other patients. Susan told Bonnie to undress while she found a gown and a robe.

"Unless you'd rather go upstairs for your own things?"

Bonnie shook her head. She was trying to pull her knit blouse over her head, and shivering. Poor thing.

"The nurse will be back any minute," Susan promised, trying to help the girl, who seemed to be getting sicker by the minute.

But, finally, she had Bonnie in bed. She tied her hair back with some string, and found an extra blanket. The girl's eyes were enormous, and her color was a ghastly green-white.

"Mrs. Aubuchon?" she would say, as if she wanted to ask Susan something, or tell her something.

"I'll try to locate Mrs. Gann," said Susan. "You try to get warm and rest."

"Yes, ma'am. Only—I think I should tell you something."

Susan folded the girl's cothing into a neat pile. Gann would know what to do with them.

"All right, Bonnie," she said, sitting on the foot of the cot-like bed. "Let's get it said."

Bonnie shivered again, and Susan reached for her hand. She must find the nurse!

This Bonnie—as a student, her name had come up a couple of times in faculty conferences. Bonnie was not one of their good girls. She made fair grades, but she constantly broke rules. It was pretty well decided that she would not be allowed to return the next year. Meanwhile, her parents were recently divorced. Her father was a career military man, an officer stationed in Okinawa; her mother was in Europe, but she expected to be back in the States by Easter, and probably Bonnie would spend that vacation with her.

Susan turned her attention back to the girl in the bed. "What's wrong, Bonnie?" she asked.

And Bonnie began to cry.

"Oh, now, look," said the Dean. "We won't get far that way." Her tone was kind. But there were times when to console a girl was a mistake. "I don't think there is anything wrong with you but the flu. Of course I could call the doctor."

"Oh, no!" said Bonnie. "Oh, no, Mrs. Aubuchon." She sat straight up. "I've—I've been to a doctor. He—he said I was pregnant."

Oh, dear. Exclusive school or no, this development had occurred before, though generally the Dean was not the first to know.

"Well, Bonnie . . ." she began.

"I knew it for myself," said Bonnie, speaking rapidly. Now she no longer shivered. Red spots of color had come into her cheeks. "This afternoon—or, rather, late this morning—I went to—to another doctor. And now I am not pregnant. But what he did made me sick. He said I might feel bad."

Susan stared at the girl in disbelief. Then she sprang to her feet. "Bonnie!" she cried. "You couldn't have . . ."

But she had. Susan could tell that she had. The girl had cut classes, she had gone to some doctor. . . .

"Whom did you go to?" she demanded, not expecting that the girl would tell her.

But Bonnie did tell her.

"I went to your husband," she said readily.

Susan could only gape at the girl.

"But— Why did you go to him?" she asked. "Surely not because he was my husband! You didn't make a claim upon him because of the school?"

"Oh, no," said Bonnie reasonably. "He knows I am living here at the school, but I went to him because he is that kind of doctor. I mean, he helps girls like me."

"I can't believe this," Susan whispered. "I can't believe this."

The girl shrugged and lay down again. "I guess I'm sicker than I should be," she murmured.

"Bonnie!" Susan cried in her fright and her terror. "What do you mean? That my husband is *that kind of doctor?*"

Bonnie's wise eyes stared at her blankly. "Didn't you know?" she asked. "A lot of girls and fellows know. He charges a lot."

Susan stopped listening. The girls in the Institute knew that the man to whom the Dean was married . . . But Susan did not know. She had not known. Rupert was a heart specialist. He said that he would succeed Malcolm Anderson as Chief of Cardiovascular Surgery.

Was that all a lie? No . . . He did serve at the hospital; he did have heart patients. Did his fellow doctors know what other work he did? Oh . . .

Mrs. Gann came in then, a big, rawboned woman with a toothy smile, a hearty, no-nonsense manner. "Well, well, well!" she cried. "What have we here?"

Susan turned. "Bonnie became ill," she said stiffly. "She had a chill. I got her into bed."

Mrs. Gann lifted Bonnie's wrist. "Mhmmmn. Probably the bug. Did you give her anything? Aspirin or something of that sort?"

"No. I, too, thought it was a flu." Bonnie's big eyes watched them. She probably had counted on Susan's not giving her, or the doctor, away.

"Look," said the nurse kindly. "You look tired, Mrs. Aubuchon. I'll take care of Bonnie. I'll keep her here tonight, and if she isn't better in the morning . . ."

"I'll call a doctor," said Susan quickly. Already she was determined that she would talk to Rupert, and he would do something. He *would!*

Feeling that she walked on wooden pegs, her brain numb, her hands icy, Susan went back to her office. She closed her desk and managed to speak acceptably to her secretary; she went through the rotunda and out to her car. Behind the wheel, she sat terrified. Afraid to turn the key, to start the car's wheels. Certainly she could not go out of the grounds, into the city and suburban traffic at this hour. She could not!

Nor could she— Oh, she could *not* go home to Rupert, accept the kiss he would give her, speak to him . . .

Unless Bonnie Devers had been lying. These kitten-girls were adept at lying. Though why a girl would tell such a story . . .

And wasn't illness—fever, chills—serious? Could Bonnie be very ill?

Should she be taken to the hospital at once? Should Susan tell Mrs. Gann, and get her advice? Maybe Bonnie would tell her.

No, Susan didn't think so. She had told Susan because the Dean was married to Dr. Aubuchon—the kind of doctor who would . . . who did . . .

She didn't know how long she sat there, frozen with terror. But it was dark, and the house was lighted when finally she drove into their garage. Rupert was at home. Well, she would talk to him at once, and get him to do something.

The garage opened into the utility room; Susan's foot stumbled on the step. She watched for the dog, but Mandy was not around. Probably Rupert had let her out.

Rupert himself met her in the kitchen. "Hey, Susie!" he cried heartily. "You're late. Get kept after school?"

She put up her cheek for his kiss, and went around him toward the bedroom.

He followed. "You're tired," he said with concern. "Maybe we should go out for dinner."

"No," said Susan, her voice thick. "No, I don't want to." She went into the bathroom and closed the door. For a minute she leaned against the wall, her head back. She had not been able even to look directly at Rupert. For now she no longer had any hope that Bonnie's story was untrue. Just seeing Rupert—his smile, his eyes, his hearty manner . . .

She came out and changed her suit for a short housecoat. Rupert called along the hall, did she want a drink? "No, thank you," she answered, her voice like glass.

She went to the kitchen and started preparations for dinner—struck with the fact that one did those things, no matter what tragedy impended. She put potatoes into the oven to bake, she set Sunday's Swiss steak over low heat to warm. She would make a salad, with fruit for dessert.

She then went into the family room where Rupert was watching the news. She waited until this was finished; then she asked if she might turn off the set. He got up to do it; he was generally a good-natured man about the home.

"Where's Mandy?" she asked.

"I let her out. She'll be coming in."

"Yes." Susan twisted her fingers together. Her housecoat was of silk, in a paisley design, the background was blue. "Rupert," she said, assuming the voice which she used when discussing an unpleasant matter with one of the students. "Something came up at school today. A girl—"

And she told him the whole story. Rupert leaned back in his chair, listening, interrupting only once when she told him of Bonnie's fever and chills. "Oh, damn!" he said then. Susan had hoped against hope that he would tell her . . .

He got up, went to the bar and mixed a drink. "How sick did you say the girl was?"

Susan stared at his back. It was all true; he had made no attempt to deny anything. Once he had said he had married her because of the contacts to be made through her position as Dean in a school for rich girls—girls from rich families. What had he charged Bonnie Devers? Susan shuddered.

"She had chills and fever," she answered his question.

"And you put her to bed."

"Yes."

"She'll probably be all right tomorrow."

"But what if she is?" cried Susan tensely. "You still did a dangerous thing, an unlawful thing!"

"Oh, Susie, Susie!" He spoke tolerantly.

"You hurt her. You might have killed her. And certainly you have hurt me, Rupert."

"Now, how do figure that out?" he asked.

She would not mention her disillusionment. He would call her naïve, unrealistic. "You have said that you liked my position at the Institute. Can't you see that what you did to Bonnie threatens my work and reputation as well as your own?"

He drank from the glass in his hand. "My goodness, how dramatic we are," he drawled.

She sprang to her feet. "The thing itself is dramatic, Rupert. Can't you see . . . ? You could be involved in a very nasty legal process! Any sort of medical examination would reveal . . ."

He came toward her, but she evaded his intent to put his arm around her. She could not have borne his touch!

"Explain to me," he said, sitting down again, "how I can be involved? Your girl isn't going to talk. She did to you, thinking that you knew about such things. But she won't talk to anyone else. No one will know that she came to me. Except you, Susan. And you wouldn't tell on your own husband, would you?"

She gasped. "But I may have to tell!" she cried. "Can't you see that, Rupert?"

He drained his glass and put it down. "No," he said coldly. "I cannot see it. But—here, sit down on the couch, and I'll tell you, show you, a sure way to avoid involvement in this thing, whatever develops tomorrow or the next day."

She stared at him and, fascinated, she did sit on the couch, not close to him, not really back on the cushion. What tricks and devices did he have?

He nodded, as if reading her thoughts. "It won't take much," he said. "And I think you will agree to do it."

She was doubtful, but she would listen. If he could salvage anything . . . Yes, she would listen.

"All right," he said, reading acceptance in her face. "Tomorrow morning, you do what you told your nurse you would do. You call a doctor to see the girl. I'll give you the name of a man to call. Now he may or may not examine her enough to know what has happened. But if she goes bad, he will probably say that there has been an operation, but that he did not do it. Which he didn't.

"And you, Susan Aubuchon, Dean of students at the Institute, can testify that he was the only one to attend the girl. It will be his word against yours, and I can promise that your word is the best, and will be, while that of the doctor I select will not be."

For a long minute, Susan stared at him, repeating in her mind what he had said, what he meant. She felt nausea in her throat. She was actually sick with horror. "I'd despise myself," she said hoarsely, "if I would lend myself to such a scheme."

He stood up. "And I'll despise you if you don't!" he said roughly. "For you would be the biggest fool on earth."

Susan leaned forward and held her head in her hands. "I guess you can count on me to be that fool," she said.

He moved then, and fast. He went to the hall closet, got a coat; she heard the front door slam, hard, behind him.

He did not return. Susan scraped their dinner into the garbage disposal; she ate some toast and drank a cup of tea. She wept intermittently, not for what might happen, but for what could have happened in their marriage. Finally she prepared for bed. Not realizing what she did, she took out one of her old tailored flannel robes. Because she felt cold, she put Alma's knitted red and white slippers on her feet. She turned off the lights and stood for a long minute at the window of her bedroom. She knew—she had known for three days— that she was bearing Rupert's child. Now . . .

She saw Felix's car coming into the Lynch drive; she saw him get out, a tall, slender man. He wore a white turtle-neck sweater and a dark blazer. The garage door was not working properly, and he stood revealed in the car's headlights.

A week ago, Felix had offered to help her against some trouble he had not identified. Well, now the trouble had come; she probably would need help. She could trust Felix.

He was a good man. If her child could have such a father . . . How lucky Esther was!

The night was a long one, and hellish, every minute of it. Even Mandy had deserted her; probably she had followed Rupert to wherever he might be. There was no sleep for Susan, though she tried. She lay down in bed and determined not to think. Tomorrow, routine and her sense of duty would take care of things. But now . . .

She got up again and wandered through the house, trying to sit down and read—and not think.

She took a sleeping pill, and wished she had not. She wished nothing had happened. She wished she had handled things differently with Rupert. She wished—

It was a night of doubt, and fear, and loss realized—a terrible night.

Rupert returned about four o'clock. He shucked out of his clothes and got into bed beside her. He offered no explanation. He neither spoke nor touched Susan. She lay trembling.

At seven, the alarm sounded. Susan shut it off and got up. She would stick to routine . . . She felt terrible, she looked terrible. But she bathed, brushed her hair into its usual smooth black cap. She put on a gold-colored sweater, a dark brown skirt, and went out to the kitchen to prepare breakfast. Rupert would be out . . .

She thought.

Yes, she heard him showering.

He came out, quite as usual, freshly shaven, his hair neatly combed. First thing in the morning was the only time he appeared that way. He made jokes about the number of cowlicks he had. He was carefully dressed in tan, almost yellow, slacks. With them he wore a double breasted sports coat of gray and the same buff color plaid. He fetched the paper from the front of the house and came to the breakfast table. Susan poured his coffee and put his eggs on to boil, set the timer. He put his hand on her shoulder and said something about the rain having stopped.

"Have you heard any word on Anderson?" he asked, drinking his orange juice.

"No. Is he still gone?"

"Well, he isn't at the hospital these days. And you should hear the talk!"

The timer sounded, and Susan put the eggs into two white porcelain cups. She liked hers a bit more firm.

Rupert cracked his with quick slashes of the knife, and

seasoned them. He gossiped amiably about Malcolm Anderson, telling what was being said—ridiculous stories! He even said it was told that he was hiding up in Mr. Kimberlin's suite.

"Not really, Rupert!" Susan protested.

He laughed. "No, not really." He ate his eggs quickly, as he did everything. "I tried that suggestion out at the hospital, as a joke, you know. And they proved it was impossible."

"Don't they know where he is?"

"I don't think so. They are really concerned. Kimberlin is in a bad way. And, boy, do they have security up there! You just try to get into the elevator and punch that button."

Susan said nothing.

"Don't you want to know what happens?" he asked her.

She shook her head. She knew that Rupert was extremely jealous of Malcolm Anderson, and she was beginning to guess why. Once he had talked wildly about the way Dr. Anderson had tried to keep Kimberlin from selling him a house on the Lane.

So far as Susan could tell, Dr. Anderson had few friends. But he had been very pleasant the night of the Lynch party. If he chose to go into hiding, he must have his reasons.

Rupert had his own explanation. He was hiding from Abby Bennett, he said. Abby was "quite a dame," he said. She had decided to make a play for the whiz-bang surgeon of cardiovascular diseases—his voice flattened to a brassy twang. "If he doesn't want to be caught, I don't blame him for hiding. Did you notice that dress she wore to Felix's party? *Woweee!* Talk about topless!"

It had been cut low, not topless. . . . Susan said nothing.

She tried to eat her egg; she managed only some toast. Should she tell Rupert that she was pregnant? Not yet, she decided. Not until she knew more about what she meant to do about their marriage.

He read his newspaper, and finally stood up to leave.

Susan looked up. "Rupert," she said, "did Mandy come home with you this morn—last night?"

He buttoned his jacket. "Mandy?" he asked. "Isn't she around?"

"No, she isn't. I think I'll go look for her."

"You stay here. I'll do it."

He went outside. She could hear him whistling, then talking to someone. He, and she, had said no word that morning about Bonnie Devers, nor about their quarrel of the night before.

113

She looked at the disordered kitchen and breakfast table with distaste, and decided that she, too, would look for the cocker. Mandy loved Rupert, and would come to his call, but . . .

She went through the garage. Rupert was on the driveway talking to Felix Lynch and Lionel, the yard-houseman from the Kimberlin place.

"Oh . . ." said Rupert, seeing Susan. "Come here, darling." He held out his hand.

She looked from one man's face to the other. "Something has happened to Mandy?" she asked.

"Yes . . ." Rupert put his arm loosely about her shoulders. "She's over there under the hedge. Don't go look at her."

But Susan pulled free and went to kneel beside the hedge, to look down at her gay little black dog, so quiet now, her hair matted with leaves and wet grass, foam about her muzzle.

"Rupert . . ." she begged. "Was she . . . ?"

"She was poisoned, yes." He attempted to draw Susan away.

"But how? And when?" Preoccupied with her own troubles, Susan had let Mandy . . . all night!

"It happened last night. Someone put poison out. Probably poisoned hamburger. Lionel says one of Mrs. Elis's cockers is very sick; the vet says it is dying And Abby Bennett's Scottie is sick, too."

"Could we have saved Mandy?" Susan asked, consenting to stand up.

"I don't think the vet can save the others," said Lionel. "The boy that helps me—we'll bury your dog for you, Miz Aubuchon."

Susan tried to smile at him. "Thank you, Lionel. I'll bring a blanket out."

Of course the word went swiftly up and around the Lane. Who could have done such a cruel thing? Strychnine, Dr. Aubuchon thought. And was quoted. But who? *Who?*

Within each house now, various ones suspected someone as having placed the poisoned meat about—someone who was disliked or hated for another reason. Against her will and reason, Susan suspected Rupert. To hurt her for what she was thinking about him, or to divert her attention . . . He had left the house the night before, very angry at her.

Esther came out to see what was going on, and she thought it could have been Felix. The way he went out at

114

night without explanation. The cranky way he was about *her* going anywhere!

Lionel told Margaret Elis about Susan's dog, and she came up to Aubuchon's to express her sympathy and her own concern. She was sure her cocker would die—and in agony. When it had been only her dog, she had suspected Lester. He thought the dogs were a danger to him when he was trying to get about on canes. It was the sort of thing he might do.

No one mentioned his suspicions to another, but mistrust was alive in the group that clustered in the Aubuchon driveway.

Was Dr. Aubuchon sure it was strychnine?

He could do an autopsy, he offered.

Dapper in his yellow and gray spring clothes, he was not contrite, if guilty. Though he had seemed to like Mandy.

How did one prevent such a thing? asked Susan, thinking that she would have to start for school very soon.

"You'd have to find another doctor for that," Rupert told her. "Maybe Mac Anderson would know. If so, it would seem he is needed here even more than he is at the hospital."

Margaret turned to look at him. She did not like waspish men. What kind of doctor was this Aubuchon? "Dr. Anderson is greatly admired," she said coldly.

"Oh, he is," Rupert agreed. "He is."

The hospital agreed with her, too. With each day of his absence from his normal duties, not to be seen in the halls, his name not on any o.r. schedules, the talk increased. The personnel discussed his disappearance in every hall, room, and corner of the complex. The telephone girls, the workers in the diet kitchens, nurses, orderlies, aides.

The clerks in records, and admissions, talked. Someone was going to have to take over as Chief.

"Who? Mitchell?"

"Mitchell's only resident."

"He knows Anderson's work."

"It will be someone from Staff. I heard that Aubuchon was in line."

"Did he tell you?" There were rude noises of derision. Aubuchon could not do it!

"He's a doctor on the staff," said the referrals clerk stubbornly, "and he has seniority."

"Yes, and a character that's bound to bring him recognition."

Rupert Aubuchon happened to be in the right place, at the right time, to hear this. He went down the hall, his face so grim that people turned to look after him. "Who broke his yo-yo string?" asked an intern.

Susan helped Lionel wrap Mandy in the blue blanket which had always covered the pillows in her basket, and watched him carry the little dog away. She must reward Lionel; he was a kind man. But that morning, no matter how heavy her heart, how troubled her mind, she must go inside, get ready for school, and *go*.

She hoped Rupert would just go on to the hospital, but he had not yet driven his car out of the garage.

Feeling sick, because she was pregnant, or because she grieved for her dog, or because of what she faced at school, Susan straightened the kitchen, the bedroom, and tried to remember what she had done with her raincoat. It had been raining yesterday. . . . Hadn't she worn it home? A fine rain was beginning to fall again. She would look and see if she had left the coat in her car.

She smoothed her hair, found her purse and gloves, checked on the door locks—all routine—and went to the garage. Rupert was there, wiping her car's windshield with a cloth, ready to do his own.

"Are you all right?" he asked, not unkindly.

"Yes. I think so." She was pale, but quiet.

"I hope you will take the advice I gave you yesterday. I put that doctor's name on your seat."

Susan opened the car door, picked up the sheet of prescription paper. She held it toward Rupert. "I shan't need this," she said.

"What are you going to do?"

"I'll take each thing as it comes. I will do nothing just to save us. To save myself."

He gazed at her for a long minute. A small woman, dark-haired, her high cheekbones and enormous eyes made her face exciting as conventional beauty would not have done.

Then, believing her, he shrugged and went to his own car. "Don't you need a raincoat?" he asked.

"I must have left it at school yesterday. With so much on my mind."

He turned. "Look, Susan . . ." Color had swept into his face, his eyes shone.

"I don't want to talk about it, Rupert."

"Well, you had better talk about it! And remember that any scandal about me will splatter all over you!"

"That is the first thing I thought of," she said coldly, settling herself behind the wheel.

"You won't like it!" he shouted.

"No," she said. "I've already found out that I don't like it."

She backed out, went around the drive, and out to the Lane, to the road, to school. She would keep reminding herself to do each thing routinely. Signal, lights—each thing.

It was almost noon when a big man in yellow-buff slacks and a gray and yellow plaid sports jacket drove up in front of the school and parked his car. Adjusting the yellow scarf at his throat, he looked up at the main building. Then he went inside and looked all about the rotunda, the circular entrance lobby, up at the tall glass windows, at the wall plaques, the painting.

Through an open door, he could see into the library; he could have asked directions there. But here to his right was a door, and above it a name plate. *Dr. Carlton Michael George. Headmaster.*

Rupert Aubuchon sucked in his cheeks, nodded his head, and went over to that closed door. Did one knock, or just go in?

He did both, knocking quickly, then turning the doorknob immediately.

He expected to find a secretary, and he did find a desk in the vestibulelike outer office. Behind that empty chair was an open door, another desk, and this time, an occupant—a gray-haired gentleman, slender, his face patrician, fine-boned. This man looked up at Rupert and rose.

"May I help you, sir?" he asked.

Rupert smiled engagingly. "I hope so. I am out of my depths in a girls' school. But I am looking for my wife. I wanted to take her to lunch."

"Oh?" The Headmaster came around the desk and toward him. Rupert would try to find out who his tailor was. The way those gray trousers broke at the instep ... Of course, *style* was for shorter trews, but those pants!

"I am Dr. Aubuchon," he was explaining to the gentleman. "My wife ..."

"But of course! Our Dean. How do you do, sir?" His lean, clean hand was being extended.

Rupert's hand was clean, too, and a little soft from so much scrubbing, but he felt it too big, too gross.

He again mentioned his idea about lunch.

"You can ask her," said Dr. George cordially. "She has

117

been rather occupied this morning. She has a sick girl in the Infirmary, and while her office is across, over there"—he pointed his elegant hand—"she may not be there."

Rupert had counted on someone, not Susan, mentioning the sick girl. "Could I help out?" he asked. "Take a look at her if you don't have a school doctor?"

"Since we are largely a day school," said the Headmaster, "we do not have a doctor here on a regular basis. Of course there is a nurse. And if you would be kind enough . . . I am sure it would relieve Mrs. Aubuchon and the nurse both. You see, the girl's parents are out of town, and . . ." Already he was leading the way out of his office, across the rotunda to a side door, and then across a graveled space to a smaller red brick building.

"The Infirmary is here," he explained to Dr. Aubuchon. "And you may find your wife . . ."

They did not; Dr. Aubuchon was relieved. Dr. George introduced him to the tall nurse who said good morning.

Her patient, she said, was in here. . . . She opened an inner door.

"May I use your stethoscope?" Dr. Aubuchon asked. "My bag is out in my car."

Bonnie was sick, all right. Feverish. She recognized the doctor, and moaned a little. He took her temperature, her pulse, and asked what had been done.

He came back to the Headmaster, still waiting in Mrs. Gann's office.

"I think she should be in the hospital," he said. "If you like, I can take her in my car, at once."

This was quickly agreed upon. The doctor himself carried the girl out; the nurse would tell Susan when she returned from a meeting of the student council. Such a strong man! said Mrs. Gann.

"I'm afraid you lost out on lunch with your husband," the Headmaster told Susan.

Bonnie had not spoken a word. She lay in the back seat of Rupert's car, her eyes closed. She heard the doctor say he would hurry.

He did hurry. It was raining. She could hear the tire treads suck against the wet streets. She moaned a little and rolled her head. Once the doctor turned to look at her, and started to say something.

Then he grabbed wildly at the wheel, the tires shrieked beneath them, the car hit something, bounced high in the air, took off across an empty space and down an embankment, turning over and over.

At two o'clock the word came to the school, brought by a policeman in search of the doctor's wife. Dr. Aubuchon, he told the Headmaster, had been killed, and a girl—no identification there. Dr. George told who she was. A student, sick—the doctor had been taking her to the hospital.

He himself carried the word to Susan, determining that she was in her office, then going there at once. She listened quietly. Rupert and Bonnie had been killed. Instantly. A terrible accident.

"An—accident," whispered Susan. She got up from her chair and went to the window. And she wept. From shock, yes, as Carlton George thought, and with grief for the man she had married less than a year ago.

"She was dreadfully shocked," Dr. George explained to others in the school. Others who were shocked, and meant to be kind to her.

She wanted— Oh, desperately she wanted to believe that her husband had killed himself and the girl in an accident! When she had been told, at noon, that Rupert had taken Bonnie to the hospital, she had hoped that he was going to take responsibility for the abortion. She still clutched at that hope. But there had been an accident, and now . . . Oh, poor Bonnie! Poor girl!

Others believed that it was an accident. The police report would read that way. And to believe it would make all the difference in the world to Susan. If she could think that Rupert had been going to do one last thing for her, that fate had stepped in . . . She could perhaps keep her good memory of him.

Always, weaving in and out of the horror, there was that memory of the man she had married, a woman with small knowledge of men. From Rupert Aubuchon she had learned about love, and desire. Her own love, and her own desire.

She remembered her first awareness. Her eyes were on his face, she saw something stir in his eyes. She knew, without his touching her, that if he should kiss her she would not resist. He had stepped closer. He clamped her in one arm, and pulled her to him. She went easily, and he smiled at her. He bent and fastened his mouth on hers. . . .

At the great medical center with its eleven teaching hospitals and nine clinics, every day was a busy day. When, in one of those hospitals, someone complained about the busyness, notice was taken. When that hospital was the cardiovascular unit, the blame, that rainy day, was laid on the bustling little doctor who went from ward to ward, from floor desk to the doctors' lounge, to scrub, complaining, complaining.

Dr. Bennett had patients in the hospital. He took close care of those patients, visited them every day, sometimes twice a day. He still had an old-fashioned idea that it was proper for any Staff doctor to read the chart, or visit in the room, of any patient in his hospital. This, some of the staff found not so commendable. There were arguments about it—with Dr. Bennett, and about him and his ways.

"Some surgeons do not follow up their cases," a resident would point out. "Old Bennett is right. They should."

"See if you have the time when you are a successful heart surgeon. See what arrangements you'll make then."

"I probably shall see."

"Old Bennett is a fuss-budget. Did you hear about his set-to with the Nursing Services Chief?"

"A recent set-to?"

Everyone laughed.

"This time he was insisting that he be allowed to see the Kimberlin chart. He thought it should be kept at the desk."

"Isn't it?"

"Seems not. Seems, too, that Kimberlin and Bennett are friends. That he has, for years, attended the family as a physician."

"But isn't Mr. Kimberlin in here for an implant?" asked a first-year resident, a woman doctor.

"That's right," the man agreed.

"Then wouldn't he be Dr. Anderson's patient?"

One of the men leered at her. "Do you think for one minute that would stop Bennett?" he asked.

She nodded. "The poor old man. Someday we'll be old."

"With sense enough, I hope, to step out before we get senile."

"Fussy, not senile," someone corrected.

"Fussy *and* senile," retorted the first speaker. "Did you hear about his complaints that he couldn't sleep one night because a cat in the house kept running up and down the stairs?"

"I heard it was a dog."

"Does it make any difference? He's fussy. And lately he's made a nuisance of himself talking about his disgruntlement because he has not been asked to attend Arthur Kimberlin.

With Anderson vanished into thin air, he thinks he should be permitted to step in."

"But he's no surgeon."

"Tell him that he can't do anything any young whipper-snapper can do."

"But he isn't a surgeon! He wouldn't be allowed on surgery!"

"And he'll tell you that surgery is not the answer to every problem. Give him a chance. He'll tell you. He talks to everyone."

"Poor old man," said the woman doctor, putting her coffee cup into the bin and going to the door.

She was back almost at once, her eyes popping, her jaw hanging down. "Guess what's happened!" she cried to the young men in white and green.

"Bennett did some surgery."

"Oh, shut up, Riley!" cried the young woman. "This—they told me out at the desk that Dr. Aubuchon has been killed."

She got their attention. Most of the men were instantly on their feet, clamoring. One man wise-cracked, "Who killed him?"

The young doctors wanted to know details, and there were not many to give. It had been a car wreck ... No, he skidded and went off the road. Out in the county ... He and a girl he had with him. Oh, *stop that*! She was a patient, wrapped in a blanket, wearing pajamas. . . .

"I think men are disgusting. Of course she was a patient!"

First word had come in over the radio. The news spread through the hospital like mist. There was surprise, shock, and disbelief. Everyone knew Rupert Aubuchon, in one way and another. He had been a man to get round.

There was some pity. "Isn't he newly married?"

"Yes. And to a very nice girl."

"How come ... ?"

Dr. Bennett heard the news when he came up to the surgery floor. And he reacted in a more professional, ethical manner than most. He said the news was tragic. A young man like that. As it happened, Aubuchon was a neighbor of Bennett's; he had a fine home and a lovely wife. Oh, this was too bad. For so young a man—had to be in his forties—Aubuchon had achieved seniority on the staff. This was a loss.

Within half an hour, Dr. Bennett was in the office of the Chief of Medical Services, asking to see Dr. Straub. He had put on a fresh white coat, his eyeglasses were polished to a fine glitter. He was composed, for him. Dr. Bennett, his wife told, was never still, even in his sleep.

"Did you make an appointment, Dr. Bennett?" asked the secretary, looking at her book.

"You know I don't have an appointment. But I still want to see Dr. Straub. My business is urgent."

"Well ..." She got up. Dr. Straub was in his office. He could decide for himself how busy he was.

She was gone for five minutes. She came back, somewhat slowly. She could not repeat to Dr. Bennett that "One might as well settle this business once and for all!"

She sat down at her desk. "You may go in, Dr. Bennett," she said quietly. Let her boss tell him that he had to be quick, let her boss tell the nice little man ...

With Dr. Aubuchon dead—and it seemed he really was!— the secretary to the Chief would be making some quick schedule adjustments. She felt bad about Aubuchon. Many of the girls in the hospital were crazy about the man.

Dr. Bennett bounced confidently into the Chief's office. He said he supposed the Chief knew about Aubuchon?

Dr. Straub nodded. He was a large man, with a polished bald head, and what the hospital staff called a fishy eye. "Regrettable," he said now. "The staff will do the usual things. Flowers, a representation to attend the funeral. He left a young wife, I understand."

"Yes. We know her. They live near our home. On what is called Kimberlin Lane. I think she teaches at the Institute."

"Ah-hum. Bennett . . . ?"

"Yes, I'm busy, too. But Aubuchon's death has brought cardiology to something of a crisis, hasn't it?"

"How's that?"

"Well—with Anderson missing, as he has been for days now. No explanation. I could see why no one was named Chief, since that someone would have had to be Aubuchon. But now, it does seem evident to all concerned that I shall have to serve, and we might as well get things lined up. There is work waiting, needing to be done. The implant team needs a head to go on with that work. There are critical cases waiting."

Dr. Straub got to his feet. "You are talking nonsense!" he said bluntly.

"But, Dr. Straub ..."

The Chief of Services went to a filing cabinet and took out a folder. "This says the team has been operating right along, Dr. Bennett."

122

"Oh, yes, but—"

"They seem to be able to function without Aubuchon, or you. They are very well trained. And until Dr. Anderson's return . . ."

"Return from where?" snapped Dr. Bennett.

"From a well-earned rest and vacation. He asked not to be disturbed. We'll respect that request. I am sure you will agree that a heart surgeon works under great pressure."

"Any heart specialist works under pressure, Dr. Straub."

"Yes, he does. Tell me— How long have you been a specialist? Were you certified?"

"I was certified by a courtesy vote, sir. No one thought a man of my years of experience would need to take the examination."

"Oh, yes, I remember. You were a good general practitioner when I came here as an intern. I don't know why you didn't stick with that. But—speaking of Aubuchon, as we were—I never could see why he didn't stick with one or even two of his specialties. He was a pretty good heart man, he was a fair country surgeon, and he could have been better had he confined his activities to that field. But he didn't, and now . . .

"Now, as for you, Dr. Bennett, I don't really believe you think you could take over as cardiovascular chief. Do you? So far as I know, you've never done open heart surgery."

Dr. Bennett's chin set stubbornly. "I've opened a chest."

"On an emergency basis. Though as I recall . . ."

"The trouble in our service, Dr. Straub, is that Anderson has things tied up. He has acquired a name for himself. I've attended just about all his lectures and demonstrations. But unless you're on his team, no one else gets a chance. His theory is to train other teams."

"He does that."

"For other hospitals, maybe. Not here. Here, it's his team or nothing. And with him gone . . ."

"His team has been working. I told you that. He has two fine, qualified surgeons, and his Resident is outstanding."

"Don't you agree that they—the Service—needs a Chief?"

"Until I learn different, Dr. Anderson is the Chief. But thank you for coming over, doctor." He opened the door, and Dr. Bennett went through, affronted, puzzled, angry—so angry that he could not think of anything to say or do, except to go home.

He came into the house, bustling, having left his car on the garage apron. He went through the kitchen, took two cookies from the jar there, started for his room, heard the typewriter, and went into the sewing room which Abby had appropriated for her own use.

She looked up and took off her desk glasses. Her father smiled at her. His daughter was a lovely girl. He liked having her at home and was convinced that being nice to her would keep her there.

"Where's your mother?" he asked, his mouth full.

"Playing bridge. D.A.R. meeting. Something of that kind. She's gone most afternoons."

"Mhmmmn. Well, Abby, I am expecting an important telephone call. If the phone rings, let me answer it."

"All right," she agreed. "You're home a little early."

"No office hours today." He started out, and was actually down the hall a way, then he turned back. "Had you heard that our neighbor was killed this afternoon?"

Abby's hand went to her throat. "Not . . ." she began.

"Aubuchon," said her father. "Drove his car too fast on a wet road. Killed instantly."

Abby was shocked. "Poor Susan!" she cried. "I'll go over there."

"Oh, yes, but later. The thing happened around noon. She may not be at home. And if she is . . ."

Abby put her fingertips to her temples. "This has been a terrible day," she moaned. "And the days before it. What has happened to Margaret Kimberlin's paradise? Margaret Elis's, I mean, of course. Did you know that someone put poison out for the dogs last night? Strychnine, Dr. Aubuchon said. Why—" Her eyes widened, the pupils dark. "I was talking to him only this morning! He— Oh, Dad! This is terrible! All these things happening. Their dog died, and mine. I don't know about Margaret's."

This was all news to him, and he sat down on the couch, ready to discuss the matter of the dogs, and of Dr. Aubuchon's death. He agreed that much would need to be done. The hospital, too, would need some readjustment.

He finally departed, leaving his daughter sure that he would certainly now have to fill Malcolm Anderson's place at the hospital. And this deeply concerned her. Her father was too old for such a responsibility. As for the delicate surgery needed by Arthur Kimberlin, her father should not be asked to do that on his old friend! Could she find some tactful way to sidetrack these developments? Would her parents consent to go with her on a trip? Could she herself set out to find Malcolm? And bring him back? Would there be some way to

124

appeal to the hospital people, to ask them to save her father's life? She felt that his involvement might indeed mean that. She would talk to her mother, not realizing that her mother, like herself, was unaware that Dr. Bennett lacked both the skill and the knowledge to take over as Chief of Cardiovascular Surgery, that he could not, possibly, operate upon Arthur Kimberlin.

At dinner, Dr. Bennett was still talking about all that had fallen upon him because of Aubuchon's death and Anderson's absence. "I'm going to get right to work on that team," he planned. "They haven't done any work of importance for days. I'm sure there are cases waiting. But they have been dragging their feet, making Anderson's disappearance an excuse. Of course they wouldn't let Aubuchon do his sort of work."

"Wasn't he a good doctor, Dad?" Abby asked.

"Sometimes he was lucky. He went to the right schools, he had an enormous practice. But his ethics ... Well, speak only good of the dead. However, young lady, I can assure you that your father's ethics, and his character, are all right!"

She smiled at him. "Where is Dr. Anderson?" she asked.

"Nobody seems to know, or seems ready to say if they do know. Personally, I think he's stirred up this mystery for publicity reasons—publicity purposes."

"Oh ..." Abby protested. "That doesn't sound like Mac."

Her father shrugged. "Other heart-geniuses have used that means. Their reputation does not reflect their super-ability half as much as it does their good press relations."

"Won't he be back soon? Dr. Anderson, I mean."

"Don't ask me. Ask one of your newspaper friends."

Abby scarcely heard his sarcasm. "You don't think his absence could be permanent?" she asked.

"I don't know that, either. He already has a couple of cases in the hospital where two days may prove to be too long."

"Is Arthur Kimberlin one of them, Doc?" asked Mrs. Bennett.

"Oh, yes. I haven't been on the case, but Anderson seemed to think an implant was his only chance. Then there is another patient, a man. Named Holman. His wife brought him here— Oh, they've been in the hospital for some time, now, waiting for Anderson to get around to them. She's been a most devoted woman, stays with her husband every minute she can. She's taken him to various heart specialists. Houston, Rochester. The other day someone mentioned South Africa, and she staunchly said she would consider that if Dr. Anderson did not show up soon. My solution would be to have the team go on and do the surgery on both of these men."

"If Dr. Anderson has said they both need transplants . . ." murmured Abby.

"His term is: would they benefit by an implant? That's different from a transplant, Abby."

"Yes, I know. I'm sorry."

"He was ready to do one on Arthur Kimberlin. Holman—I don't believe he'd actually said. Of course, if it would give the man a *chance,* I'd order it, and I may have to."

"I wish you'd not need to take the responsibility in Arthur's case," said his wife.

"Well, I'd rather not. But with Aubuchon gone, the team will look to me. And we may have wasted too much time already."

Abby ate her dinner thoughtfully. Her parents talked about what Susan Aubuchon would do now, about the house, the doctor's possible estate.

And Abby thought about Malcolm Anderson, trying to figure where the man could be. She thought she understood him quite well. He was not an easy man to know—but in her short acquaintance with him she had found times when he would relax and talk freely to her. He had done that on his first meeting with her, that snowy Sunday when they had come in to the fire and talked. Then he had talked about the work he did, his ideas and ideals for it.

At other times . . . Not too long ago, she had managed to entice him—her lips quirked at the word, but Mac had used it. "You enticed me over here for breakfast, and I find I have to cook it myself."

She had enticed him, and they had cooked breakfast—on an outdoor stove. Bundled up against the chill of an early spring morning, they had cooked sausages and pancakes on the griddle. Malcolm had taken over the fire, which was inclined to smoke and smolder, or burst erratically into flames. He had gone at the thing scientifically, or so he claimed, and eventually he did develop a bed of rosy coals. Abby had been content to watch him, behaving in a womanly, domestic capacity—ready to fetch and carry, to compliment him on the first pancake, and to listen absorbedly when he talked about his work.

About the row he was having with the hospital administrative staff over a system called Total Hospital Information System.

126

"Or computerized medicine, to you," he said, wrapping his pancake around a sausage, sitting astride one of the benches to eat it. The sun was burning off the frost, and he opened the collar of his jacket.

She was skilled at interviews and knew how to keep the man talking.

"No!" he cried. "I don't like that sort of thing. Oh, for routine medicine I suppose it would work out. Gall bladders, upper respiratories, broken bones. But when you are dealing with the chest—the lungs, the heart—the source of life, you see? They claim this system will let us add a hundred more patients and not increase the hospital staff by a single number.

"It is supposed to improve patient care. The Administration claims it will put all of our departments—we must have upward of twenty—and all the nursing stations into instant communication. For a general hospital, that will be fine, though I hate the term data processing brought into a place of healing and supposed compassion."

Malcolm Anderson had a mobile face, a particularly expressive mouth. He frowned when he talked, and gestured with his hands.

"Of course," he said, "I can see the advantage of messages and orders relayed clearly and accurately, the service charges entered automatically against the patient's account. *That* is very important!"

Abby laughed obligingly and the doctor nodded.

"I'll agree," he said, "that in an institution the size of our Medical Center, there can be place after place for error. Conveying information should not be at the mercy of human motion, no matter how furious and well intended. Take this, for instance." He got up to refill their coffee cups and pick up an orange which he peeled expertly. Abby watched his hands, fascinated.

"A patient comes in," he resumed. "The examining doctor writes out an order, the nurse reads it, fills out a requisition slip to show what is required. Say it's a gall bladder X-ray and a g.i. test. Then she must fill out another form so breakfast is not sent to the patient before his g.i., and a prescription for pills to take for a good gall bladder picture. These forms are put into a box on the nurse's desk, and it is hoped they will be there when the courier comes and, it is hoped, gets them to the right department.

"And we'll assume the requisition does get to X-ray, a charge is put to it, and the thing is delivered, by courier again, to the accounting office. It is hoped the requisition slip is not, by then, too smeared, rumpled, et cetera, for the key punch operator to read.

"But, you see, anywhere along the line, the order could have been lost, or misplaced, or misread. The patient could get the wrong drugs, and of all disasters, he could be billed improperly.

"Now, with the computer in action, the doctor needs only to make the diagnosis. Gall bladder tests! He selects that card, drops it into a slot, and *whiz-o!* Diet kitchen, X-ray, the pharmacy, *and* the accounting office are all alerted and go into proper action. Nobody gets the wrong bill, nobody gets the wrong pill." He smiled at Abby, and gave her half of the orange.

"But you don't approve of the system?" she asked.

"Only to a point. My work—even the examination of the heart is never a routine thing. Oh, an entering patient, if not as an emergency—just someone coming in for me to examine—is routinely put to bed, his diet light, no visitors allowed. The computer can handle that. But the examination, the methods used, the machines and medications—oh, no. I've never known one case just like another case, and to be handled as if it were.

"Dr. Aubuchon—you know him—thinks that I am just being recalcitrant. He thinks heart pictures follow a pattern just as X-ray, EKG, oscilloscope monitored—and out comes a diagnosis. No, I believe he makes his diagnosis first." He spoke dryly. "And for the sort of surgery he does, that may suffice."

"What . . . ?" asked Abby.

"He does heart surgery, some chest. Repairs a hole in the cardiac sac, things that have become routine. Though he is not always successful.

"But in my work—myocardial revascularization—we've had to move slowly; our mission has been to establish the feasibility of the surgery, and to obtain sufficient results to convince the skeptics—among them, large and noisy, your Dr. Aubuchon!—that we are in a new era of coronary surgery.

"And that sort of careful examination, et cetera, does not lend itself too well to computer systems. And I have been spending some precious time lately trying to convince the Administrator that his total-whatever is not, and should not be, applicable to the tenth floor of Thoracic and Cardiovascular.

"For instance, Abby, I now have a man in the hospital. He

has a distressing heart condition. He is not getting enough blood to the heart and some sort of internal mammary procedure is indicated.

"But my surgery, the sort this man's wife is clamoring for me to do, has to be selective. You see, a relatively small number of patients have distinct lesions that lead themselves to direct coronary surgery. I want to save lives, not to experiment. I want my patients to benefit by the improved selection techniques. I can't seem to sell this to Mrs. Holman.

"She claims that she *knows* her husband can be helped. She wants me to schedule him for surgery day after tomorrow. And I just won't do it."

"And you won't accept the total computerization of your service," murmured Abby.

Malcolm had agreed wryly, then he said he was surprised at the amount of talking he had done to her about his profession and its problems. Abby herself was surprised.

She was still debating whether to say so, when he rose to cook another "last" pancake, and turned to ask her if by her absorbed interest, and this breakfast, she perhaps was courting him. He asked the question bluntly, pointing the turner at her accusingly.

Abby had laughed and said that, frankly, yes, she had some such thing in mind. She had had to find some way to get to him.

He stared at her, his eye-pupils retracting into hard brown marbles. "Don't you read me well enough," he demanded, "to know that I would want to do the man's part in any courtship?"

She had answered him; she had tried to cajole him. He seemed to be furious.

He said he should go home at once, but he would not leave a girl who looked like Abby to clean up a sooty stove, especially when this one belonged to the Kimberlins.

He put powered sugar and blackberry jam on his pancake, rolled it up and presented it to her. "Eat that while I scrub and brush," he ordered gruffly.

"And get jam on my face."

"On you, it will be becoming." He began to work furiously, putting on gloves to save his precious hands.

"Don't bother to court me any more," he told her, as he began to carry their gear up the hill. "Because the truth of the matter is: I would not want a wife as ornamental as you are."

Abby had puzzled often about that morning. He had gone

home, still in that fine temper, or making a good pretense of it.

She had done no more "courting." Something else had caused him to depart permanently. He was a complex man, she could do a wonderful book on him, but it would take work. Research. And without seeing him, or able to talk to him, to get him to talk . . .

Where had the man gone? Was his disappearance her fault? If so, she might have a lot—too much—on her conscience.

Abby looked up and waited until her father had explained to his womenfolk the complexities of closing out a medical office. "I understand Aubuchon's practice was pretty varied," he said.

"But I thought he was a heart specialist," said Mrs. Bennett.

Her husband cackled. "He thought he was, too!" he retorted, pleased with his joke. He said it again. "He thought . . . Is something wrong with you, Abby?"

She shook her head. "I was just wondering about the hospital," she said. "With Dr. Aubuchon dead, and Dr. Anderson away . . . Is he really needed, Dad? Anderson, I mean."

"I know whom you mean. Well—Anderson does some good work. But ours is a big center. He's one of the Staff. We'll manage."

Early in the afternoon, the rain had stopped. Margaret Elis, grieving for her little dog that had died, worried for the other one, worried about her grandfather in not a too different way—he, too, had always been kind and loving—she wanted some physical work to do—something that would take her out of the house.

Lester, for the past day or two, had taken to speculating upon her grandfather's wealth and his will. He made lists of relatives, questioning her as to cousins of her same rank. He scribbled sheets of paper with numbers and sums.

She had to get away from him, lest she turn on him and call him every name for an unfeeling, cruel man! She didn't want her grandfather to die! She wanted him to get well, to return home, where she could care for him and be a companion to him. She . . .

She went down to the little greenhouse and watched Lionel, who was tending to his flats—low trays of green plants, neatly marked. He told her where and how he would plant these. "I got way more'n we can use," he said. "And there's snapdragons and mums needs to be thinned out. I reckon some of the neighbors could use 'em. I was plannin' to take some around, but today things got ahead for me."

They had. The dogs, and . . .

"Could I take the plants around?" Margaret asked eagerly. "I was trying to find something to do, to get me out of the house a little."

"Yes, ma'am." Lionel was a wise person. Lester had thrown too many things at him for Lionel not to understand Margaret's problems.

For an hour, he let her talk to him while, with the boy's help and Margaret's, he prepared a little cart of plant slips. He told her which set should go where. "They all got new flowers beds," he point out. "It's gonna rain some more, so it's a good time to plant. Miz Bennett, she won't want any. Her yard is old. She got peonies and stuff that don' make trouble.

"Now Miz Aubuchon, she'll be real glad to have some, but I'll save hers to Sat'day, when she'll have time to plant 'em."

"Of course," Margaret agreed.

"But the others— You take this big lot to Miz Lynch. Mr. Felix's wife ain' goin' be interested. You ever see that lady's fingernails, Miss Marg'ret?"

Margaret nodded. She had seen them—long, and pearly white. "You meant Felix's mother," she said. "I understand. Yes, she'll want flower beds."

So she took her first offering down the road to Alma, who was her friend and would want flowers. But on that warm, damp afternoon, Alma did not have much to say.

She thanked Margaret.

"Lionel did all the work."

"I know. And I am glad to have the flowers."

She did not ask Margaret in. She did not seem to want to talk. Reserve, tension . . . Whatever ailed Alma?

Margaret went back up the road again, and across to Malcolm Anderson's home. The orchard trees were in bloom, and bees hummed. The cleaning woman answered the door. The doctor was away, she said.

Margaret stated her errand. "I thought you might like plants for the flower boxes, at least."

"Yes, ma'am, I would. I'm doin' some spring housecleanin' till the doctor gets back."

She was friendly enough. She asked about Mr. Kimberlin, and Margaret talked to her for ten minutes while transferring the plants from the little blue cart to the back stoop of Malcolm's house.

She could not give much information about her grandfather, she said. He was being kept in bed, quiet—and he was accepting that edict, though Margaret was sure he would rather be at home where he could see the apple trees in bloom. Yes, she thought his condition was serious. There had been mention of an aneurysm, and a vascular implant. But she was ignorant of medical things. "I've always been healthy."

Though her grandfather was not allowed visitors, she could see him every day, briefly. She looked up at Dr. Anderson's housekeeper, smiling. "That helps me," she said. "Not him."

"With the doctor gone," said the older woman, "who is Mr. Kimberlin's doctor?"

"I think the whole hospital staff," said Margaret, standing up straight, ready to move on to the Kendrick house.

"I wonder," said Teresa, "if maybe you folks, or other people, think Dr. Anderson's being gone isn't right, with Mr. Kimberlin so sick."

Margaret turned back quickly to reassure this kind and loyal woman. "I've been puzzled," she admitted. "I've heard some people at the hospital say he had no right to disappear. But then I've heard even more people express concern for him. They fear he himself may be ill, or perhaps have had an accident. Because no one seems to have heard anything from him."

"I haven't," said Teresa. "He left me a note and told me to care for things until he returned. Dr. Bennett stopped by to question me. I think he feels he should be looking out for Mr. Kimberlin."

"He does feel that way," Margaret agreed. "But maybe they are too-close friends. Mrs. Bennett seems to think that would make caring for Grandfather difficult. Dr. Bennett is not young anymore."

"No, he isn't," agreed Teresa. "Well, I hope this all comes out all right. We all have our troubles, and maybe Dr. Anderson is tending to some of his. He'll be back."

Margaret nodded, and went on down to Kendrick's where she left the plants and a note. The men of course were not at home, and their maid had left.

By the time she reached home again, word had come of Dr. Aubuchon's death. Lionel told her, sure sorry for that nice Miss Susan! Lester also told her when she came into the house, pulling the scarf from her hair, wondering just where to start to be kind to Mrs. Aubuchon.

The news made her very sad. Not entirely for the dead man; she had not known Dr. Aubuchon at all well; he had not seemed to be the type for a woman like Susan to love and marry, but that certainly had been none of Margaret's affair. She had last seen him at the Lynch party, and now she tried to remember him more clearly.

Lester was talking about him, not being kind. Margaret heard him, his tone of voice—now and then a word came through. She had learned to shut her ears to Lester's talk. But, very likely because of the death on the Lane, unhappiness descended upon her. She went up to her room and changed her clothes, freshened her make-up and brushed her hair. She would try to get in touch with Susan. She wished she could talk to her grandfather about the way she felt Not grief for the man, whom she scarcely knew, but grief at the blight, the smog which lately seemed to linger, and often thicken, in the air about her. She had declared, upon coming here, that she had attained heaven itself. But here was heaven, not for the first time, failing to produce its typical attributes.

What had happened? She could look about, walk about, and see all the things that mean heaven to her in this place—the woods, the fern house, the orchard in bloom.

Of course her grandfather's illness had cast its shadow, but she had come to this house, knowing he was not well, that things probably would get worse for him. She had accepted this sad situation, hoping to handle it.

No, her present sadness was due to a special kind of trouble. It reflected conditions which might be different, and were not. And since the day when she had dug wild flowers in the woods and overheard Mrs. Lynch and Mrs. Bennett talking about her, she had thought the failure could be her own fault. She herself had tarnished the gold, dulled the shine.

Lester had told her from the first that she was expecting too much of her heaven. He had said the atmosphere she had claimed for the place was too rarefied for mere mortals. He had pointed out that there were other angels in her paradise.

And there certainly were.

She went downstairs as quickly as she could, to prevent Lester's making the difficult journey up to find her, to talk to her. She had offered to make a bedroom for him on the first floor. There was a small, but charming room overlooking the woods. There he could have his books, his desk. This had

133

once been the servants' sitting room, and in it there was a fireplace.

He had brusquely refused. Lester was definitely one of the inhabitants of heaven to contribute to her unrest. Not an angel, of course, but it was she who had brought him into her heaven.

She should, she supposed, abandon the allegory, or whatever her fantasy was. She should return to earthly matters, accept the fact that one of the gutters of her grandfather's had blown loose, that a crack had appeared in the tile wall of a bathroom, and she and others in this place were nothing like celestial creatures.

Perhaps she should even abandon paradise and return wholly to earth. She moved restlessly about, and finally snatched her red coat out of the hall closet and went outside. If there were lights at Aubuchon's, she told Lester, she would go to see Susan.

There were no lights, no signs of life. Susan would have things to attend to. Not even Mandy, her dog, would now demand her early return home.

Margaret walked down the length of the Lane, and turned back. Dusk was falling, and the lights of the homes glowed behind their windows. All but the Aubuchon's and Anderson's. She began to think about Teresa, and about Dr. Anderson, and what could have happened to that busy, earnest man. She liked him, and she knew that he was a good doctor, dedicated to his work.

Without warning, Chris's hand fell on her shoulder, startling her. He was sorry, he said. Hadn't she heard him coming up behind her?

He wore a short, heavy coat, and the wind was ruffling his hair. He was glad to see her, his eyes said, even as he spoke nonsense about not tying a white chiffon scarf around his head the way Margaret had done.

"I came out for a breath of air," Margaret said. "I had heard about Dr. Aubuchon."

"Terrible, isn't it? So vital a man. Of course he drove like a bat out of hell. But having that girl with him . . . I suppose poor Susan has all sort of unpleasant things to attend to. If I knew where to reach her, I'd offer to help her."

"So would I," Margaret added. She had not heard about the girl in Dr. Aubuchon's car. Chris told her. A patient, it was said, whom he was taking to the hospital. He probably had been, too. The accident had happened on that road where it crossed above the Interstate. But of course there

134

would have to be inquests—and all sorts of unpleasant things. He was sorry for Susan. Just the identification of the bodies . . .

Margaret said "Yes . . ." and started to walk on toward home. She wished Chris would turn back. If Lester was watching out of the window, and he probably was . . .

Again the mood of grief, of tarnishing unhappiness, engulfed her. "I have to get home," she told Chris, drawing the collar of her coat up closer about her throat.

"I know, but I found the plants, and I wanted to thank you. They are wonderful. I'll plant them by moonlight. Do you think I have enough for all around the patio?"

"If not, Lionel may have more."

"Good. Maybe I could go up with you now and ask him."

"No!" She spoke brusquely, and Chris frowned a little.

"Margaret?" he asked. He would have touched her, but she drew away.

"No, Chris . . ." she said breathlessly.

"I love you, Margaret. You know that."

Yes, she did know it. "I love you, too," she cried, "and we've already meant too much to each other. We . . . We . . ."

He stood looking at her sadly. She had dropped her head, not able to watch the hurt in his eyes. "Has Lester been making trouble?" he asked.

She shook her head, not looking up. "It's not that . . . Oh, he would, certainly. But I—I know for myself that we—"

He stepped closer to her. "This can't be wrong, Margaret," he said firmly. "If we love each other."

"It can't be good, either," she said, her voice breaking. "Until—unless—I am free."

"And meanwhile?"

"Meanwhile— Please, Chris! Please help me!"

His broad thumb smoothed the tears from her cheeks. "I'll help you," he promised, his deep voice vibrating through her whole body. This was a man who loved her. A man . . .

She walked down the road, knowing that he watched her. She went into the house, knowing that he could see her against the lighted hall.

She hung her coat away, and her scarf, went into the small, pretty powder room to smooth her hair, dust powder on her face. Lester, too, was watching her. When she came out again, he said that dinner was ready.

"For long?" she asked, surprised. "Have you been waiting?"

"No."

They went in, and Lionel served their dinner. Chicken pie, a fruit salad—she ate without knowing what she ate.

Lester, of course, was talking. He asked her if she was not going to see her grandfather that day.

"I went this morning."

"I don't remember your being gone."

He did.

"I went into the city to see him, and I did the marketing. This afternoon Lionel gave me plants and I took some around to everyone on the Lane except Susan Aubuchon. A half hour ago, I went out again to speak to her if she was at home, but she wasn't."

Lester made no comment. "How was your grandfather this morning?"

"Cheerful. They keep him very quiet, and I never stay long."

"Do you think he might get well? I thought when the old coot went to the hospital this time, he sure would die."

She said nothing.

"Do you think there's a chance he won't?" her husband asked, leaning toward her.

Margaret sighed. "Lester . . ."

"Yeah, yeah. I know the routine. But doesn't it bug the old man?" This last year, Lester had lapsed, slipped, into slang. He never had used it when well. "Doesn't it bug the old man?" he asked. "Anderson's being gone from the job?"

"He's not mentioned it," said Margaret. "We don't talk much."

"You're keeping it from him, eh? Or you think you are. Though he probably knows. But he knows he's helpless, too, poor devil."

"Lester . . ." Margaret said wearily.

He smiled. "All right! What does give with the Anderson deal? Where is he? What's he up to?"

"Grandfather is being taken care of, I'm sure."

"Yeah, but things are said . . . Sounds to me like he's off on a drunk."

Margaret smiled at him.

"I know you think he's a tin god," said Lester, "but there are other opinions about him. I've talked to our neighbor, Dr. Bennett, and I've talked to the doc who got himself killed today. He was a queer sort of fellow, but I guess he was a good doctor. Anyway, both of them think something went haywire with Anderson. Bennett says he isn't anything like the genius his reputation has built him up to be, and Aubuchon said he hoped you knew that it was against the law—he meant legal, not ethical, though maybe that, too—for a doctor to abandon a case. Did you know that?"

"I think we should take into consideration, Lester, that Dr. Bennett, at his age, cannot be the keen doctor a man in Grandfather's condition needs. He doesn't do surgery, for one thing. As for Dr. Aubuchon . . ."

"Yeah, yeah. He was bird-dogging all right."

"I am sorry he was killed. He was a young man, as things go in his profession. And his wife is no older than I am."

"Good-looking gal, too. I can't help but wonder what, or who, caught up with Aubuchon."

"Oh, Lester!"

"The wise guys hereabout say he did some doctoring for the local Mafia. Now that can be a good racket, if the man plays it right. But if he doesn't . . ."

Margaret gave him a warning look. Lionel was ready to change the plates. She asked the servant if he had had any word from the vet about her dog. Lionel said that he had not. He poured coffee and departed.

"I wonder," Lester mused aloud, "who poisoned Aubuchon?"

Margaret laid her silver teaspoon carefully on the flower-wreathed plate. "Lester!" she said firmly. "I know it does no good to ask you not to speak so of people. You yourself poison everything your interest touches upon. Now, I know you are constantly in pain, and I am sorry for you in that regard. But other people have pain, too; other people have troubles, and they find strength to bear them if not quietly, at least without ugliness. Have you *ever* tried to make a life for yourself, to handle your illness and pain like a man? Must you always slash out and seek to hurt others? I often wonder, if people were as uncharitable as you are, what they would find to say about you?"

Lester stared at her balefully. "Let's start with what you find to say, my sweet and charitable wife."

Margaret stood up. "The best I could say," she said tensely, "the very best!—is that, sick or well, you are a poor substitute for a man!"

Chapter 4

On that Wednesday of rain showers, clearing, and rain again, Esther Lynch found, to use her own term, that she was fed up. Weeks and months of living in her husband's home, run by her husband's mother—nothing done for Esther's comfort or pleasure. Now the old lady was saying that she couldn't get up at all hours and cook herself a hamburger or something in the middle of the afternoon. She should eat meals when they were ready.

Felix, appealed to, asked her why she didn't try it his mother's way.

She had told him, and she repeated it now. She did not *like* his mother's way! She did not like much of anything about being married to Felix Lynch, and the things she did like, she wasn't getting a lot of, lately.

My God, Felix was out at all hours, he got telephone calls ... The characters who came to the house ... Alma had caught Esther listening at the study doors, which were louvered, and she had all but pulled the girl away by her long yellow hair!

"I have a right to know what he's up to!" Esther had told the old woman.

"You'll get the rights Felix wants you to have," said Alma sternly.

"Are those men members of that gangster bunch?"

"They could be. They could not be. It is none of your business, or mine."

"I sure don't want it to be mine," said Esther.

But she became increasingly determined to find out just what Felix's business was, and to show Alma that she could not boss Esther around.

That day—Alma was up to her elbows in baking bread. Lunch was a bowl of her idea of soup, with cheese and crackers. Esther went into Felix's study and looked around. By one o'clock she was in a state of pure terror, and she called Nathan at his office to tell him that she had to see him! She was scared to death! Yes, of course something had happened! All right, if it hadn't, he *could* beat her! My God, she was in danger of her life as it was!

All right. She'd wait for him at the gate. She didn't want to take the car anywhere—the old lady asked questions, and *questions!* She probably was in on the thing . . . Oh, she'd tell Nathan what thing when she saw him! An hour? All right. At the gate.

She flew upstairs to dress. If she was going to see the police, and she was! she wanted to look her best. Such things bore weight. And of course Nathan needed an eyeful; he'd been fairly cross about taking an hour or so off work, though Esther didn't really think he had much of a job. He was talking about going back to the University next fall, or even into the army. Esther should be doing a little work on that. Now, let's see . . .

Brown panty hose, very silky, very rich brown, over her handsome legs. Her clunkiest shoes with gold buckles. Her brown dress with the white stripes, all widths, going around and around—very sexy, specially with Esther's pale, long hair, brushed and brushed, until it glistened. The rain had stopped, but she had better take a raincoat—she could leave it in the car—though the kelly green job was not bad. Nathan once had said she looked cute in it.

She got out of the house without having to tell Alma some story—which was just as well. Alma never believed her stories, and always said she didn't. Really, Felix was going to have to make other arrangements, though God knew Esther would not do the work in this big house! She waited at the gate for less than five minutes, but she asked Nathan what had kept him.

"Get in," he told her brusquely. "What is all this about the police, and being in danger, and stuff?"

"I'll tell you. I'll show you." She opened her large purse. "But let's not hang around here. Somebody who knows us is apt to come by."

"Okay." said Nathan. "I'll drive a way—find a place to park, and you can show me those papers. Meanwhile, talk."

She talked. She told him what Alma—Felix's own mother—had said about his belonging to the Mafia.

"I don't believe it."

"It's true, Nathan. I have proof." She patted the notebook she had brought in her purse. She told about the phone calls, the men who came to the house, the times Felix went off at night— She mentioned Dr. Ottolini. "I think he's one of them, too. It's called Cosa Nostra."

"Esther, you shouldn't be telling this stuff on Felix!"

"Alma said I was in on it, as his wife. But I don't want to be in on it, Nathan. I don't want to be a gangster's wife. I can tell you, I'm going to walk out on him. Even if the police don't do anything."

He pulled to a space along the curb of a quiet suburban street. He took her papers and the black notebook. "Shut up," he said. "Let me go through these."

He unfolded the papers to read them, he folded them again and glanced at the notebook. Then sat thoughtful, his young face pale, his eyes troubled. He could take Esther with him and talk to his father. But with Felix also in the company, and Ottolini—if he really was involved . . .

He started the car. "Put this stuff back in your purse," he said. "We'll show it to the government. I guess the police should be our first start. I only hope your volunteering to give this information will save you. And I hope I can find a way to explain my part."

"You're helping me," she said, snuggling against his side. "I've only been married three months, so I couldn't be very active."

"Yeah, and you look like a dumb blonde." He drove away.

"Nathan!"

He grinned. "Beautiful, but dumb," he said firmly. Then he looked worried again.

They went to the County Office Building, parked the car, and went into the huge, resounding lobby. Esther enjoyed the appreciative whistles and stares which followed her progress. Nathan said her makeup was too heavy.

"You've enjoyed it before," she reminded him pertly.

He was cross today. Not, he explained, because she had taken him from his work. "Kimberlin can spare me," he said bitterly. But he did not like any of this business she was into, and when, in the lobby, they ran into Susan Aubuchon, he blurted to the white-faced woman that they were in the courthouse because he'd just found out that Felix Lynch was an operator for La Cosa Nostra. "We thought we should report it to the police."

Susan frowned and rubbed her fingers across her forehead. "You must be wrong, Nathan," she said. "Esther . . ."

"Oh, no," said the girl. "We're not wrong. We know it's so."

Susan shuddered. "It can't be true," she said. "If I were you, Esther, I'd go back home and appreciate the good husband you have. I wish—I wish I had—"

Her voice trembling, she told them of Rupert's accident. "I had to come here. There are papers—I have to claim his body."

She was so *white!* Nathan took her arm and led her to a bench against the marble wall. She said a policeman was going to come for her. "I—I went to the restroom. Really, everyone is being very kind. It's just—there's so much—"

"Maybe we should go with you," Nathan suggested.

Susan tried to smile. "You sound like your father," she told him. "But no— You kids go home. Don't— Oh, here's my man."

"He probably went to the restroom, too," Esther told Nathan, watching Susan walk away with the tall man in uniform.

"Don't be flip," Nathan growled at her. "She's in terrible trouble."

"Oh, I know that. She was very upset."

"She could be right," Nathan said thoughtfully. "Felix does seem like a nice guy."

"Now you listen to me, Nathan!"

He listened. And finally he said, all right, they'd take the papers to somebody. But he didn't think a desk sergeant in a police station ... The sergeant could direct them. Yes. Yes, he could. He had never felt so young.

They asked directions of a man in uniform who seemed to be a guard or something and was watching things. The police desk sergeant said they'd better talk to the inspector. He pointed to a door. The man inside this office looked at Esther's papers; he listened to her excited story. He asked who Nathan was.

"Just a friend. He drove me here. I don't have a car."

"You do, too, Esther!" Nathan told her crossly.

"Oh, sure. I have one I share with my mother-in-law, and she is in this Nostra thing, too, you see. My God, she doesn't even talk English!" She leaned back in the chair and crossed her legs.

The inspector nodded and spread the papers out before him. "I take it your husband doesn't know you have these records," he said thoughtfully.

"My God, no!" cried Esther. "He'd kill me!"

"Quit saying 'My God,'" Nathan told her gruffly. "Maybe we shouldn't have brought that stuff to the police, sir?" he asked the officer anxiously.

"Oh, I wouldn't say that. You were taking a risk, of course. These things ... Look. I think you should stay right here in this department. But I am going to consult a federal man."

Nathan stood up. He wanted no part of any such deal, he said. He was needed back at work. He had no beef against Lynch. Esther had asked him to drive her here ...

The man at the desk said for him to sit down. He would telephone ... He did telephone, speaking tersely. "I think we have a situation here," he said. "Could someone come out? Yes. Fine."

He put the phone down, gathered the papers and the notebook together, put a rubber band around the stack, and put the packet into his desk drawer. "There will be a wait," he said. "I am going to ask you to sit in the outer office."

"I don't suppose we have a choice?" Nathan asked.

The inspector smiled. "No," he said quietly. "Not at this point."

They went to the outer office where they sat on two very shiny, very hard chairs. Nathan told Esther he did not want to talk. She did talk, however, mostly about Dr. Aubuchon's being killed. He had been quite a man, she said. Well, no, he'd never been anything but proper with her, newly married and all. ...

Nathan snorted and took off his raincoat.

It took an hour for the federal man to come out from the city. He came through the outer office, a tight-faced, slim man of fifty years, with a keen quick glance for the blonde girl and the unhappy young man with her. Nathan, with each minute, was more and more anxious to be out of the mess which Esther had stirred up. These women! He didn't care if he never saw one again. Once inside, he was going to ask to have his father sit in on any discussion. Chris Kendrick would probably beat him with a barrel stave for getting into this, but Nathan thought he would welcome such direct action.

They waited again. And then, to Esther's astonishment, who should walk into the waiting room but Felix! Her own husband! Why, the dirty, double-crossing so-and-so inside! Keeping her sitting on this such-and-such hard chair ...

Felix nodded to Nathan. "I suppose she got you to drive her here?" he asked. "This all wasn't your idea, was it, Nathan?"

Nathan had stood up. "No, sir. Today was the first I'd heard of it. Esther just told me she was in some sort of jam."

Felix looked at his wife. "Yes," he agreed. "She was."

He went inside. Esther asked the policeman at the desk if there was a little girl's room. He grinned at Nathan and said there sure was. And he summoned a police matron to escort Esther. This frightened Nathan more than anything that had happened. Were they under arrest? he asked.

"Not that I know, sir. But you're supposed to be here when the inspector and the FBI man want to talk to you."

The FBI no less. A "federal man." Well, he was one. He sure was!

It was after four o'clock and getting dark. Rain was trickling down the windows again in a brief shower. But finally the policeman at the desk said they were to go "in."

Esther reached for Nathan's hand, and he jerked it away. "Behave yourself!" he said. "If you know how."

He opened the door, and she went through. Felix, looking like a handsomely carved statue, stood against the window. The federal man asked them to be seated. He now had Esther's papers. He looked at Nathan.

"I understand you are a friend of Mr. and Mrs. Lynch," he said, "and a neighbor. That you drove Mrs. Lynch here today."

"Yes, sir. When she showed me that stuff—"

"Dynamite," agreed the federal officer. "All right. Now I think it only fair to tell you that you two young people have stirred up a mess of trouble for a lot of folks."

"We know that," Esther spoke up. "The Cosa Nostra is dangerous."

"So is the government," said Felix, his voice like ice.

Nathan looked at him. "Could my father come here?" he asked.

"He could, Nathan," Felix answered, his tone softening. "And he will be told about all this. But for now—in case you are worried along certain lines, I shall look out for your interests. As well as my wife's." He shot a glance at Esther, who slumped back into her chair, looking sulky.

"You mentioned the Cosa Nostra," said the federal man. "You brought in these papers and records, Mrs. Lynch. Did you steal them from your husband's safe?"

"From my desk, in my home," said Felix. "I thought them safe there. I didn't know she even had heard of La Cosa Nostra."

Esther leaned forward. "Your own mother told me you belonged!" she cried. "And that it was a bunch of gangsters."

Felix gulped and turned full about to look out of the window. "My mother has not approved of my marriage ..." he said woodenly.

There was a silence. Esther shifted uneasily in her chair.

"He's a Dago, you know," she blurted defensively. "He carries a gun!"

The federal man gazed at her. "We know a great deal more about the man you married, Mrs. Lynch, than you seem to do. For instance, we know that he is about as loyal as an American can get. For some time now Mr. Lynch has been helping the government investigate, apprehend, and bring to justice members of a crime organization that, without the vigilance of men like Felix Lynch, could seriously interfere with our governing processes. He and a number of men like him have been, and are, members of a secret council for the purpose of contraverting the efforts of La Cosa Nostra. Mr. Lynch's particular efforts and talents have been directed against the infiltration of local labor organizations by these subversive people. He began in the Kimberlin industries; his work has led him to other industries and other labor organizations. He is what we call a labor specialist, and the anti-strike council to which he belongs is operating effectively, though hampered by a lack of funds and the need to work with a certain amount of secrecy.

"What you have done today, Mrs. Lynch, has certainly threatened the work of your husband and the council."

For most of the time this man was speaking, Nathan had sat on the edge of his chair. Now he spoke eagerly. "I don't think she's talked to anybody else," he said—not to champion Esther but to reassure the authority represented here in this room.

"Have you talked to anyone, Esther?" Felix asked sternly.

"No," she said readily. "I wasn't proud of the gangster idea. But your mother—you'd better muzzle her."

"I think she knows the work I do," said Felix quietly. "Her efforts in your direction were misguided, though my mother does not often make mistakes. I shall talk to her about this one."

"She never has liked me," said Esther sulkily.

"And I can understand why!" cried Nathan. "What were you trying to do, anyway, Esther? Get Felix killed?"

She glared at him. Then, one at a time, she looked into the eyes of the of the other three men in the room.

"Disloyalty in a wife . . ." said the federal agent thoughtfully.

And Esther screamed. She shrieked. She called names, she made threats and promises. When she had reached a peak of hysteria, Felix strode across the room; he seized her arms, and he shook her. He shook her hard; her hair streamed away from her head, and her head hung limply on her neck.

"Give it up, Lynch," said the police inspector then.

Felix glanced at him. "She isn't sorry for what she did," he said. "She just hates being exposed to me, and to young Kendrick here. She likes her men blind."

"Felix Lynch . . ." Esther began tensely.

"Mrs. Lynch!" It was the FBI man who spoke, and when she looked at his face, at his cold eyes, at his stern mouth, the fight died out of her. "That's better," he said. "Because I can promise you we intend to watch you. You are not to speak of today's happenings and revelations. You are not to interfere with Mr. Lynch's work ever again."

"Don't worry," said Esther. "I've left that guy as of now. Him and his mother!"

"Well, that's up to you. But remember—and you, too, Kendrick, there is to be no talk, careless, angry, or otherwise, about Mr. Lynch and his work for La Cosa Nostra. We would hope to maintain his great usefulness to us."

Felix stood shaking his head. "She really blew the works," he said in a tone of wonder.

"I don't think so," said Nathan. "She's too dumb to have got anything out of this except that you don't belong to the Mafia."

Esther sobbed, and hunted in her purse for her comb. The men in the room smiled, though grimly, at each other. A dumb woman, their smiles said, could be as dangerous as a gun.

Felix touched Nathan's elbow. "I'll take you kids home," he said.

"You're going to take me home only long enough to get my clothes!" Esther threatened him.

"Whatever you want. But for now . . ."

Out in the lobby, not crowded any longer, Nathan said in a wondering tone that Susan had told them that they were crazy to think Felix could be a member of . . .

"Susan?" asked Felix sharply.

"Yes, Susan Aubuchon. She was here when we came this afternoon. Her husband was killed, you know."

Felix was shocked. No, he had not known. He asked for details. Nathan told what he knew. "And she said we were crazy to bring any such information about you to the police."

Felix drew a deep breath. He was inordinately pleased that Susan believed in him, as his own wife did not. Of course, Aubuchon's death was a shock, but the guy was no good. He had dabbled in every sort of shady sideline to his profession. His death could be a break for the nice girl who had committed the error of marrying him. If he had killed himself by driving too fast on a slick road, it was only one of the ways there had been open for him to be killed.

At the hospital the open-heart surgical team was at work. Their patient was going to be a young girl, and they were debating whether to use the blood from the lung machine through a long leg artery or to subject the child to the additional chest surgery which use of the subclavian would require.

The girl was eleven years old, and strong; she probably could take the extra chest surgery, and certainly they would get more oxygenated blood. However, the leg artery would be easier to repair, and that was an item with these men. Gretchen, their patient, would, they hoped, have need for healthy blood vessels for years to come.

The six men huddled like a football team, their capped heads together.

"We could always ask Dr. Bennett," said Bill Alt.

Somebody made a rude noise.

"Hadn't you heard? This afternoon, he told Chief of Services he was ready to function as our Chief."

"Over my dead body," said Hank Mitchell, the resident.

"He was doing it over Aubuchon's," cracked Dr. Cameron.

And everyone groaned. "That was not nice, Cameron," said Chuck O'Neal.

"I am sorry, but Bennett is being such a nuisance these days. We try our damnedest to consider his age, we try to maintain an ethical position within our service, but, damn it, the man is not able to handle a case like Kimberlin's, and make no mistake. That is what he is angling for. Personally, I believe that nothing short of a quick, merciful blow will do for him. Somebody suggested that he be allowed to go in and see Kimberlin, read his chart, things like that, but I believe Mr. Kimberlin knows him pretty well, and just seeing him in anything like a professional capacity would probably scare the old man to death."

"You're for telling him bluntly . . ."

"Not me. And not so much bluntly as persuasively. But someone really should quiet him down. He is going around telling the patients that the department is at loose ends. They—"

"Meaning, he's telling Mrs. Holman."

"Meaning Mrs. Holman, and other patients. They think their hearts are in bad hands, or no hands at all."

"They should be shown a picture of what Bennett's hands could do for the department."

"Still, he's an old man, and he's a good enough doctor within limits. I wish there were a way . . ."

"Could we appeal to his wife?"

Dr. Cameron shook his head sadly. "I know Mrs. Bennett," he said. "She is a lovely lady. Pretty. The Dresden-doll type, and of course she is getting old, too. She believes completely in Dr. Bennett. She knows that he is a fine heart specialist; he has a certificate to prove it."

Three of the men growled.

"On paper, the grandfather's clause reads okay," Dr. Cameron mused. "But in practice it has proven to be a mistake to give certification to older men."

"Nobody expected them to go on for the time Bennett has done."

"That's true, I suspect. And perhaps there isn't anything we can do about Bennett."

"Well, I for one am ready to keep him off the Kimberlin case by force if necessary," said Hank Mitchell.

"Yes, he must be kept away. But could we do it without hurting the old fellow?"

"He has a daughter, as well as a wife," said young Dr. King. "A damn good-looking girl; I'd be pleased to talk to her."

The other men laughed.

"But King may have more than one idea," said Mitchell. "Maybe any one of us could talk to her, perhaps we could even say that Anderson was on the case."

"If she knows Mac, that should chirk her up."

"Over Bennett, it would help Kimberlin, too," said Dr. Richardson.

"Yes, indeed!" agreed Dr. Alt. "Yes, indeedy. Gentlemen, shall we get to work?"

The rain was coming down persistently by the time Margaret had finished her unhappy dinner with Lester. She always was more upset than he was when she allowed herself to quarrel with him. He knew this, and seemed pleased when he could provoke her into that sort of emotion. This evening he went contentedly into the library, turned on the TV, and lit a cigar. He seemed interested in the program, whatever it was.

Margaret got her red coat out of the closet. "Lionel," she said, going to the dining-room door; he was straightening the chairs, and placing the candelabra again on the hard, polished table. "Will you tell my husband, if he asks, that I have decided to go to the hospital again this evening? I should not be long."

"Yes, ma'am. I could drive you."

"Thank you, Lionel. You've had a long, hard day. I'll be back early."

"Yes, ma'am. But be a little careful. The streets are wet."

She smiled and said she would be careful, then she went out to the garage.

She did mean to go to the hospital, but as she approached the end of the Lane, she thought that perhaps Chris would go with her. There were a lot of things she needed to say to him; before dinner she had been abrupt and unkind to the man. If he were at home . . .

He was. She could see the top of his head above the chair where he sat reading in the living room. Even if Nathan were at home . . .

She turned into their drive, and, leaving the lights on, she went up to the front door. Chris must have heard the car, or seen the lights; he opened the door before she could ring.

"Oh, Chris," she said. "I thought—it's raining again. I may be a little nervous about driving because of Dr. Aubuchon. Would you want to go with me to the hospital?"

He stood looking down at her, and his eyes smiled. "Sure," he said then. He turned his head and shouted along the hall. "Nathan?" he called. "I'm going to drive Mrs. Elis to the hospital."

She heard Nathan's voice, and Chris came outside.

"A raincoat?" she asked.

"Won't need it in the car . . ." He touched her elbow. "I'm glad you stopped," he said, putting her into the right-hand seat

"Yes. I—"

He got behind the wheel, backed the car, and drove it carefully through the gates. "Nathan had a row or something with his girl this afternoon," he said. "He doesn't want to talk this evening."

Margaret turned her head.

"I don't know which girl," Chris answered her unspoken question. "But something has sobered him down. He told me at dinner that he guessed young people would do well to listen now and then to the old folks."

Margaret smiled faintly. "I wanted to talk to you," she said.

"Good." He slowed for the highway traffic.

"I don't know where to begin."

"Take your time. Do you really want to go to the hospital?"

"Yes. Just to check, maybe not to see Grandfather. He's probably asleep."

She did not know where to begin with Chris. She knew that she did want to take some sort of definite stand with him, neither to tie him nor to offend him. She hoped he would understand her position. She had thought maybe she could talk to him a little about Nathan. Perhaps not mention the petty cash, but she would speak of his involvement with Esther Lynch. That girl . . .

If Chris didn't know how often, and how intimately, Nathan was seeing Esther, he should be told. Maybe he could save the boy. Or maybe whatever she said would mean a break between father and son—which would be very bad.

Oh, dear. She realized that Chris loved his son just about as intensely as Margaret loved Chris. He would hate her for being the cause of any break between him and Nathan.

He would probably listen to what she had to say, then he would look at her and ask her why she was telling him these things. He could even ask who she was, to be so virtuous.

Well, indeed, who was she? But still—he must know—before the boy got into real trouble with Esther and hurt his father more than her telling him would do. If she could just think of the right thing to say!

Chris drove into a space close to the Heart Building's front doors. "We're lucky," he said.

"They don't encourage evening visitors here," she explained. "Are you coming in? I won't be long."

"I'll stay out here, I think. Take your time." He took his pipe from his jacket pocket and watched her as she went inside, spoke to the woman at the desk, then disappeared down a hall which led to the elevators.

She was not gone for long. "They were busy up on the surgical floor," she told.

"Is that where Arthur is?"

"He's in the penthouse, but the elevator . . . Of course, Dr. Anderson plans surgery for him."

"Is he back? Anderson, I mean."

"I don't think so. At least, I haven't seen him, and no one

149

said he was back. But they were doing open heart surgery on a child."

"At this hour of night?"

"I don't believe those surgeons up there know night from day. And I think there may be an emergency of some sort, as well. There was a great deal of bustling about, and Dr. Bennett came racing down the hall."

"He races everywhere. How was your grandfather?"

Margaret smiled. "The phrase is: his condition is stabilized."

"D'you know what that means?"

"Not really. But it does mean that he was not the emergency."

"Good."

It was also good, Margaret felt, just to sit beside this man, to feel the warmth and strength of his arm and shoulder, to hear his quiet, confident voice. She wished . . .

"Shall we sit here for a minute?" he asked. "Or maybe go somewhere for a drink? I have something I very much want to say."

She looked up at him in surprise.

He nodded. "Yes. Before dinner, this evening, our communication was not good. Static or something got in our way."

"I know. It's been a disturbing day."

"It has. But I do want to say this, Margaret. Tonight. Now."

She drew a deep breath. "Let's just stay here," she said.

"All right. Then I'll get it said. It should not take long. Simply, it is this: I want you to marry me. As soon as possible, I want you to be my wife. I want things made right between us."

Oh, dear! She put her hand on his sleeve. "Chris, darling . . ."

"You need not mention his name!" he said gruffly. "I know he must be got out of the way. And that will not be pleasant."

She sat shaking her head. "You have no idea . . ." she said below her breath. "You can't have, Chris, or you wouldn't speak of anything ever being right with us."

"Oh, but that's nonsense!" he cried, sounding angry.

"Lester . . ." Margaret began, then fell silent for want of words she would care to use in describing her husband.

"I know all about Lester," Chris assured her. "He married you when you were a girl, and he was, I presume, a young man, able to get about, to support you. To be nice enough

150

for you to love him. Don't mention the marriage vows to me, either. They work both ways, those words about 'in sickness and in health.' He promised to love you, and cherish you, sick or well. Has he done it? Can you honestly say that sadistic, self-centered man cherishes anything but his sourness at the trick which life has played on him? Has he 'loved' you—in how many years?"

Margaret sat with her head bowed. Chris was right. Yet, he was wrong, too. She loved Chris. Oh, she did love him! She could be a good wife to him, help him and Nathan. And those things were right, but they were wrong, too.

"It is very hard," she said, "for me to get on firm enough ground to know what it would be right to do. I love you, I want to be your wife, and the mother of your children. And yet, I cannot see myself taking the first step toward divorcing Lester."

"You don't have to keep him in the house where he hurts you, ten times a day!"

"I have promised him, and myself, that when he becomes unable to care for himself, he will go into a nursing home. I've promised Grandfather that."

"The man can outlive us both."

"Yes, he can. And there may develop some way— Chris, I can even think that someday he may want to divorce me."

The big man snorted.

"But he may, Chris. If Grandfather should die and leave me any amount of money. Or even if he had this surgery and lives, Lester may decide that he can get a lot of money from the Kimberlins."

Chris thought about this. "He could do that ..." he decided.

"I'd hate to see him get any of Grandfather's money."

"Just forget that sort of thinking. Your grandfather would think it cheap at the price. I've heard him on the subject of Lester Elis."

"Yes," Margaret agreed. "So have I."

"Can we work on that a little?"

"No, we can't. He'd see right through anything I'd do. As for you, he knows that you are a threat to him. I won't ask you to stay away from the house once Grandfather is home again, but we do have to be careful, Chris."

"Do you mean he'd name me in a divorce suit?"

"Or refuse to sue for a divorce if he thought I had you waiting to take his place."

Chris whistled. "He's a real stinker, isn't he?"

Margaret sighed. "I'm afraid he is," she agreed. "So—I believe the only thing in our favor is time, Chris. Do be patient, and give me that time. I couldn't bear it if you got tired of waiting, because I do love you. I do!"

He put his arm about her and drew her close. He bent his head and kissed her long and tenderly. Out on the wide, rain-blackened drive, two young people, their hair hanging dankly, their coat shoulders stained with the rain, yelled and cheered. "Go to it, Pops!" the boy shouted.

Chris sat erect, smiling. "Wait till they are my age," he told Margaret. "They'll begin to get some idea of what love is all about."

He drove her home then, going clear into the garage. "I'll skulk around in the shadows," he promised, "until you get safely into the house."

Margaret pressed his arm warmly and ran toward the side door. Only when she was inside did she remember Nathan. She had not mentioned him to Chris.

The light green walls and passageways of the big hospital had no windows, but the fact that this was a rainy night added its ounce or two to the air of the surgical floor that Wednesday night. The open-heart surgery had been going on for hours, and this fact always built up tension. And tonight, other things were happening.

At eight o'clock, Mrs. Holman had come running out into the hall, calling shrilly to the nurses at the station. Her husband, she cried—something was wrong!

The nurses had been watching the monitors; they knew that Mr. Holman was not doing well. They had known all day that fluid was developing in the lung tissues, and efforts had been made, were being made, to improve his heart action and the circulation of his blood.

But Mrs. Holman knew better than to run, and scream, in the halls. The coronary unit was functioning; there were two nurses and a doctor at her husband's bedside. The floor nurse mentioned these things.

"But he collapsed!" screamed Mrs. Holman, in spite of what she knew, and had promised to observe, of hospital decorum.

"We'll need a doctor for her," murmured the floor head to the intern.

"Maybe I can . . ."

"She knows you're an intern. She knows entirely too much!"

"I'm sorry for her."

"We are all sorry for her. Mr. Holman isn't going to make it this trip. I think I'll phone and ask Dr. Bennett to come over. Maybe he can explain things to her."

"Nothing less than Anderson will satisfy her. She wants his team and rull surgery, right now!"

"Will you phone? I'll keep her from going back into the unit. Tell Dr. Bennett what goes on."

Dr. Bennett agreed to come back to the hospital, in the emergency. He asked how Holman was.

The intern glanced up at the monitor. "I think he is already dead, sir. We are keeping it from his wife. She is very upset; we thought you could explain to her just what happened."

"After someone explains it to me," snapped Dr. Bennett. "But I'll be over. I suppose there will be a post?"

"Yes, sir. That's a rule for Dr. Anderson, on admission."

"Anderson should make a few more rules. Well, don't hold me here talking. I'll get on my way."

The intern set the phone down and shook his head. Did all the characters have to be up on the cardiac-surgery floor?

Dr. Bennett arrived at the hospital and came in on the run. He got into a white coat and went up to ten. The floor head was glad to see him. "We have an open heart just coming out," she told him.

"The *team* took care of that case!" Mrs. Holman told the doctor, her voice dry and harsh. "They could have saved Elmer, but they didn't get around to him!"

"Now, Mrs. Holman, your husband . . . Look. Let me explain just what was wrong with Mr. Holman's heart . . ."

The little woman stared at him balefully. Her face was streaked with tears. "I brought him here to get well!" she cried. "Instead of that . . ."

Dr. Bennett was sympathetic. He patted her shoulder. He let her talk. "I am sure the best cardiac procedure was followed," he told her.

"Oh, don't give me that stuff!" She took a fresh tissue from the box the nurse had provided. "If Dr. Anderson would have operated—and he would have! He planned to. Instead of that, he went on a vacation! With Elmer ready to die! Try to explain that to me, Dr. Bennett!"

"Well," said Dr. Bennett, "the way you put it . . . Though I didn't know that Dr. Anderson was planning to operate on your husband."

"Well, he would have. And do you know what?" Mrs. Hol-

153

man leaned toward him her face drawn, her eyes wild. "Dr. Aubuchon told me, just a few days ago—Monday, I think it was—that it was illegal for a doctor to abandon a case, to go off and leave it."

Dr. Bennett was tempted. That young whippersnapper, Anderson, did not have the right to drop out of sight the way he had done! But— He patted Mrs. Holman's shoulder, and shook his head at Hank Mitchell, fresh out of surgery, who had come straight down the hall to say what he could to Holman's wife.

"We won't talk about legal matters, Mrs. Holman," Dr. Bennett said soothingly. "But we can take the matter up with the medical society's grievance board. They'll know better than I do."

Dr. Mitchell faded from the scene. He went, fast, to the floor desk. "Better get Straub up here, and quick!" he told the nurse in charge.

She stared at him. "The Chief of Services, Dr. Mitchell? It's after nine o'clock."

"I don't care what time it is. Get him up here!"

It was going to take the Chief of Services to straighten out this mess.

By the time Dr. Straub arrived, Mrs. Holman had been told that her husband had died, and had been taken in to see him. She put on a scene, and because of it, a nurse took her to a room and tried to get her to go to bed for the night. This she refused to do or even consider. Dr. Bennett was asked to administer a sedative; she would at least talk to him.

"After this," said the resident fervently, "I hope we can get a rule against wives on the floor. Whew! This sort of thing takes it out of me more than— She's so damned unreasonable! She knows all the answers, and we can't say one thing different to her."

"She should go home."

"Trouble is, she's from out of town, and there are no friends or relatives close."

"She keeps talking about suing the hospital."

"I know. Over Anderson's absence."

"But . . ."

Dr. Mitchell put a finger to his lips. "That's why Straub was sent for. He knows where Mac is, and why. It's up to him to talk to Mrs. Holman."

"He can have the job," said the other doctor. "I don't believe I'll strike for Chief of Services."

"I imagine he is having second thoughts."

Dr. Straub arrived, pink, bald, meticulously dressed. He was taken to Mrs. Holman's room and introduced. He said a few appropriate words to the bereaved woman, he said that the hospital would do all it could to facilitate her return home.

"With the body of my husband!" she said bitterly.

"He was a very sick man when you brought him here," Dr. Straub reminded her.

"We came here because Dr. Anderson told us he could cure Elmer."

Dr. Straub's eyebrows went up. "Did he actually write you such a letter?" he asked.

"Oh, no, but he said we could come here, and when we did, he told me that he could help Elmer."

"You've been here how long?"

"Four months."

"That's a long time. Now I've been told that you blame Dr. Anderson for your husband's death tonight."

"He wasn't here to operate, to save him!"

Dr. Straub nodded. "Mrs. Holman," he said, "we keep very careful records here in this hospital, and Dr. Anderson is particular—above the average in such things. Knowing that you were blaming him, before I came to you, I checked his records, and in no place do I find any prognosis for cure, or even for implant surgery."

"You are saying I am a liar."

Yes, this was a dangerous woman.

"No," said Dr. Straub quietly, "I am saying that you have let your own wishful thinking make you believe things that differ from what actually was the case. Dr. Anderson did all he could for your husband. He let him stay here at this crowded hospital for a long time, trying to help him. When he had to go off the case—and I can promise you that his reasons were good—other doctors took care of Mr. Holman. Competent, well-trained men."

"I've been told all that, doctor," said the weary, grief-stricken woman. "But Dr. Anderson still had no right—he should have stayed and taken care of Elmer. He understood the case, the medicines being used. Things like that."

"Did Dr. Anderson ever tell you specifically that Mr. Holman was a candidate for implant surgery?"

"Maybe not in those exact words. You doctors don't make promises straight out. But he would have done it. I know he would have."

"I am sorry you feel so, Mrs. Holman. Now, could I help you in any way? Perhaps take you to your hotel?"

"I'll leave when Elmer leaves."

Dr. Straub would not mention the autopsy. She knew there would be one, he felt sure. "I think it would be better for you to go to your hotel now," he said. "I can send a nurse with you."

"I don't need a nurse. I don't need any help. Unless you can produce Dr. Anderson so that he can tell me what reason was good enough for him to walk out on Elmer and me."

"Doctors are human, Mrs. Holman. They need rest. They have personal affairs which demand their attention. They have problems. Always, when they take a few days for their own affairs, they must leave patients who do not want them to go. I truly do not think that Dr. Anderson's being gone or being here would have affected this case. Your husband had the best of care. His condition was such as to be beyond that care."

Finally, he got away. Finally, Mrs. Holman called a cab and went to her hotel. Both were unhappy.

But the quiet of midnight settled upon the hospital. The shadows stabilized in the long green corridors; people in white moved on whispering feet. Silence enfolded them all— the operating rooms, the empty bed in the coronary care unit where Elmer Holman had made his struggle for life, the intensive care unit where, behind plate-glass windows, an eleven-year-old child was responding to the care of the nurses and doctors who attended her, the penthouse suite where the white-haired industrialist slept on his high white bed, a nurse silently beside him.

A sudden sharp noise, the dropping of a pan, the crash of glass, the unthinking whistle of an orderly coming on duty, from time to time showed that the hospital was a place of life as well as sickness and death.

Chapter 5

By the end of the week, the sun was out again, the skies blue, the grass green, and the flowers blooming. Margaret Elis sat beside her grandfather's bed and told the white-haired man that the sparrows had moved into the Martin house.

"It's just a damned apartment," said the sick man vigorously. "A housing project."

She laughed gently. "You're losing your color," she told him. "Can't you be wheeled out on the terrace? Or could I bring you a sun lamp and some glasses?"

He smiled faintly. "I used to be proud of my warm, healthy glow," he said.

"I'll ask about the sun lamp. I like my men healthy and handsome."

"You do, eh?"

"Yes." She sat thoughtful.

He watched her. Green suit of thin wool, a crisp white blouse. "You're a handsome girl, Margaret," he told her.

She said nothing.

"Don't like to be told you are handsome?" he asked.

"I do, of course. Knowing that you are buttering me up."

"For what?"

She shook her head and again sat silent, though Dr. Mitchell had said she could talk to her grandfather. "He gets bored, and irritable. Don't get him excited, but let him gossip if he wants to."

Today—

"Are you unhappy, Margaret?" he asked unexpectedly.

She looked up quickly. "Because you are ill . . ." she began.

He dismissed this with a wave of his hand. "I meant, are you unhappy, or happy, in your new home here?"

She smiled at him. "I've told you, it is heaven."

"Yes. You did tell me that."

"Now, with the lilac bushes in bloom, and the roses . . ."

"Are you happy?"

She sighed and tried to smile. It was not a very good smile, she knew. "You are guessing that I am not," she said.

"Guessing, yes."

He waited, but she said no more.

"Is it Lester?" he asked.

"Well, not exactly. Oh, he is difficult. But like your illness, I knew when we came here, that he would be difficult."

"Yes. You did know that, didn't you?"

She leaned toward him. "Grandfather," she said earnestly, "do you think it would be a terrible thing if I should divorce Lester?"

She thought he might be surprised. But he was giving the matter careful consideration.

"I thought I could handle things," she said. "Wait."

He nodded. "I understand. I myself have found the man impossible to live with, and I've said so. But divorce— Yes, I think it might be a terrible thing for you to do, Margaret. For yourself. Lester relies on you quite a bit, my dear. And the day will come when you'll say to yourself, 'He was not to blame for the fix I got myself into.' That means guilt, which is a hard thing to live with." He smiled at her. "Perhaps harder to live with than Lester, though I'll grant you that he is damned hard to have around.

"Of course you should be able to get a divorce. You would have no trouble finding witnesses to testify to his brute ugliness. And his health—I don't imagine he can fulfill his duties as a husband."

Head down, Margaret nodded. "I've done for Lester," she said softly. "I've put up with him. But, now— Oh, Grandfather, I may have to do this! I may have to marry Chris, love him, help him. I want to do that, so much!"

The old man nodded. "I've seen that growing between you two," he agreed. "And I've been sorry that things were as they are. But, Margaret, my dear, Chris is a strong man; he doesn't need your help. On the other hand, Lester is weak, in health and in character, and he does need help. Obligations, legal rights, are not the whole thing. The strong must help the weak, though there is not much fun in it, of course."

"Now, I am old, and I am sick, but I still remember how it is with a strong young woman who loves a man. She wants that man at all costs. But I would hope to show you at least one of the costs in this thing you are considering. And that will be the thought that will come to you: that you turned your back on the weak man who, despite his denial, does need you."

Margaret sighed, and she sighed again. "I know you are

158

right," she agreed. "But I can't help but regret the loss of my heaven."

Her grandfather stretched out his hand, and she took it. "Your heaven is still there, my dear," he told her. "The things that made you feel it was heaven when you came here as a child, when you came here to live. The flowers, the dogs scampering through the woods."

"Not the dogs, dear," she said. "Last week, someone put out poison, and killed the little scampering dogs. Mine, Abby's, and Susan Aubuchon's."

Her grandfather was shocked.

"It was bad," Margaret agreed.

"Do you have any idea who the monster could be?"

"I decided not to entertain any such ideas. The damage was done. Susan plans to get another dog."

"And you could."

"Yes. And you're right, Grandfather, everything is still there."

"I suppose flowers and dogs are about all one should expect to get from an earthly heaven," said her grandfather. "Your happiness with Chris would be an extra bonus."

Margaret got up and walked to the window; she stood looking out at the roofs of the city, the houses, the trees, the tall buildings, the busy streets far below her. "It must be awful," she said, "to live long enough to know so much."

"You're damned right!" said Arthur Kimberlin. "It is awful. For me, and for you. Look, my dear, why don't you make friends with Susan Aubuchon? You two young women probably need each other."

Margaret turned. "Do you know about Dr. Aubuchon?"

"That he was killed. Yes, I know. A young life wasted."

She came back to the chair. "I could read that in a dozen ways," she said.

"You could. How is Susan? What plans does she have?"

"I've done what I could for her. She is very brave, and sensible. For one thing, she isn't making any drastic plans just now. No changes, I mean. She has gone back to her work at the school, she works in her flower beds. I went to the funeral with her. Of course the school people have been very good to her, but she asked me to stay close, and I did. That was a difficult performance. Reporters, cameras—the curious."

"And gossip."

"Oh, yes. There was a girl killed, too, you see. I also went to that funeral. Susan cried. Bonnie had been a student at the school. She had had an abortion—and the talk asks who performed it, who was the father of the child—things like that. I suppose this goes on at school, as it does on the Lane. Though we mean to be kind."

"Of course."

"Then there is a lot of talk about Dr. Anderson."

Her grandfather stirred. "What about him? What gossip, I mean."

"Oh, they talk about his continued absence, of course. And now it seems that some patient has died, and his wife is suing, or threatening to sue, him and the hospital for abandoning the case. That is supposed to be a bad thing."

"Could he have saved the man?"

"Perhaps not. The autopsy showed that he didn't have the proper heart lesion, or artery lesion, for the surgery Dr. Anderson specializes in. Something like that. I read about it in the newspaper, but I didn't understand a thing."

"Mac's a good doctor," said her grandfather. He was looking tired.

Margaret stood up, came to the bed and kissed him. "I'll see you tomorrow, darling," she said.

He did not answer.

It was that same evening—Margaret had dropped in to see Susan for a few minutes, and to ask if she would come up the Lane and eat dinner with her and Lester.

Susan shook her head. "I mean to eat a proper dinner, Margaret," she said. "I really do. Look." She led the way to the kitchen. "See? I have lamb chops set out to thaw, and potatoes."

Margaret picked up one of the small pink balls. "You won't get fat on this," she said.

"I'll eat two. Make a salad."

"And dessert?"

"Oh, I could have ice cream and a slice of cake which Mrs. Lynch sent me."

"Esther says she puts garlic in everything. Does she?"

Susan laughed. "Not in cake. Felix brought me two slices last night. I ate one, and it was delicious."

There was gossip on the Lane, too, that Esther was promising to leave Felix. That he had an eye for Susan . . . Margaret tasted a bite of the cake. It was white, with a caramel icing, and it *was* delicious. "I may stay and eat with you," she teased Susan.

"Oh, you may! And I'll put you to work. Do you know what I am doing?"

"Haven't the least idea."

"I'll show you. I worked all day yesterday at it. I got out all of Rupert's clothes. I thought I'd select the badly worn ones and find someone who could get some use from them. Then I thought maybe there might be an intern or a medical student who could use his good things."

"He had a lot of clothes," said Margaret, surveying the heaps and piles on both guest room beds.

"Yes, he did," said Susan. "There are white uniforms, too, at the office. If Dr. Anderson were at home, I'd ask him."

"Couldn't Dr. Bennett help you?"

Susan's face brightened. "Yes, he could!" she said eagerly. "I'll ask him."

Margaret recognized some of Dr. Aubuchon's clothes as things she had seen him wear. A certain fleece-lined coat ... Susan did not seem saddened by her task. She had gone on to explain about the complications of closing a doctor's office. Narcotics alone were a problem.

"Do you have a good lawyer?"

"Yes. Felix told me of one. He's been wonderful."

Felix again. Well, they'd make a fine pair. Better matched than ... "Look, I'll have to go," said Margaret. "Call me if you need me. And I'll be seeing you."

"I know you will," said Susan shyly. "You've been so good."

"On orders from my grandfather. He said I should make friends with you."

"How is he?"

Margaret told her as she went to the front door and outside. She had only reached the main roadway when she heard the running feet behind her, and turned. Chris and Nathan were jogging. They caught up with her. Chris wore a gray sweat shirt and trousers, Nathan had a red t-shirt and white shorts.

"Will you join us?" Chris asked, bobbing up and down in place.

Margaret laughed and looked down at her black pumps. "In these heels?"

Chris went on ahead of her and around the circle. As she continued toward her home, Margaret watched the two men. She had reached the high hedge and overly thick evergreen shrubbery before Bennett's when Chris came up to her again. "Nathan chickened out," he explained, wiping his face with the towel slung around his neck. He glanced around and behind him, then leaned forward swiftly and kissed her cheek.

161

Startled, she stepped back, and his hand caught at her arm. "Don't, Chris . . ." she said.

"It's getting dark. No one can see us. You're nicely camouflaged in your dark green."

"Sometimes you sound and act younger than Nathan."

He laughed. "I can outjog him, too. But he's a good boy, Margaret. Lately he's been doing fine, and planning to go back to school."

"I'm glad, Chris."

He peered at her. "You don't look very glad."

"I am glad about Nathan. But sad about you and me, Chris. I've decided that you should forget about me."

His hand drew her toward him, close, and closer. Holding her, he kissed her hard, and long. "That's how I should do about you," he said gruffly.

She pushed herself free, and stood away from him. "No!" she cried, shaken by his strength, his passion. "No, Chris! You must listen to me!"

He stood in the shadows of the prickly yews, and studied her face. "I'm listening," he said, his voice deep.

"Well, it's this. You know how I call living in Grandfather's home heaven, the woods, and the Lane—all of it. But—" She lifted her head, regaining her poise. "Lately I have realized that the things which I love, the things which brought you and me together, now must keep us apart."

"Things," said Chris.

"Yes. My grandfather. Lester. The Lane itself. The friends I have made here. In fact, heaven itself."

"Have you been talking to someone?" he asked. She knew that she had hurt him.

"Yes," she said, "to myself. The answers are not too happy, nor definite. But one thing comes through clearly. I won't wait for you, Chris, and I don't want you to wait until I am free."

"Margaret . . ."

"I love you," she said quickly. "I wish I were free to show you how much. But until I am, Chris—there should be nothing."

He nodded. "You've been talking to the wrong person," he said gently.

"Or to the right one."

"I love you, Margaret," he said earnestly. "And I would say that you are asking us to pay too high a price for your heaven."

"The price was paid, Chris, before I ever knew you. And a

bargain has to be a bargain. I wish these things were not so true. But there must be some comfort in the fact that I have my heaven still, and you have your son."

"But, dammit, woman, those are things we could share!"

She bit her lip. "No," she said firmly, "we can't. Not now."

Abby Bennett had watched the act of the play being performed on the Lane, astonished at how much drama could be featured in the lives of these quiet, well-behaved people. She had not dreamed ... But then, she did know that her ideas had become provincial, that she had lost sight of the fact that the middle west, the middle class, could know passion, tragedy, and even high comedy.

Or, if she had known it, she would not have attached drama to the lives of her parents, such dear people, growing old gracefully.

Gracefully? She laughed. Not her father. That sprightly cricket of a man was hopping about in so many directions. He was up at five-thirty in the morning, off for the hospital by seven, where he would pick up breakfast. He talked importantly about the responsibilities which had fallen upon him. Abby got only a vague idea of just what those responsibilities were. Lectures, she supposed, in the medical school, patients—and lately he had talked a lot about surgery, drawing pictures for his daughter and wife of aneurysms and heart valves. He brought home a plastic model of the heart and tried to show them just what ailed his old friend, Arthur Kimberlin.

Arthur Kimberlin. That was the main source of Abby's worry. Then had come the lawsuit about another patient ... Holman? Yes, that was the name. The suit was against Dr. Anderson, the hospital, and the cardiovascular department of that hospital. She asked a dozen questions. Was her father involved in the suit?

He was on the staff, yes, he said curtly. He thought perhaps his womenfolk should not be told enough details that outsiders could question them. The hospital was maintaining a "No comment" attitude to the press, and this would make reporters try to discover, in any way they could ...

Abby recognized the technique, and smiled grimly at the idea of her family being the target of high-pressure news investigators. She herself could cope. So could her mother. "The doctor never tells me a thing!" was that lady's best line. But her dad?

He was getting old; he had always been a great talker, and

163

lately he had had a compulsion to establish himself not only as a heart specialist, which he was, but as the best, the key surgeon of the cardiovascular staff at the big teaching hospital. His urgency on the subject seemed about to burn the old man up, and Abby did not want that to happen. She did not want him to take on too much; she did not want the hospital to take him at his own word and forget his years.

The lawsuit promised to be the decisive straw. He talked about it all the time, blaming the other staff doctors for not thinking enough of their patients, or of the patient's family. They wouldn't stop and explain things, he said. He had known surgeons who never went to see a patient after the surgery was done. He hated to think of one of these working over his old friend, Arthur Kimberlin. But that would not happen. Dr. Bennett was now in a position . . .

What position?

Running up against still another of his answers, "I don't want you to be bothered, Abby," she decided to get bothered. She would go to the hospital, and in her best snooping manner, she would find out why such a large institution must rely on one old man to get them out of their troubles, legal and surgical. And if that situation was as ridiculous as it sounded, thought about sensibly, what *was* happening to her father? A capable doctor, and alert—but at his age—and the thought of his being responsible for his old friend's life—the whole thing was unbearable. She would get things straightened out; there must be someone who would talk to her.

And when she knew what was going on, then she could . . ."

She dressed carefully in a spring suit the color of a teal duck's feathers, her ash blonde hair was brushed to a soft glow, her gloves and shoes were impeccable. She drove to the hospital, parked her car, and went into the tall building which was devoted to the department of cardio and thoracic diseases. There was a directory in the lobby, and she studied it. Then she asked if she could be directed to the Unit Administrator.

The woman at the desk pointed her pencil down the right-hand corridor. "Mr. Kammeyer," she said. As if, every afternoon, pretty young women came asking for the Unit Administrator.

Abby had chosen her day; on Wednesday, her father served as physician at a correctional institution, a charity which he enjoyed and talked about importantly. "If he were

164

anything but my beloved father," Abby told herself, smiling, "I'd call the old duck a pompous ass."

She was still smiling at this thought when she opened the proper door and went into Mr. Kammeyer's office. She was glad he would not be a doctor; their closely knit league could be baffling, she knew.

The gentleman happened to be in the outer office talking to his secretary, and when Abby stated her mission, he identified himself, and asked her to come in. He indicated the door to the inner room.

Mr. Kammeyer, was a very tall man; he looked like a Norseman, with blond hair, pink and white skin, friendly blue eyes.

Abby sat down and lifted her own dark eyes to this man's face. "I am Abby Bennett," she said. "My father is Dr. Bennett, on your staff."

Mr. Kammeyer nodded. "Oh, yes. Been with the hospital a long time."

"Yes, he has," said Abby. "And lately my mother and I have been concerned about him. He seems to be working too hard, and to be under some tremendous pressure. At his age . . ."

"You're right. Dr. Bennett has continued to work long beyond the age of retirement welcomed by most doctors."

"I know that. Though he seems well, and certainly alert."

Mr. Kammeyer nodded.

"I have worried about the pressure he seems to be under, and because he talks about it so much, my mother and I suspect that this is due to his concern for his long-time friend, Mr. Kimberlin, who is evidently very ill here in the hospital."

"Yes, he is a patient."

"We live next door to Mr. Kimberlin," said Abby. "We know that he is critically ill with some heart condition."

"Coronary insufficiency, yes."

Abby leaned forward. "Is my father attending him?"

Mr. Kammeyer leaned back, and his expression became wary. "Well," he said, "Our heart service is set up in what we call teams, Miss Bennett. That means a group of doctors who work together. As a team, they make the diagnosis, determine treatment, do possible surgery, and so on."

"Is my father on the team attending Mr. Kimberlin?"

"Your father does not subscribe to team medicine, I'm afraid. But he probably has talked to you about this."

"No. He doesn't talk to us specifically about his work at

165

all. If his attitude means that he carries, alone, the burden of Mr. Kimberlin's condition . . ."

Mr. Kammeyer stood up. He had been polite, even kind—beyond, really, Abby's expectations. "If your father is Mr. Kimberlin's friend and neighbor," He said, "you must be, too. Would you like to go up to see him this afternoon?"

His question took Abby completely by surprise. "Is he able?" she asked, stuttering alittle.

Mr. Kammeyer smiled. "Well, he is a sick man. A very sick man, and he is facing surgery. But, yes, I think he could see an old friend."

Abby was surprised. Her father had indicated . . . Walking along beside tall Mr. Kammeyer, she decided that, for the time, she would shuck free of all the things her father had said. Not that he was untruthful; he never could be! But the few, selected things he revealed at home certainly had given the impression . . .

For one thing, he talked about there not being any other doctor, but this place swarmed with doctors! The registry board must contain three dozen names! White garments were about in the halls, they were in the first elevator, they were in the second hall, along with nurses and other people in green as well as white. Some of them were surely doctors!

She and her guide reached another elevator, and this one was operated only with a sort of key arrangement. Inside, it was like almost any elevator, but it did have a button labeled Penthouse. This struck a familiar note; her father had said that Arthur Kimberlin was isolated in the penthouse suite.

"He doesn't have much company," said Abby, her voice quavering, "I suppose."

"No, he doesn't," the Unit Administrator agreed. He gestured to her to step out. "This is Miss Bennett," he said to a white-jacketed man who sat at a desk in the hall. "I think she might see Mr. Kimberlin." He turned and held out his hand to Abby. "You'll be all right now," he said. The orderly was talking into a phone.

"You certainly have been kind," Abby told her guide. "And I am awed by your tight security."

Mr. Kammeyer smiled at her, stepped back into the elevator, and disappeared behind its silently closing door.

"This way, ma'am," said the orderly, rising and leading the way.

The room they entered was a sitting room, tastefully furnished, with oyster white curtains pulled halfway across the wide windows. There were green plants set about, a blue carpet on the floor, a beige couch and a blond wood coffee table. There was a dark blue armchair, an oyster white one, not quite so deep nor so large. There were current magazines, and good pictures on the walls.

"Miss Bennett?"

Abby whirled and gasped. For the man who spoke, the man who had come up behind her, was Malcolm Anderson.

In the flesh, looking entirely his quiet, self-controlled self, his brown eyes steady, his jaw and mouth a bit stern. He wore white hospital clothes—shoes, trousers, white jacket. There was a name plate on his pocket.

"When . . ." Abby stammered. "When did you come back? Where have you been?" She could feel the prickles of surprise, of astonishment, cold on her skin.

"I've not been away," said the doctor's rich, steady voice. "I have been right here."

"But—I heard you had disappeared, that something was wrong with you, that you were on vacation."

"Let's choose the last one," he said, smiling a little. He motioned to the couch. "Won't you sit down? Will you have some coffee?"

She sat down weakly, but shook her head at his suggestion of coffee. "They said I could come up here to see Mr. Kimberlin."

"He doesn't have visitors. I left the word downstairs to send you up here if you came." As if he had known that her father would have talked wildly about Kimberlin, about himself, about Malcolm Anderson. It had been partly to isolate Mr. Kimberlin from the well-meaning old codger that Mac had brought him to the hospital and isolated him from all but a select few. Bennett, while Mr. Kimberlin was at home, had advanced some disturbing medical ideas about the case. The only way to keep him away from his old friend here at the hospital had been complete seclusion, with Dr. Anderson secretly in attendance.

"I've been taking my vacation right here," he now told Abby. "I use this suite—I have my own room and bath here. The Chief of a service can claim certain privileges."

Abby nodded. "It is very pleasant," she agreed. Her tone and manner were cautious until she knew what was going on. "If you needed a vacation—and I suppose you did."

"Yes, I did. At any rate, a break. I stayed here because I had some important work to do."

"For Mr. Kimberlin."

"That was a part of it. Yes."

"Couldn't you have done your work and stayed in your own home? The orchard was lovely this spring."

He nodded. "I'm sorry I missed that."

"You could have had it, and been only an hour away from the hospital." By now she was defending herself against the concern she had felt about this man.

"Only an hour away from four surgicals a day," he agreed.

"I understand the hospital is into a lawsuit because of your disappearance."

"Yes. I regret that. But it is never easy for a doctor to take a break."

"I suppose not. Didn't anyone know where you were?"

He laughed. "Yes. About two dozen well-trained personnel who respected my need for a breather." He sat on the couch beside her, turned to face her. His thick brown hair, his steady eyes, the quiet of his strong hands, there so close . . .

"I wish I had known," said Abby simply, directly.

"I couldn't risk telling anyone whose job did not depend on his discretion. You see, Abby, I did need to get away. Because of Mr. Kimberlin, mainly, I could not leave the hospital. So I retired to what my team irreverently calls this nunnery."

Abby laughed.

"Yes, the term is valid. I accepted it. A nunnery would give me what I had to have. I had a personal problem to work out; to do that I needed time, physical rest, a change from my usual rigorous schedule. I couldn't leave Mr. Kimberlin. Nor Mr. Holman, if the truth is known and told. My team knew where I was, about four nurses, a couple of orderlies, and a bewildered kitchen staff who must have made their guesses as to who was eating the broiled steaks and all the coffee that has been coming up here."

"Did you get a rest?" She felt odd. She was glad to see him, and a certain exhilaration was taking over, that he would admit her to the charmed circle and talk to her.

"I got a rest," he agreed. "A let-up on the hectic routine of my normal days—seeing patients, ward walks, surgery. I've been keeping better hours than I usually do. And besides thinking about my own affairs, I did some work I have been wanting to do for some time. I worked on a lecture series for class instruction through closed-circuit TV. In the room next door, I have quite an impressive electronics setup. TV camera, tape recorder, a place where I can select and edit film made during surgery or diagnostic tests. I got those lectures boiled down to a good script, beginning with a case history, tabulating the tests made, telling how they were made, and the results. The diagnosis bit was brought out, and the results. When I refused a case for implant surgery, when I accepted it, and why in each instance. Then the surgery is shown in detail. P.O. care. Prints of all this can go to any medical school, chest surgeons convocations—for information and instruction."

"But, Malcolm, that will be a wonderful contribution!" She knew now why she was excited.

"I hope so. I have wanted to do it. There just was not time in my busy days."

"So you took a vacation." She was laughing.

And he grinned. "It really was one," he told her. "I have the satisfaction of getting the job done. Mr. Kimberlin knew what I was up to. In fact he financed some of the expensive material and paid a technician who knew what he was about."

"But that's wonderful! How many lectures, or cases . . . ?"

"I have ten done. Complete. Mr. Kimberlin's is up to the actual surgery."

"Was Mr. Holman one?"

He met her gaze. "You're a keen one," he said.

"I'm interested."

She saw something like a shadow cross his bright brown eyes. But he answered her readily enough. "Holman was a case," he said. "He presented a fine diagnostic problem. He had had a muscle resection—that's where the diseased tissues of the heart are trimmed away. I decided, and told Holman, that I could not do an implant."

"And he read it 'would not.' "

"His wife did. I think Elmer trusted me. The autopsy bore out my decision."

"Is that on the lecture film, too?"

"It is."

"It's sure to be a smash," she said dryly.

"It will clear me and the hospital about any court suit for malpractice."

"Yes. And that's fine in itself, Mac. I truly mean that."

His hand covered hers. "I know you do."

"There's been a lot of confusion in your hospital while you were gone."

"I know, and that's too bad. But when I got the cooperation I did from Mr. Kimberlin, and the Chief of Medical Services . . . Mr. Kimberlin really has got a kick out of going the whole way on tape, tests and X-rays . . . he jokes about

169

nude movies. He made me promise to go all-out for the surgery on him—pump, artificial heart and lung—the works."

"Will you?"

"Yes."

She stood up. "Malcolm Anderson," she said. "I think you are wonderful."

"Don't tell anybody."

"That you are wonderful? I shan't say a word about any of this. But you should pray that I'll learn to be a better actress than I think I am."

"I pray all the time. Good-by, Abby."

"Good-by." She wished he would kiss her. He did not.

Abby kept her promise of silence, and she hoped that Malcolm knew that she did, because within twenty-four hours, word began to go about, first on the Lane, then in the newspapers, that implant surgery was scheduled for Arthur Kimberlin. In the newspapers there were intricate drawings and detailed discussions of what revascularization meant. Dr. Anderson was extolled as a young wizard of heart surgery. The pictures of him did not do him justice, Abby thought.

One resourceful feature writer detailed the surgical techniques perfected by Dr. Anderson and mentioned the team of men who worked with him. Pictures of these doctors were shown—young men. "Dr. Anderson is on vacation and perhaps will not do the actual surgery on Arthur Kimberlin."

With some hesitation, Abby discussed this article with her father. He professed distaste for newspaper publicity of the sort. "You never catch any of my work being advertised," he said virtuously.

Later that same day, Abby heard her father assure Alma Lynch that of course Mr. Kimberlin was in good hands. "I've not left the case, and shan't," he said earnestly.

"Oh, dear," thought his daughter. She was realizing that she had not used her opportunity to talk to Mac about her father's attitude to the situation, his sad and perhaps senile aberration. She had not asked him, either, why he had expected her to come to the hospital and had set up a procedure. Could she go to see him again? She wanted to—but no. Malcolm could have got in touch with her. Once Mr. Kimberlin's surgery was completed—within a day or so, she believed—he would return to normal living, he would again be on the Lane. She would wait.

Even Esther Lynch read some of the stories about Dr. Anderson and Mr. Kimberlin. And she ventured to ask Felix what was being thought and said at the plant about his chances.

"Kimberlin is a pretty big and sprawled-out operation," Felix reminded his wife. "I don't get around much beyond the lab section."

"Yeah, yeah," said Esther. "I know how you don't get around."

Since the exciting afternoon at the county building, Esther had lived in the house, pleased to know that Lynch had chewed out his mother for telling that he was an operative of La Cosa Nostra. Alma professed innocence. "How was I to know different?" she asked blandly.

"Next time you don't know different, Mamma, don't talk about it at all. Understand me? Please?"

Alma thenceforth did little talking "at all" to Esther. Felix had chewed his wife out, too, but good. Frightened at the revelations, morbidly shaken by Dr. Aubuchon's death, Esther had withdrawn into a long fit of sulks. For days, she scarcely left the house.

But this evening she did talk to Felix about Mr. Kimberlin. Alma had gone next door to sit with Susan for a while. Esther was in the living room, looking through some magazines. Felix came in, and she began to talk to him.

"Look," she said now. "That mistake of your mother's— the police bit and all—did word of that get around the plant?"

"Not unless you've talked about it."

"Golly, I didn't talk. I didn't see anybody, for one thing. And I'm not proud that you might be doing that sort of work."

For his own information, Felix would have liked to question her on this last point, if point it was. But he picked up the newspaper, and wished he might have gone with his mother to see Susan.

"Look, Esther," he said abruptly, "at the courthouse the other day, you said something about leaving me."

"Yes, I did," she said, stretching her long legs before her, wagging her sandaled feet back and forth.

"I think it would be a good idea," said Felix.

"Split, you mean?"

"That is exactly what I mean. Our marriage was a mistake."

"And how!" she breathed fervently.

"Yes. And how. You thought I was good-looking . . ."

"And rich," Esther purred.

171

He laughed. "I thought you had a seductive woman's body."

"Don't I?" she asked boldly.

"You know you do. You work on it all the time. But you don't like living here."

"I don't like your mother."

"The feeling is mutual, I'm sure."

"Yeah."

"So I think the two of us should break up, and as quickly as possible."

"On what grounds?"

"Incompatibility. If that won't do, there are others."

She looked at her fingernails. She was using a new polish and it seemed okay.

"I think," Felix continued steadily, "that you might move out tomorrow."

"Just like that."

"Mhmmmn. Just like that. You can go to the hotel, or find a small apartment. You can get a job."

She sat up straight. "Oh, now, wait just a minute, Buster!"

"You can meet more men if you're working. Just as you met me."

She sat shaking her head. "Boy, if you aren't a cool one."

"Not always, Esther. I certainly wasn't cool when I married you."

"No. Not for about two weeks. Then Mamma got busy."

He ripped out an oath that made her blink. "You keep my mother out of this!" he roared.

"All right, Mamma's boy. But if I do divorce you, there's two things I gotta say. One, don't bring your next wife into the same house with her, because the woman's not been born yet she'll think is good enough for you. Second—" She stood up, and swung her long hair back from her face. "Second, you're going to pay me dearly, Felix Lynch."

Felix regarded her steadily. "I expect to pay," he said.

"And I guess you know, when I leave tomorrow, or whatever, that Nathan Kendrick will be leaving with me."

"Does Nathan know that?"

She flushed. She had not seen Nathan since that rainy evening when he had driven away from the county building and she'd had to go home with Felix. "He knows," she said truculently. "He loves me more than you ever did, and I love him more than I ever did you."

Felix nodded and stood up, too. "Then that's all arranged," he said briskly. "You can move out tomorrow."

"In the car?" she asked.

"In the car," he agreed. He would get Alma another one—and handle her vigorous protest on the matter.

The next morning, Abby Bennett found a problem on her hands. And the problem was her mother, who was upset about the doctor. "He didn't sleep a wink last night, Abby," she told her daughter tearfully. "I am sure they are going to operate on Arthur Kimberlin this morning. He would get up and go over some papers he has. He calls them operational charts. All about the heart-lung machine, and the pump. He had a list of names. The team, he said. And he checked them off. He said he had to leave early this morning; he had had an idea. Each member of the team should have a physical examination—something about eyesight and reflexes."

Abby put her arm around her mother. Mrs. Bennett had not yet combed her white hair, she had no lipstick on, her housecoat was unbecoming. "Come and sit down," she said, "and try not to worry. Dad has handled his professional problems apart from his family for as long as I can remember."

Mrs. Bennett sniffed. "He hasn't been seventy-six years old for as long as you remember, and he never had to operate on his best friend before. He just should not do it, Abby! It will be too hard on him."

Not for worlds would Abby suggest that her mother not believe in what she thought she knew to be true. Malcolm Anderson would do the surgery. Abby was certain that he would. "Did Dad say he was going to operate?" she asked.

"But he never says anything like that, Abby. You know he doesn't. But with Dr. Anderson still gone, he'd think he should do it. Who else is there? Dr. Aubuchon is dead—and anyway, he would have been unthinkable. I've heard your father say that much! Oh, Abby, I know your father is a good doctor. At least, he has been."

"Of course, Mother."

"But he's *old,* Abby. And the trouble is, he doesn't think he is old. He doesn't know it. He keeps walking fast, and running up stairs—and I truly don't believe he knows he's too old to do a long operation. You know what I think? I think I'll get sick, so he'll have to come home and take care of me."

"Oh, now, Mother . . ."

Mrs. Bennett sighed. "He probably wouldn't come," she conceded. "But I am worried, Abby."

"I know you are." Abby twisted her thick curl of hair around her finger. If she could think of something to say, or do!

"Your father is an honorable man," her mother was telling her, "but he is old, and Arthur Kimberlin is his close friend. They've been like brothers. I suppose you're thinking about ways to solve the problem. You aren't old enough to realize that some of life's problems cannot be so neatly solved as those you work out on your typewriter."

Abby laughed and stood up. She leaned over to kiss her mother. "I'm going up to dress," she said. "You had better dress, too. You'll feel better."

"Then I'll certainly dress," said her mother tersely.

Professing errands to do—a new typewriter ribbon, she wanted to look for some navy blue shoes—yes, she would pick up a list of things at the market—Abby drove off into the morning sunlight. It was a warm day.

She went directly to the hospital. She would see Dr. Anderson and speak to him about her father, as she had failed to do on that other afternoon.

Now— She hoped that she could see him. If she went through the same routine . . .

The Unit Administrator was not in his office, but his secretary recognized Abby; she consulted a list and said she would take her up to surgery.

"I know the way . . ."

"I'd better take you. Unauthorized personnel aren't welcome up there."

Abby nodded. She and the secretary both put on enveloping white gowns, and they went up in the elevator. The secretary consulted with a nurse behind a desk, and then took Abby to a small room.

As she was waiting, she had stood, fascinated, in the hall. Things certainly were busy! Gowned, capped, masked people went this way and that; she flattened against the wall for a stretcher, she stepped aside for a dolly loaded with green tanks; she smiled at a red-headed young man who greeted her, "Hi, beautiful!" and then she followed her guide to the small room. In it were shelves of books, some instruments, a small desklike table, and two chairs. She said, yes, she would wait.

She looked at her watch, but made no estimate of the time she expected to wait. She was studying the titles of the books on the lower shelf, and shaking her head in disbelief, when the door opened and still another person, tall, swathed in green, came in. But she knew his eyes. They were distinctive under any circumstances. Brown eyes, the pupils as round as marbles against the whites.

"I forgot to say something the other day," she hastily told Malcolm.

He was standing and looking at her. "Yes?" he said.

"I really came that day to talk to you about my father."

"Yes . . ."

"Then I was ready to urge you—someone—not to let him attend Mr. Kimberlin. I was going to mention his age, their long friendship, various things."

"I know both men quite well, Abby." He was not cold, exactly, but waiting to hear what she would say.

"I'm sure you do. Today I am going to ask you to say that my father will be on the team that does the surgery for Mr. Kimberlin."

Her request startled Malcolm Anderson. He leaned toward her and searched her face. "Abby," he said gently. "Your father can't take such a place, he can't do surgery."

Abby nodded. "But can't you let him think he is scheduled? He knows he can't do the work, and he won't do it."

The hospital knew it, too. They would think, those who knew that Anderson was available, they would think he had flipped. And how would old Bennett be handled in the meantime?

He touched Abby's shoulder and the thick curl of hair which lay there. "I think I know what you are hoping to accomplish," he said. "And I'll help if I possibly can."

She smiled at him. "Thank you, Malcolm," she said softly.

Felix Lynch had to tell his mother about his showdown with Esther. There was the matter of the car and the way Esther had gone off with it, with clothes hanging from a rod, and shoes and boxes piled helter-skelter into the back seat and the trunk.

"Is she leaving?" Alma asked her son.

Felix nodded. "She is leaving. Don't talk to her, Mamma."

"I watch that she doesn't take what is not hers."

"You stay out of it. Find something to do. That's what I plan."

Felix went outside to cut the grass. Alma went into her kitchen. Tomorrow she would clean that upstairs, air it good. Perfume, powder. *Wheesh!* For now she would cook. She felt good, and she would cook. Within an hour the whole house

175

reeked of garlic and wine and cheese, the aroma drifted through the open windows.

Felix came to the porch. "Mamma!" he called. "What are you cooking?"

"Spaghetti, and a chicken for risotto, and I made . . ."

"I'll take some spaghetti over to Susan. She's just come in late from school. She'll be glad she won't have to cook her own dinner."

His mother answered something and he waited. Within minutes she brought out a round blue dish, and lifted the cover to show the contents. "You should put on a shirt," she admonished her son.

He laughed and loped across the connecting lawns to Susan's back door. He knocked loudly and called her name; she came, laughing.

"The dish is hot!" he cried, hurrying past her to deposit the casserole on the counter.

"Your mother?" she asked, lifting the lid.

"Who else cooks like that?"

"I can't think of a soul."

"She knew you were late coming home."

"You told her?"

"Well—I saw you, and I thought about all that New Math and junk you teachers labor to stuff into the kids' heads, and—anyway . . ."

"Sit down, won't you, Felix?"

"I will if you will, though Mamma thinks a man should put on a shirt when he calls on a lady."

Susan smiled. "Not with your muscles," she said.

Felix rubbed his bare, brown arms. "You look a little tired."

"I am tired. But not from teaching New Math. We've given up that national disaster."

"It was one," Felix agreed. "Unintentional, perhaps, but a monstrous hoax just the same."

"Yes. The biggest mistake since John Dewey's ideas for permissive education. We are now reaping the harvest of that change. Really, though, I left the school early this afternoon. I've had a session with the lawyers and an office management chap about closing out my husband's affairs. It was a very complicated thing."

Felix nodded.

"One doesn't sell a medical practice any more," Susan told him. "But what with his narcotics license, and the supplies— they have to be inventoried—his equipment and furnishings must be appraised; there is the matter of what to do with his patients' records. How to collect unpaid bills . . ."

"Will there be money enough for you, Susan?" He was being kind, not curious.

She brushed a wisp of hair back from her face. "I think so, Felix," she said. "Rupert earned a lot of money, but he had extravagant tastes. Often he would borrow ten or a hundred dollars from me. But I think enough can be realized. We'll need to do something about his office lease. I will say that the other doctors have been most kind to me."

"Why not?"

She flushed. "Do you remember, Felix, that you offered to help me, and that was before Rupert was killed. Did you guess . . . ?"

"Not that he'd be killed as he was killed, Susan. But I did know that he had a complexity of interests, and that sort of setup can be dangerous, if only to a man's blood pressure and his temper."

She sighed and nodded. "Did you know that he poisoned the dogs on the Lane the night before he was killed?"

Felix made a sound of regret, protest, and sympathy.

"He did," she said. "He was angry at me for something I would not agree to do. He was frightened because he knew I would do as I thought right. I—I suspected he had poisoned the dogs. And I found the strychnine container in the pocket of his fleece-lined coat after—after—"

"He probably had many pressures upon him, Susan."

She nodded. "I am sure that he did." She looked up pleadingly at Felix, her dark eyes wide. "Do you think I will have to know all the complexities, Felix?"

He smiled at her. "You're a cute girl, Susan," he said warmly.

She flushed with pleasure. "Now what has that to do with it?"

"From where I sit, without my shirt, it has a lot."

She was confused. "How old are you, Felix?" she asked.

"I'm thirty-one. Why?"

"That's my age. I'm past thirty. And I thought I was old."

"Oh, no!" he cried. "Oh, no! What do you plan to do, Susan?"

"I'll finish the term. Then— You see, I am expecting a child in September."

He leaned forward in his chair and took her hands into his. "Are you glad, Susan?" he asked.

She studied his face. "When I first knew," she answered, "I

was in despair. I had learned of things which I feared his child might inherit, or learn from his father. But now, when I think of the way Rupert may have died, when I can convince myself that he died when trying to help that girl, I am able to be proud of him. I always knew that I had loved Rupert when I married him. And then there came a time ... But the manner of his death tells me *why* I love him, and so I can carry on, strong in that knowledge."

Felix still held her hands. "The times when you believe will remain," he said gently. "And you may be right, you know. Aubuchon was a charming man, and clever." He talked this way, hoping that she would think he agreed with her. Here was a proud woman, gathering straw, and with such wisps as she could find, she was endeavoring to build her life anew.

To divert her with other failures and doubts, he told her about himself and Esther. "We mistook excitement and passion for love. I should never have married her. Girls like that don't even want marriage, Susan."

"No," she agreed. "And some men don't need it either."

"I am not one of them. A good marriage sounds wonderful to me, and I wish I could have it. Esther has left, but there are threats she has made—I can't let her wreck Nathan Kendrick's life, so I'll either take her back or bankrupt myself paying her off. My only hope is that Nathan may have learned his lesson. She almost got him into some frightening trouble. He seems a smart kid ... But, no, I can't let Esther . . ."

"But aren't you forgetting yourself, Felix? You can't live with Esther unless you love her."

He sighed. "We'll manage," he said. "Somehow. Good days must be ahead for you and me both, Susan. They can seem far off, but they must be there."

That morning, after Malcolm had left her at the hospital, Abby went out into the crowded hall of the surgery floor. Oh, she corrected herself, not so much crowded as completely busy. There was room to walk, and people from whom to ask directions. But everyone seemed intent on doing important things. Really it was good to stand and watch the organized disorder. The men, the women—all seemed to have a place, a function. Even the shrouded patients on the carts ... She had talked enough to Malcolm Anderson to understand the growth of heart surgery, the advance in helping people with heart defects and diseases, to know that these patients were important links in the growing chain. Not that they were sick, but that they had the will, sometimes the faith, or even the fear, to let the doctors take their painstaking steps toward cure.

It really was inspiring. Abby moved toward the desk, her eyes bemused with her thoughts.

"May I help you?" asked the nurse on duty.

Abby nodded. "You remember—I am Miss Bennett. I was wondering if I might see Mr. Kimberlin."

"Visiting hours . . ." the nurse began.

Abby smiled. "I happen to be here now."

"Yes. And maybe you could see him. Not now, I'd think."

"Could I wait somewhere? Out of the way?"

"There's a lounge." The nurse's pencil pointed. Abby thanked her and went down the hall. Malcolm, or somebody, was making things easy for her. The lounge was deserted; there was a coffee machine and a tray of cups. Behind the glass doors of a vending machine there were sandwiches and sweet rolls.

With intentional carelessness, Abby left the door open, then selected a chair out of the center of the room from which she could watch what was going on in the corridor. A great deal seemed to be building up out there. A whole phalanx of men—six at least—came along and stopped just outside the door, talking earnestly. Somebody's head light had gone out. "If that ever happens to the Chief . . ."

Head lights?

Now there was a six-way discussion of electric cables. There should be a way to get them out of the line of traffic. One man had tripped over the electrocautery.

Abby hunted in her purse for her pen and small notebook. She'd write the scraps down; eventually they might form a sense-making pattern.

Three times she saw her father cross the door. Impossible to mistake his size, the forward lean of his shoulders and head. Other people walked briskly; Dr. Bennett ran. He scampered, he scuttled between obstacles. In the state of quiet tension which was clamping down on the surgical floor, Dr. Bennett alone bustled about.

He talked to everyone, and at the minute his main subject of complaint seemed to be the schedule board. How, he demanded, could Dr. Anderson be operating if he was still away?

"That's a fair question," said the man whom he had accosted. Not disrespectfully. Really, these hospital people were courteous to her father. They might turn their heads and

179

look after him, they might, and did, lift an eyebrow. But it was, "Yes, doctor." Or, "Yes, sir," always.

He actually came into the lounge with two other men. Abby made herself small behind the back of a second chair. She wanted to stay where she was.

Her father was intent on showing these two companions that all the schedule boards were wrong. Here in the lounge, the board was behind the coffee machine counter.

"See there," he cried. "I knew it would be wrong, too. There it is: Internal Mammary Implant. Twelve noon. Surgeon, Malcolm Anderson. Did he return in the night?"

"I don't think so, sir," said the taller of the two men.

"Then he's still away," said Dr. Bennett, "and I think someone should have warned me that the team would be in charge. As of course we can be. I'm on that team, you know." He spoke happily, archly. "My name isn't there, but by seniority alone, I'll be in charge."

"If you are taking charge, sir," said one of his listeners, and he spoke gravely, "what will you do should Anderson show?"

"Oh," said Dr. Bennett, "he's a good man. The team will cooperate."

He raced out of the room, saying that he had things to check.

The two men watched him go. "He's flipped," said the taller one.

"I hope," agreed his friend.

The surgical floor was busy, the activity rising to a peak. Up in Arthur Kimberlin's room, there was activity, but measured and calm. He was being prepared for the surgery which he had been awaiting, and he accepted each preliminary step with interest. Malcolm Anderson had explained to him what would go on. There was a recording device ten feet from his bed.

Now Dr. Anderson, and his resident, Hank Mitchell, were going through a check list.

"Is that a new intern?" Dr. Anderson asked, pointing to the papers.

"Yes, sir. New on cardiac. He's second year in surgery."

"All right. I suppose he will have only two things to do: one to watch and learn, the other to hold the retractor. But make it a point, Hank, to tell him that, if he falls, to try not to fall against me, and that he could try pinching his leg if he thinks he might fall."

Dr. Mitchell made a note. "How are we going to handle the Bennett situation, doctor?" he asked, glancing at the bed where Arthur Kimberlin lay drowsy.

Dr. Anderson spoke in a guarded tone, his head turned away. "I haven't assigned him a specific duty. I think he'll clear the situation himself. If not, if you watch closely, you'll see that I'll manage."

"Like the intern," said his resident, "I'll be watching and learning. Are we ready to go?"

Abby remained unnoticed for an hour which she enjoyed with enough mixed feeling, she told herself, to make a steamed pudding. And then, when she was absorbed, head down, bent in writing something in her little book, her father charged into the room and came straight over to her. What was she doing there? he demanded.

"The nurse said I could wait here."

He nodded. "Plenty of drama going on. We're operating on Arthur Kimberlin, you know."

"I've found out. Or deduced. No one told me. But from all the preparations . . ."

"Yes, it's a big thing. Look, would you like to observe?"

Abby sat straight up. "Watch the surgery, you mean?"

"That's what I mean. You're a writer, you're doing books all the time. Sure, you can observe. I'll take you up. Be right back!"

He charged out. Abby went to the lavatory; she drank a cup of coffee and ate a sandwich. Right or wrong, the schedule board said twelve noon. And nothing else was listed. Open-heart surgery, she believed, took a long time.

She had butterflies, not only in her stomach. There was her father, and Malcolm . . . She had seen surgery done but not this sort. Since childhood, she had called this patient "Uncle Arthur."

But when her father came for her, she went willingly with him. This door to which he took her opened on a space, a runway, that circled a half-dozen rows of benches spiraling downward to form a circle about the operating amphitheater. Having thought about Malcolm's surgery so much, Abby was a little surprised, let down in fact, by the small size of that theater and its crowded condition. There was an operating table, of course, with the apparatus for anaesthesia at the head of it, lights in clusters, and, protruding from the ceiling at the far side of the room, there was a television camera. There were tables of instruments stacked in gleaming rows,

shining pans of all sorts and shapes; there was a compli-
cated-looking machine with glass tanks, and tubes. Oh, there
were all sorts of gadgets! And people! People in caps and
shapeless green robes, shuffling about in what looked like
ticking pillow cases. Abby, on the third bench, put her elbows
on her knees and tried to make sense of what was going on
under the glass, or plastic, dome which separated the operating theater from the observers, of whom there were a lot.
Students, she supposed, but some older men, too, who probably were doctors. Everyone was interested, not talking much
though they could not be heard on the floor, just as the workers there could not be heard up here.

Abby settled herself on the hard bench—there was no
back to it—and watched. She saw the patient brought in and
swiftly, skillfully transferred to the table. His head was covered with a cap, he seemed to be sleeping. The anaesthetist
came in and twiddled valves, examined the patient's eye, constantly observed his dials, and the flashing polliwog of the oscilloscope. He had some bladderlike bags which he watched
and seemed to manipulate as if he were breathing for the patient. Maybe he was. "Heart-lung machine" must be a mean-
ingful term.

There had been some painting and marking on Arthur
Kimberlin's back and chest; now the green-swathed people
who had done this stepped back, and a new group came in.
The phalanx. Abby gasped. Her father really was with them.
He was there! Unmistakable. Oh, but he should not be. Abby
should not have meddled.

He went straight to the table; everyone seemed to watch
him. A nurse whisked away the towel which covered his
hands, and then—six inches from the patient's side, he stood
frozen. Abby could see his arm shake. Someone spoke to
him, and he turned away uncertainly. A nurse held his arm,
and he disappeared from Abby's view.

"What was all that about?" asked the man behind Abby.

"They did it all polite and proper," said someone else.

Abby gulped and blinked her eyes. Yes, the thing had been
done gravely, correctly. Her father, that night, would explain
what had happened. His old friend . . . a sudden faintness . . .

She leaned forward again. A tall man, swathed, unrecogni-
zable to those who did not know him well, had stepped to the
left side of the table and was beginning the difficult task of
cutting through the chest.

"Anderson?" said the student behind her.

She turned her head. "Who else?" she asked sharply.

She leaned forward and watched. The operation took hours, and she was unaware of passing time. She found out about head lights and cables and the fatigue experienced by the men who held the metal retractors; she saw one team serve, a second handle the artificial heart apparatus, she saw the heart lifted, turned, and craned her neck to see the delicate stitchery which patched the injured artery.

She saw it all done by that steady, strong man.

"Of course it was Anderson," she told the student behind her when at last they were finished. "There's only one man that good."

He smiled at her. "He's good," he agreed. "Can you stand up?"

"Why not?"

"Better take my hand. Together we might make it."

Arthur Kimberlin had asked Margaret not to stay at the hospital during his surgery. And certainly not to let the family come. "I've done enough of those death watches," he told his granddaughter. "Tonsils, appendix for your father when he was fourteen . . . Don't do it, my dear."

"But if I want to be there?"

"Try to think of something else you want. Mac will tell you about it when it's over. I'm hoping that not many know it is finally happening."

"All right," she agreed, kissing him. "I'll pull weeds tomorrow."

"Good girl! Now go home and eat supper which is more, I understand, than I'll be allowed to do."

"But you'll get a pill."

He made a face, and she managed to smile at him from the door. If things went wrong, that was a good way to have parted. If things went well, she could greet him, smiling again.

She kept her word. She attended to her household duties that day, she ate lunch with Lester and talked to him about various things. After lunch she changed to her gardening clothes, got her tools, and told Lionel that she was going to pull grass and weeds, very carefully, from under and around the shrubbery.

"Yes, ma'am. Did you talk to the hospital?" His eyes were troubled.

"I did. And all was going according to plan."

"Miz Bennett told cook her doctor is goin' to operate."

Margaret smiled at him. "I don't think so, Lionel."

"Yes, ma'am. I'm prayin'."

"Oh, yes," said Margaret. "So am I!"

She held herself to her task, knowing that she would be told at once should any word come from the hospital. The sun, the warm earth, were better than sitting up in the penthouse at the hospital. Her basket of weeds did not fill very rapidly, but she really had not expected it to. She often knelt, or sat, thinking.

She heard footsteps coming along the drive and peered out from under the junipers to see who it could be. "I'm here, Chris," she called softly. "If you wanted to see me."

"Yes," he said. "I did. What are you up to?"

"Pulling weeds and worrying about Grandfather."

"Is he . . . ?"

"Yes, he is. In good spirits, and in good hands. Malcolm Anderson is doing it."

"Knew he would. Mr. Kimberlin will come through this and have been given several happy years."

"I hope so."

"Margaret . . ."

She looked around at him warily.

"I only wanted to tell you that I am going to leave the plant and the Lane."

She was surprised and concerned. "On my account?" she asked.

"Partly. I've found that I can't stay near you and be patient. I've accepted a job in a government research project."

"You'll sell your house?"

"Yes. For a time I won't really need a house. Nathan has enlisted in the Marines."

She sat back on her heels. "He hasn't! I thought . . ."

"School, yes. But he enlisted. Says he'll get his military service done; he can make Officer Candidate School if he wants. After boot, of course, which will be good for him. I just wish I could be his top sergeant."

Margaret laughed.

He grinned. "Be soft in the head there, too, wouldn't I? Those kids—I talked to Nathan last night. I told him that I tried to look at his age group realistically, that I saw their beauty, the strength of their healthy limbs. I said that I envied him the years and the opportunities which lie ahead for him.

"There are an awful lot of young people these days, Margaret. And they argue. Dear Lord, do they ever argue! I've

184

been told they are smart, and I guess they are, some of them. All young people are bright. Smart. We were, some of us.

"I talked to the kid and he talked to me. Really talked. He told me he had snitched cash from the drawer in his office, but has paid it back. He told me he had got in too deep with Esther Lynch, and that Felix had saved him from making a fool of himself there. It seems . . ." He broke off and bent toward Margaret to study her eyes. "You know all this?"

She flushed. "I couldn't tell you."

"No. I wouldn't have taken that well, would I? But, Margaret—well, this way, I have my son back. And I still love you deeply, dearly."

"Yes, I know."

"Someday . . ." he promised.

"Yes. Someday. Keep in touch, Chris."

"You know I will." He stood erect. "Last night," he said, laughing, "I heard myself ask Nathan whatever had happened to the nice girl he went around with at the U. He asked me if I meant the one I had called silly. And I said yes, that we all make mistakes."

Abruptly, he walked away from her, without touching her. Margaret watched him go, the tears running down her cheeks.

By evening, by dinnertime, everyone on the Lane knew of the successful surgery on Arthur Kimberlin. Dr. Anderson had done it; he had been closely in attendance on the old man. "To keep Bennett from doing the transplant, do you suppose?" Chris Kendrick asked Felix Lynch.

"I won't quote you," laughed Felix, "but it's fine news."

A week later the newspapers told of the lawsuit filed by Mrs. Holman against Dr. Malcolm Anderson. There followed two paragraphs about the city's most distinguished heart surgeon. The suit was for abandonment of a patient who had died.

"Would he have done such a thing?"

"It seems he did."

The hearing was set for the twentieth of April, and Dr. Bennett asked Abby if she would go with him. He was to be a witness, he said.

She agreed at once. She wanted to go. If she could help her father by her presence . . . Should she tell him that Malcolm had never really left?

He would be furious with her for not telling him sooner.

He was excited enough as things were. Going to the courthouse that afternoon, he drove so recklessly that she determined to tell her mother that the doctor must not only retire, he must stop driving a car.

The hearing was held in a small courtroom of an aging building that showed the wear and tear of the sorts of people who for years had gone along its marble corridors and had sat in the chairs of its courtrooms.

There were thirty or forty people present; her father identified various ones to her—doctors, lawyers ... "I didn't bring my own attorney," he said, laughing.

"Maybe you should have."

"I'm an old hand at testifying, Abby. It's called forensic medicine. That's Mrs. Holman coming in now."

Abby looked at her curiously. She was a small, very thin woman, with leathery skin, short-cropped hair, a suit of bright red plaid—a trousered suit. With it she wore a black blouse which was unbecoming, and dark glasses, which surely were not needed in this room lighted by indirect ceiling lights, and two green-shaded lamps on the judge's bench.

Dr. Bennett even pointed out Malcolm Anderson to Abby. "I know him!" she cried impatiently.

"Thought you might have forgotten, he was gone so long." The little doctor positively cackled, for heaven's sake!

Abby studied Malcolm. He was wearing a hound's-tooth checked coat in brown and white, a brown handkerchief, a loosely knit, cream-colored shirt. His face was calm and strong.

Things proceeded. She had attended other trials and hearings. The charge was read. Abby listened and wanted to cry out that Malcolm could not have done those things! She whispered this to her father. "They say he did," the old doctor answered her.

Abby was annoyed with him. She wished she had endeavored to tell him all she knew and to persuade him that Malcolm could not be accused ...

Very soon in the proceedings, Dr. Bennett was called to testify. He walked briskly up to the witness chair, and Abby smiled even as she shook her head. The little cricket of a man, lovable and irritating—he was enjoying his minute in the limelight.

He identified himself. Yes, he was a heart specialist. Yes, he was on the staff of the University Medical Center, and other hospitals, too!

He had practiced medicine for fifty years. He knew Dr.

Anderson. Of course he did! The young man had been made Chief of Surgery of the Thoracic and Cardiovascular department. That meant chest medicine, he explained to the judge, thumping his own flat chest.

Then—Abby never was sure that he'd been asked so to testify, but he was telling of his long friendship with the Kimberlin family. He said they had homes next door to one another, and had lived as neighbors for thirty years or more.

He said that, yes, he knew that Dr. Anderson had—well—disappeared. "But I knew he was somewhere around," he continued pertly. "I was not asked to attend my old friend who was in the hospital, gravely ill. My feelings were hurt and my pride offended. I was not allowed to see him because it was feared I would express my grievance to Arthur, and this would certainly have upset him and have had a bad effect.

"Some people might have been fooled. I think Dr. Aubuchon was. But Dr. Anderson—we call him *Mac* at the hospital—he was there—somewhere. Night and day. Didn't come to his home for two weeks. He was the right doctor for that case; he admired Arthur Kimberlin. Although all sorts of talk went on about his disappearance, most of the hospital staff knew he must be available. Otherwise, another specialist would have been named. Some jokes were told that he stuck around to see that I'd stay out. I've studied to be a heart specialist, you see. But my one try at opening a chest didn't turn out well. They knew Mr. Kimberlin would not be exposed to my surgery, or should have known it. Of course nobody called me an old fool to my face. I am not an old fool."

Abby felt her eyelids sting with love, with pride, for her father. He spoke with dignity.

"I am a good doctor," he said, "and Anderson is a good doctor. He did not abandon Arthur Kimberlin; he did not abandon Elmer Holman. I cared for Mr. Holman who had been told, and whose wife had been told, that implant surgery was not possible for the man. There were four or five doctors in his room when he died, all of us under orders from the Chief of the Service, Dr. Anderson, yonder."

His testimony did not conclude the hearing, but at its end, Malcolm came over to thank the old man. "You got me out of a bad hole, sir," he said sincerely.

Dr. Bennett bridled with pleasure. "My daughter," he said, glancing at Abby, who stood beside him, "my daughter would want me to help where I could. As the judge said, there were no grounds for a suit."

187

Malcolm smiled at "his daughter." "I'm going out to my house," he said to her. "Could I take you home?"

This suited everyone. Dr. Bennett had work to do. Abby had come in his car. Happily, she went through the dingy corridors at Malcolm's side. Happy. She knew that all was well between them.

She waited on the front steps of the courthouse while he fetched his car, thinking of Malcolm as he had been in the operating room during the surgery for Mr. Kimberlin. He had worked, a strong man, knowing his craft, sure of his skill, working confidently with the ones who assisted him and trusted him.

From that first snowy day of knowing this man, Abby had been curious about him, always interested, and sometimes puzzled. But observing him in surgery, all these feelings had polarized into the simple emotion of trust. He could do that delicate, difficult work; his hands knew, his mind knew, exactly what move to make. And with trust there came to her the most overwhelming emotion of all; perhaps it was the sum of it all. A woman's love for a man, of a man. Abby now stood waiting for this man, a gentle smile on her face, her eyes dark with joy.

She was sure that he read her face when he put her into his car, and she did not care. All sparring and maneuvering was done with. This man could lead the way.

Going down the Lane, he asked if she had ever seen his house, been in it?

"No . . ."

"Would you like to see it?" He turned into his own drive. "My housekeeper will be gone."

The house was of white clapboarding, the wide front door opened into a generous hall from which stairs rose in an arc. To the left was a big living room, with a Chinese painting above the fireplace, deep chairs and couches. Beyond this room was a glassed-in dining porch that overlooked the orchard. There was a big bedroom, with twin beds; the spreads matched the green and gold figured draperies at the windows; there was a luxurious bath, in green.

Without pointing out a thing, or even speaking much at all, Malcolm led her across the living room again to the kitchen, compact, complete. Its windows, too, looked upon the orchard trees.

"There's a bedroom upstairs," he said tentatively.

Abby's foot was on the first tread.

"The stuff up here," said the man behind her, "is family inheritance."

The "stuff" was collector-type mahogany—a wide, four-poster bed, cushioned rockers, two tall chests, a hand-woven bedspread. There was another bath. Abby closed the door of it, and turned to Malcolm. "I love your home," she said warmly.

"I hoped you would," he agreed. "I suppose, if things worked out, a study could be arranged. A place for you to write."

Abby smiled at him. "If things work out," she said gently. "If I write, there would be a place."

"If you write . . ." he repeated.

"Just now," she said, "my idea of a full life would be to keep a house like this, to be the wife of a busy man, and in time to be the mother of five or six children."

"Five or *six?*" he asked, looking dazed.

"I'd be a good mother."

"Yes," he agreed. "I think you would be."

Another man would have kissed her then. Malcolm stood looking down at her. "I was afraid of you, Abby," he said readily. She sat down in the red-cushioned rocking chair and watched his face and his gesturing hands. "I was afraid of your wit and your beauty. And your considerable understanding of what went on. Today"—he smiled ruefully—"that same understanding got me out of the jam I was in."

She endeavored to speak.

"I know what you did," he said. "Abandonment suits are not nice things for any doctor. Today, and the two weeks I spent in close attendance on Arthur Kimberlin, have taught me a few things I needed to know. I can now see the other side of the medical coin. But mainly those two weeks gave me the time to think which I needed, and profited by having. I was able to consider whether I wanted to be a man alone, following one arrow-straight line, or if I wanted to be a man complete."

He paused, looking intently down at the girl in her red suit, at the thick curl on her shoulder, the shadow of her lashes across her dark eyes.

"You wanted," she said softly, "to decide if you could risk making love to me."

His right hand swept out into a wide arc. "Oh, making love—that question was easy. I could, and would. But marriage was what I had in my thoughts, Abby. I had to ask

189

if you were too clever, too beautiful, to be a doctor's wife, and put up with all that this means."

"Something had made you doubt that?" she asked, rising to stand before him.

"Yes," he said. "The article your father said you were writing about me."

Abby turned away from him and walked over to the small-paned window. Her father? Talkative ... "Wouldn't you marry me," she asked, "if I did write such an article?"

He remained where he was, five feet behind her. "Let's put it this way," he said. "If I marry you, I would be most unhappy to be the subject of such an article."

She turned. "Is that an ultimatum, Malcolm?"

"I don't know. I spent two weeks trying to decide what answer I would give if you issued such an ultimatum to me."

She smiled. "You sound like a man who has fallen in work."

"Why not?" he asked frankly.

"And doesn't it make you happy?"

"Not yet it hasn't."

Abby went to him and put up her arms, her hands clasped behind his head. "It will," she promised. "It will."

Then he did kiss her, surprising her by the strength of his passion and the extent of his surrender—surprising her, exciting her, fulfilling her.

When they went downstairs again, he said that he knew he was giving her all the power.

She glanced up over her shoulder at him.

"I am ready to do that," he agreed. "Yes, and don't smile so smugly. I am glad. Everything seems to be falling into place. The ornamental wife I feared is offering a pleasant prospect, and, as it was today, no doubt your cleverness will be helpful to me again—many times over."

She patted his arm. "Suppose we both relax," she said, "make our plans and take our happiness where it is available."

He nodded. "Today ..." he said. "I didn't think it would turn out this way. Look. What about your father? Did I accomplish anything for him, and you, letting him come into o.r. for Kimberlin?"

"Not at the time. But Mother is planning on future winters in Arizona, and our wedding will salve all his wounds. I'll bet anything he will tell everyone that he engineered the whole affair."

"Didn't he?" Malcolm asked.

She laughed. "Yes, I believe he did."

That night the full moon shone down upon the Lane, and cast shadows in Lester Elis's study-bedroom, and one downstairs where Margaret sat late, watching TV. It was good to see a light in the Anderson House. Except for a lamp in the front hall, Bennett's was dark. Abby had told her news, and said that the marriage ceremony would be simple, and soon. But she was tired and went upstairs.

Yard lights glowed at every doorway, and Susan Aubuchon stood in the radiance of hers as she attended her new puppy. Felix had brought it to her, a bundle of black fur and yipping barks.

His house was dark except for the entrance light. Across the circle, the light at the Kendrick house cast the *For Sale* sign's shadow blackly across the lawn.

Susan sighed and scooped the puppy up into her arms.

"We could be happier," she told the little dog. "But we could be sadder, too."